Those Summer Nights

Also by Laura Silverman

Girl Out of Water
You Asked for Perfect
It's a Whole Spiel
Recommended for You
Up All Night
Game On

THOSE Summer NIGHTS

Laura Silverman

MARGARET K. McELDERRY BOOKS

New York   London   Toronto   Sydney   New Delhi

V50

MARGARET K. McELDERRY BOOKS
An imprint of Simon & Schuster Children's Publishing Division
1230 Avenue of the Americas, New York, New York 10020
Text © 2022 by Laura Silverman
Jacket illustration © 2022 by Ana Hard
Jacket design by Debra Sfetsios-Conover © 2022 by Simon & Schuster, Inc.
MARGARET K. McELDERRY BOOKS is a trademark of Simon & Schuster, Inc.
For information about special discounts for bulk purchases, please contact Simon & Schuster Special Sales at 1-866-506-1949 or business@simonandschuster.com.
The Simon & Schuster Speakers Bureau can bring authors to your live event. For more information or to book an event, contact the Simon & Schuster Speakers Bureau at 1-866-248-3049 or visit our website at www.simonspeakers.com.
Interior design by Irene Metaxatos
The text for this book was set in Aldus LT Std.
Manufactured in China
First Edition   10 9 8 7 6 5 4 3 2 1
Library of Congress Cataloging-in-Publication Data
Names: Silverman, Laura, author.
Title: Those summer nights / Laura Silverman.
Description: First edition. | New York : Margaret K. McElderry Books, [2022] | Audience: Ages 14 up. | Audience: Grades 10–12. | Summary: After recovering from a soccer injury that ended her Olympic dreams and still grieving the death of her beloved grandmother, seventeen-year-old Hannah Klein must navigate a new summer job working with her ex-best friend, her younger brother, and her brother's suddenly attractive best friend.
Identifiers: LCCN 2021052658 (print) | LCCN 2021052659 (ebook) | ISBN 9781534488397 (hardcover) | ISBN 9781534488410 (ebook)
Subjects: CYAC: Interpersonal relations—Fiction. | Summer employment—Fiction. | Recreation centers—Fiction. | LCGFT: Novels.
Classification: LCC PZ7.1.S543 Th 2022 (print) | LCC PZ7.1.S543 (ebook) | DDC [Fic]—dc23
LC record available at https://lccn.loc.gov/2021052658
LC ebook record available at https://lccn.loc.gov/2021052659

○ ○ ○

**For Bubbie and Grandma,
it's an honor to be your granddaughter.**

○ ○ ○

Those Summer Nights

Chapter One

THE MORNING AIR is damp and warm. Soupy. Disgusting. I swipe a hand across the back of my neck as sweat curls beneath my hairline. The iconic neon lights of the BONANZA sign are muted in the daylight. I shift my weight onto my good ankle and let out a quiet sigh.

There is no choice to be made here. I have to go in. That was the deal I cut with my parents over the phone last month. *You need structure,* they said, *something to keep you centered and grounded.*

Grounded.

I will also be grounded until next year's high school graduation if they see fit, the only exception being my new job. I would call that an extreme measure, but for what I put them through last summer . . .

Well, I can't blame my parents.

I can blame a lot of people—Kensington's star defensive player, Lily Thompson; my ex–best friend, Brie Bradley; and certainly myself. But my parents? They are not to blame.

A car beeps next to mine. I watch as a middle-aged man walks toward the Bonanza entrance, grocery bag in hand. Maybe his lunch for later. It's time for me to go in as well. I arrived home yesterday evening and still haven't unpacked my things, but we were all eager for me to get a job, so I scheduled my interview for this morning. The interview is just a formality, supposedly. Joey, my younger brother by one year, got a job here last fall when he turned sixteen. He promised I'm a shoo-in to be hired.

And yet, my muscles tense with nerves. I have no work experience, a mediocre academic record, and zero recommendations other than the one from my kid brother. Joey is a charismatic goofball with a heart of pure gold. I'm sure the boss loves him because everyone loves him. Unfortunately, my brother and I could not be more different.

Will the manager realize it from the start? What if he asks how I spent my last year? Thank god I don't have any sort of record, but it's still like I'm marked, officially slotted into the problem-child category. And I feel like people can read it all over my face.

I shift my weight again, wincing as it settles onto my left ankle. I wasn't like this before. I was never unsure. Unsteady. I used to have confidence, used to *know* and not *think.* But everything is different now. I'm different now.

The BONANZA sign blinks at me, and I walk inside.

"No former work experience?" the manager asks.

His name is Pete. He looks exactly like a Pete, middling height, middling weight, pale white skin and eyes that seem a shade too dull, like someone turned down the saturation. I have a feeling if I saw Pete on the street tomorrow, I wouldn't recognize him.

I concentrate on these details instead of the spiral of thoughts that stems from his question. "Um, no." I sit up straighter. "No, sir. No former work experience. Well, I did a little babysitting, if that counts. . . ."

I didn't really babysit so much as hang out with Brie while she watched her little sisters, twin girls, miracle babies. Her parents had trouble conceiving for years, and then got a two-for-one special when Brie was nine.

Brie.

I cross my arms and dig a nail into my skin. I haven't spoken to my best friend since I was shipped off to Mountain Bliss Academy. Ex–best friend. Spending an evening watching *Monsters, Inc.* and baking snickerdoodles with her little sisters feels like a lifetime ago.

"Babysitting is applicable here," Pete replies with a nod. "You'll be with children all the time. Are you good with kids?"

I've never been good at anything other than soccer, and with soccer no longer an option in my life, I guess that leaves me with being good at nothing at all.

"Um, yes," I say.

Kid-wrangling is a requirement at Bonanza, a megaplex entertainment center serving our Atlanta suburb since the eighties. There's a bowling alley, mini golf, go-karts, an arcade, and more, so birthday parties and Little League celebrations are regular occurrences. My traveling team went here in fifth grade after we won the regional championship. I stuffed my face with chocolate cake, guzzled soda, and ran around all afternoon, eventually throwing up somewhere around the windmill hole of the mini-golf course.

Thankfully Pete doesn't notice my lackluster lie, as he's busy fumbling with the wrapper of his protein bar.

"Great!" he replies, finally ripping open the wrapper. He smiles at me. "Love the peanut butter flavor."

I give a weak smile in return. "Great."

"Well, your brother is one of our favorite employees, and I'm sure you will be as well. I can only offer a seasonal job for now, but if you want it, you're hired."

"Really?" My stomach flips, and I realize how scared I was of failing a task this simple. "Yes, definitely. Thanks. Thank you."

"Let's get your paperwork filled out, and then we'll get you on the floor for training."

"Training . . . today?"

As in *today*, today?

I don't have other plans, per se—being grounded and alienating all your friends clears a calendar with impressive totality. But we weren't allowed access to our laptops at Mountain Bliss, so I'm about three hundred episodes behind on all my favorite reality TV. I was planning to numb my brain for the rest of the afternoon with straight-to-camera confessionals.

"Yep!" Pete hands me a clipboard of paperwork. "Welcome to Bonanza, Hannah Klein!"

The paperwork is easy to fill out. I have to call Dad to ask for my Social Security number, and after he lightly nags me for not having it memorized, he congratulates me on getting the job. I can hear the eagerness in his voice, the hope that this will fix things. That this will fix *me*.

I don't share in his hope, but I don't have the heart to burst his bubble, either. And if getting a job is what it takes for them to let me spend my senior year at home instead of back at boarding school, then that's what I'll do.

That was the deal, at least part of it. My parents agreed that I could come back home for summer and then return to my regular public school in the fall if, and only if, I got a job.

Mountain Bliss isn't the worst place in the world. It's like the Diet Coke of boarding schools for troubled teens.

My cohorts' crimes ranged from cutting class to shoplifting jewelry from Forever 21. Our daily activities ranged from yoga to sustainable farming. And the entire place is tucked against the beautiful backdrop of the North Georgia Mountains. We even peer-interview past students before enrolling to ensure it's a safe space.

But I missed home. I missed my bed and my things. And most of all, I felt a heavy weight of guilt thinking about how much my parents were spending to keep me in line. My bad behavior draining their savings.

I love my parents, and I don't want them to worry. So I can fake it for a year, pretend things are fine, be a good little worker, act as if I'm *like, totally okay.* And then I guess I'll go off to college or something and be away from their nervous eyes.

I finish filling out the paperwork and hand everything over to Pete. He hands me a Bonanza T-shirt in return. In the bathroom, I send Joey a quick text. We share a car now that he's sixteen and I'm home from boarding school.

Got the job. Apparently my first shift is today—can you get a ride here?

Joey: Mazel tov sis! No problem, Ethan can drive us

Ethan is Joey's best friend and basically my second kid brother. They've been inseparable since they met in their preschool synagogue class. Ethan regularly sleeps at our place more often than his own home. One summer, when

I was on a traveling team, I'm pretty sure he slept at our house more nights than *I* did.

I text back great and then slide my phone into my pocket.

"Everything looks good here!" Pete says when I return to his office. "Let's get you started!"

He leads me out into the hallway. The dark carpets are grimy, plastered in decades of dirty shoes and spilled concessions that no steam cleaner can erase. The offices are in a hallway off the arcade, but Pete says he wants to start me on mini golf. "It's slow during the day," he explains. "Too hot for most of the customers. So it'll give you a chance to learn the ropes."

We pass the entrance of the arcade. From here, I can feel the cool blast of air-conditioning, see lasers and blinking lights, hear the electronic beeps and whirs. For a moment, the sounds yank me to the hospital, to images of my bubbie weak in bed, to images of myself broken and battered.

I rub my arms, shivering as I walk past a vent.

It's barely noon, so there are only a handful of people playing games, and another few in line at the EZ Eats concession stand for slices of underbaked pizza and dry hamburgers. Culinary fine arts, not exactly a strong suit of the Bonanza brand.

Sunlight hits us as Pete pushes open a pair of heavy double doors. I blink, eyes taking a moment to adjust. Then

I follow Pete down the sidewalk path toward the mini-golf course.

When we're halfway there, his phone beeps. He looks down at the screen and gives a tiny "Hmph." Then he turns to me. "Hannah, I apologize, but there's a kerfuffle at the bowling alley about the senior discount. I need to go handle it. Head straight to the check-in counter and let the employee on staff know you're new. Sound good?"

"Yeah." I clear my throat and force a pleasant smile. "I mean, yes. Sounds good. Thank you, again."

Pete gives a little wave before doing a half jog back toward the main building. I'm curious about the senior community drama, but I follow Pete's instructions and finish walking down the path to the check-in counter.

There's a family in line, a dad and his two kids. I'm not sure if I should stand to the side or cut the line or what. Awkwardly, I step behind the dad like I'm getting in line to play mini golf as well. I rub my hands up and down my jeans as I wait. The fabric is too warm for the hot sun, but Mom said it wasn't appropriate to interview in shorts.

Eventually, the dad and his kids finish paying. They walk away to pick out their clubs, and I step up to the counter to introduce myself, and—

"Oh, shit."

Last Summer

The night air is sweet and crisp. My skin tingles as I tighten the laces of my cleats. My left ankle, weakened by years of injuries, feels more secure with each sharp tug. I lock my car, then walk down the hill and toward the field, my cleats crunching down fresh-cut grass. Half the team is already here, gathered and chatting. Buoyant laughter echoes through the air. Elizabeth sets eyes on me first. She waves, jumping up and down a couple of times as she does so.

Brie notices me next, smiling at me as she adjusts her neon-green shorts. Brie is Black, and her dark brown skin glows under the floodlights. I tackle her with a one-armed hug. My strength might throw a lesser being off-balance, but Brie Bradley has the steadiness of a gymnast.

"Hey, best friend," I tell her.

She grins and wraps an arm around me as well. She smells

like peaches today. Her collection of Bath & Body Works sprays could last her through an apocalypse. "Hey, best friend," she replies.

We're at our happiest in summer, when the days stretch long and the nights even longer. No papers and teachers and group projects. Just cleats and water bottles and suntan lotion.

We're addicts. Soccer is our lifeblood, and we'd be lost without it.

"Hey, Hannah girl," Nina says, giving me a cool nod. She pulls on an eighties-style sweatband. Her light brown skin is freckled from days in the sun. Even though we're the same age, Nina Pérez has always given off cool-older-sister vibes. She doesn't let the little stuff bother her, which makes her the perfect goalie and captain: clearheaded and confident.

"Hey, Nina," I reply with a smile. "Ready to play?"

"Soon. Stretches first."

Excitement pulses through me as we stretch, like it always does when a game is close. There's nothing better–the lights, the competition, the adrenaline. A perfect pass to a teammate, nailing one smack-dab to the corner of the net, a game-changing goal, the crowd erupting around me in–

"She's doing it again," Nina says.

"Oh yeah, definitely," Brie agrees.

They're both looking at me with amused smiles. "Doing what?" I ask.

"Imagining your Olympic fame and glory," Nina answers.

I roll my eyes but smile. They're not wrong. I've made a name for myself as an offensive force to be reckoned with. If I stay on the right path and make it into a D1 school, the Olympics could well be in my future. I wouldn't be the first alumni to make it from this team to the medal podium.

Just the idea makes my heart skip.

"All right." Nina claps her hands together. "It's time."

We finish our stretches. Elizabeth asks for my help lacing her shoes. "Thanks," she says, smiling as I yank the laces. Elizabeth Mehta, our tiniest teammate, plays a ferocious defensive game that makes our opponents tremble. Our own little pint-sized glass of terror. "You always get them tighter than me."

The scrimmage kicks off slow, everyone feeling each other out, trying to sense who will play aggressively tonight and who will hang back. That's what I love most about my team. We're adaptable. To be the best, you have to constantly shift. You can't just play to your one strength—everything has to be your strength.

My eyes focus on the ball in Brie's possession. She strikes it with a hard left to Ainsley as the wind picks up and rustles through my hair. I give my ponytail a tight tug, then fall back to midfield, biding my time to make my move. I had to learn that when I was younger—there's a time to strike and a time to fall back. I used to be too eager, always chomping at the bit.

I practice patience now, watching Ainsley pass to Brie, then Brie pass to Rosie, but Rosie isn't quite in position, and in that lost second, I get in front of her to intercept the ball. And then all noise drops off around me, and I'm in a breakaway, sprinting with the ball toward the goal. Acutely, I'm aware of Carrie-Anne on my right, there for an assist while closing in on the back door. But I have a wide-open shot.

I strike hard. The loud *thwack* brings the rest of the sounds back, and I hear the tension in the air as the ball rockets toward the top right corner of the net. Nina jumps, reaches, stretches–and manages to deflect the ball with the tip of her fingers.

I deflate, but only for a moment. Nina is an incredible goalie, and I like playing against the best. We exchange grins, and I fall back to center field.

Ninety minutes later, the game ends in a 1–1 tie, everyone equally frustrated and pleased. Some girls head home, but most of us linger on the field. We collapse onto the grass in a sweaty mess, lying on our backs in a circle, our heads almost touching. The air feels cooler now. It rustles over my skin, my hairs rising up in pinpricks. I inhale and savor the scent of summer, cut grass, and sweat.

My muscles relax, and I let out a gentle hum. "Good game, Brie," I say.

"Good game, Hannah," she replies.

The smile in her voice warms me down to my toes.

I get to spend every day of summer with the sport and the friend I love most.

How lucky am I?

Chapter Two

"OH, SHIT."

The words escape my lips of their own volition.

Immediately after, I snap my mouth shut. And then there's a long pause, a knot forming in my throat, as the person at the counter stares at me in equal shock.

"Um," I say.

After what feels like forever, Brie asks, "What are you doing here, Hannah?"

Her voice is cool, detached, but I catch the hint of emotion in it. The uncomfortable tremor of coming face-to-face with the person you used to care about most and now haven't talked to for almost a year. A million emotions pummel me at once—sadness, guilt, anger—it's overwhelming. I'm not ready to see her. This wasn't part of the plan. I can't *do this*.

Panic makes my head light.

Brie shifts back on her feet as her expression holds steady. Her box braids hang down past her shoulders. She's wearing a pink Bonanza T-shirt and small gold hoop earrings. A purple bracelet with a silver charm adorns her wrist—our team bracelet. I scratch my own empty wrist.

When I speak, I stare at a spot just to the left of Brie's head and try to keep my voice neutral. "I'm, uh, back for summer. My parents said I needed a job, and Joey works here, so." I gesture down at my Bonanza T-shirt, which she just now seems to notice. "I didn't know you worked here as well."

"Started in the spring," she replies, then after a beat adds, "Postseason."

The season—the season they won, first in regionals, fourth in nationals. All without me. Mom texted me a picture from the game, a photo of Brie, mid–defensive kick, eyes bright and determined. "You should congratulate her," Mom said.

Reception at Mountain Bliss was spotty. I pretended the text never got through.

Guilt claws at me even though it's Brie who let *me* down. It's Brie who ratted me out to *my* parents. It's Brie who let years of friendship go when *my life* got flipped inside out.

And that's all true. But what's also true is that I'm not

an innocent party in the downfall of our friendship. No, Brie wasn't alone. It was mutually assured destruction.

"Right. Well . . ." I crack my knuckles, one by one, a nervous habit. "Pete said to tell whoever was working to train me, but I can—"

Brie pulls out a radio and speaks into it. "Daisey, need an AC break?"

A voice comes through the static a second later: "Like you need to ask. Be right there."

My throat tightens. Nothing says *I hate my former best friend* like relinquishing the cool blast of AC to get away from her.

An incredibly uncomfortable ninety seconds of silence later, Daisey appears from the curved path of the course, and Brie exits the check-in counter. As she passes me, I catch the scent of today's body spray, a coconut-pineapple mix, and remember a flash of our Daytona team trip, hot sand and slushy nonalcoholic drinks.

"See you around, Hannah," Brie says.

Her tone insinuates she hopes for anything but that.

As the sun rises higher in the sky, I grow increasingly more stressed.

I can't believe that of all the places in our city, Brie works *here*. What are the chances of that? She could work at Wakesville Mall or at a restaurant or at a summer camp, literally *anywhere* else, but god decided to play some cosmic joke and land us both at Bonanza.

I just want to put my head down and work. I want to forget everything about last summer. But with Brie here, a reminder will be around every corner.

With a groan of frustration, I shove a handful of tiny pencils into a basket.

"They're heavy, I know," Daisey says with a raised eyebrow.

A pierced raised eyebrow. I've been working with Daisey Liu for two hours now and have counted at least sixteen piercings, including one in her chin, which hurts to look at. But despite the unfair assumptions I made from all the metal, Daisey is really nice, and apparently we see eye to eye on how to use sarcasm: in large doses.

"Sorry," I reply, "just a long morning."

Understatement of the year.

"Evening shifts are better," Daisey replies, running a hand through her short hair. Her skin is a light tan, and her T-shirt sleeves are rolled up at the shoulders. "Busier, more stuff to distract you." She snaps her fingers. "Zips by like that."

"Sounds nice," I say. "How long have you been working here?"

"Three years," she answers. "Since Owen turned two. He was too young for Bonanza daycare before that."

Daisey is twenty-five with a five-year-old son. Bonanza might be an old, run-down place that barely pays over minimum wage, but they're famous for their free in-house daycare. It lets employees have somewhere safe for their kids to be while they work.

"And you like it?" I ask. Other than running into Brie, my first few hours as a Bonanza employee have been pretty easy—though I did have a moment of panic when it took me too long to ring up a customer. Her foot did an impatient *tap-tap* on the pavement.

"Better than most jobs," Daisey replies. "The daycare is great. And the staff here is awesome." She grins. "*Wild*, but awesome. Some of the over-twenty-one employees, well, they're hot messes."

"What do you mean?"

She shakes her head. "You'll have to check out the alley bar after close one night. Shift employees are allowed one drink each, but they play fast and loose with that policy."

I grin. "Nothing says 'kid-friendly family fun' like a fully stocked bar."

Daisey laughs. "You've got that right." She checks her watch, an actual analogue one with a slender black leather band. "Pete usually likes the newbies to move around, see where they'll be the best fit. Why don't you go check out the arcade? Or the bowling alley? You'll want to hold off on whirly ball for now—the birthday parties there are the definition of chaos."

Since whirly ball is a combination of bumper cars and lacrosse, I'm not surprised by Daisey's appraisal.

"Okay." I nod. "I should just head over and ask someone to train me?"

"Yup," Daisey answers. "Exactly. Pete is . . . Pete. He's fine. There are a lot of employees to corral, so it's usually best to take the training into your own hands. You'll get the hang of things a lot faster that way."

"Okay, thanks, for the tutelage and stuff."

"Sure thing," Daisey replies. "I'll see you around, newbie."

I wave goodbye and head off toward the bowling alley, wincing as I put weight on my ankle. It's gotten a lot better over the last year, only hurting badly when I land on it wrong. My doctor said it was okay for me to work, but I have a feeling I'll need an ice pack by the end of my shift. I grit my teeth and keep walking.

I'm used to pushing through pain—I've been doing that for years, pushing through sprained ankles and pulled muscles. Ice and heat and ibuprofen all to make it through one more practice, one more game. But with this pain, there's no scored goal or winning game as a reward.

I shove my foot down with more force and squeeze my hands tight. The sharp pain shoots up my ankle all the way to my spine, pushing everything else out of focus.

The bowling alley double doors are automatic, so I have to slow my pace while they stutter to open. Once inside, the icy air-conditioning blasts me. Hot, cold, hot, cold. I wonder how many employees get sick each summer.

I spot an employee immediately, his back to me. He's a lean guy with medium-tan skin and pushed-back black hair. A tattoo crawls out of his Bonanza shirtsleeve.

"Hey. You." I walk up to him. "I need someone to train me."

He turns to me, and I feel a tug in my stomach as his dark eyes connect with mine. *Hot.* He's hot, in what I can already tell is an utterly self-satisfied way.

His lips quirk. "Hey. *You*," he responds, eyes flicking over me from head to toe. If I had to guess, he's a couple of years older than me. Boys who live with their parents don't look at girls like that.

I used to steer clear of boys entirely—not for lack of interest but lack of time. Soccer consumed my every waking hour. But after breaking my ankle, I found myself with a lot of spare hours and energy and no way to expend it. And it turns out, making out with a string of guys can really pass the time.

It never went far with any of them, not to something more physical, not to something more emotional. I didn't *want* any of it to get serious. So I went for guys with superior attitudes and guys with video-game addictions and guys who had too many girls with first names only in their contacts list. I went for guys who had no more interest in me than I had in them.

"I'm Patrick," the guy in front of me says now. "Patrick Cho."

I stick out my hand. "Hannah Klein."

He closes his hand around mine, fingers lingering a second longer than necessary as he replies, "I'd be happy to train you, Hannah."

"Great." I take half a step closer to him. "Let's do it, then."

He laughs, eyes sparking. Then he nods toward the front counter in a motion for me to follow him. "How old are you?" he asks.

It's a bit of a creepy question to ask right out of the gate, but honestly, I'm glad he's getting to the point.

"Eighteen in the fall," I answer. "You?"

"Nineteen in the fall." His eyes flick over me again as he answers, a bit more interest in them this time. A smile tugs at my lips. Only a one-year age gap. Nice.

I'm positive he's thinking the same thing, and suddenly Daisey's description of the *wild* employees is making a lot more sense. With a rotating staff of more than one hundred people, I'm sure things can get more than a little incestuous at Bonanza. I need to keep it in line this summer, but I don't think I'd mind falling into something lightly irresponsible with Patrick Cho.

Patrick actually does a good job with training, showing me how to work the register, how to clean the shoes, and how to assign lanes so fights don't break out. *"Never* put the Birdies next to the Highnesses," he tells me, talking about two of the early-bird-special women's bowling teams. "Putting them next to each other is a guaranteed way to start a catfight."

"'Catfight' is a sexist term," I tell him.

"You're some kind of feminist, huh?" Patrick asks. He steps closer to me so his hip presses against mine behind the counter, just for a moment, before moving away. "Maybe you'll have to teach me about it."

"I am a feminist," I tell him, leaning forward so our hips touch again. "But I can think of better things to do with my time than teaching you the ideology."

His eyes flash as I move away to ring up a new customer. "I like where your head is at."

I shrug and shoot him a quick smile, then turn my focus to the customer and the archaic, but thankfully easy to use, cash register. I feel Patrick's eyes settle on me as I work, and I adjust my posture under his gaze. The guy might not be Prince Charming, but here's the thing: I don't have to actually like someone to want their mouth on mine.

To be honest, it seems as good a way as any to spend my time this summer.

Last Summer

"I think we're going to do it," Brie tells me. She sits up in my bed and hugs a pillow to her chest. Her pink Adidas are on my floor, along with her backpack, water bottle, and keys, flung to the ground like they would be in the comfort of her own room. Brie and I share habitats with ease, best-friend symbiosis.

It's dark outside, stars in the sky and crickets chirping. Figgy, my family's giant Saint Bernard, is curled up on the floor by my feet, snoozing soundly against me. I reach down and pet her soft fur. It takes me a second to process Brie's words because my mind is still on how I messed up a drill at this morning's practice. My timing was all off. I should know better by now.

I look away from dozing Figgy and up at Brie's nervous eyes. She has a fingernail in her mouth, the yellow polish almost entirely nibbled off. "Like it, it?" I ask. "Like sex."

"Yes." Brie nods. "Sex." She says the word like she's testing it out. After a short breath, she clarifies, "I think I'm going to have sex with Cody."

"Oh," I say, brain whirring.

It's strange, the feeling that Brie is outpacing me, especially because nothing about this should be a competition. And yet, Brie is about to have sex, and I've never even had a boyfriend. I've only ever had two kisses. One at a bar mitzvah party, when I was too young for it to really count, and one last year on the beach. We had just won a tournament in Daytona, and I locked lips with a shaggy-haired boy playing Frisbee. It was fine.

I'm not jealous—I don't think. Just uncomfortable. And uncomfortable at being uncomfortable. And honestly, I don't even understand how Brie has *time* for boys. With our soccer schedule, I barely have time to eat and sleep. When your heart is set on the Olympics, there's not much wiggle room for extracurriculars.

But somehow Brie found time, found a boy. They've been dating for five months now, and I've nodded along to every advancement in their physical interactions and have tried to say the right things . . . but it's hard to invest in something I can't relate to.

"I'm nervous," Brie admits, eyes vulnerable.

I remember then our first day of sixth grade. I, always confident on the field, hesitated at the double doors of Maplewood Middle School. I could feel my heart beat in my throat as kids swarmed inside. Older kids. Older kids who knew things I didn't and could make fun of me for it. I was at the bottom of the food chain when I was used to being at the top.

But then Brie slung an arm around my shoulder and pulled me close and said, "Hey, you've got this. I'm here for you."

And I knew she was right. And all those nerves went away.

I lean forward now and soften my voice. "Hey, you've got this. If you want to have sex, have sex. If you don't want to, that's okay too. I'm sure Cody will wait. He's, um, really nice."

To be completely honest, I've never understood the appeal of Cody. He's always sighing, like the weight of the world is resting on his giant, football-player shoulders. His jokes are never funny. And he doesn't even try to cover his mouth when he burps. But Brie likes him, and that's what matters.

"I know he'd wait," Brie agrees. "I wouldn't be with him otherwise. But I want to do it."

"Then do!"

Brie laughs and shoves her face in her hands. "Ugh. I'm being ridiculous, I know. I'll shut up about it all."

"You're not being ridiculous," I say. "We can talk about it more if you want."

Brie shakes her head. "It's fine. Really."

I glance down at my watch. It's late. I'm exhausted. But I still wish we'd practiced longer. My mind goes back to the drill from this morning. I need to put in more hours. The game against Kensington is coming up, and we have to win. I have to win.

"Thanks for listening," Brie tells me.

Maybe I can squeeze in an extra hour tomorrow morning before practice with the team. The field should be empty.

I pet Figgy again and tell Brie, "Always."

Chapter Three

I'VE DECIDED I definitely want Patrick's mouth on my mouth. The more I look at him, the more attractive he gets. It's like a magic trick. Now you see him, now you see him, and he's even hotter. His little amused lip-quirk makes me want to pounce.

"You good at bowling?" he asks me.

We're cleaning up the alley, picking up discarded trash, mostly cups and chip bags but disturbingly a condom wrapper as well. I use a napkin to pick that up.

I shrug. "Okay, I guess."

I haven't bowled in years. But I guess I have a natural ability with most sports. I'm comfortable with a clear objective: score a goal, knock down pins, run faster than the person next to you.

Sports have rules and regulations and boundaries and

score cards. You know the exact parameters and what you have to do to get better. You know everyone around you wants the same thing, and that makes it exciting, exhilarating—

My jaw tenses, and I yank a full trash bag out of its can.

"Damn," Patrick says. "You've got some muscles on you. Those are thirty-gallon bags."

"You should see her carry groceries into the house, three bags in one go," a familiar voice cuts in. "Heavy ones too. I'm talking cans of black beans and jars of pasta sauce."

Patrick and I turn around, and that's when I find myself face-to-face with Ethan Alderman, my brother's best friend.

But something catches in my throat as I take him in.

Um. Whoa.

Ethan . . . Ethan looks . . . *different.*

He is no longer a string bean with a Shaggy-from-*Scooby-Doo* hairstyle. It's been almost a year since I last saw him, and in that time, Ethan seems to have shot up a few inches, cut his mop of hair into a cleaner style, one where you can actually see his light brown eyes, and he's accrued muscles, muscles that noticeably fill out the sleeves of his Bonanza T-shirt. The overall effect is disarming in a way that makes heat rise to my cheeks. I'm not used to looking at my younger brother's friend in any sort of light other than *guy around my house who also likes crunchy peanut butter on his PB&Js.*

"Hey, Hannah," he says to me, his voice soft.

Ethan has always spoken softly, but now his quiet voice almost sounds sensu—

"You two know each other?" Patrick asks, his eyes flicking between us as he tries to figure out the relationship.

"Yeah, this is Joey's older sister," Ethan answers.

Patrick looks confused at first but then nods. "Right, Joey. Whirly-ball kid." Patrick's lapse of recognition throws me. Joey's primary life function is being the center of attention, so I'm surprised he hasn't made more of an impact on Patrick. I guess it is a big workplace. "Cool, cool." Patrick runs a hand through his hair. Again. Patrick has tousled his hair approximately ten times since I've met him. I'd bet twenty bucks his conditioner costs more money than mine.

I nod. "Yep. Cool."

We're all silent for a moment. Even though I'm looking away, I can feel Ethan's eyes searching my face. My skin itches under the quiet scrutiny.

Patrick breaks the silence. "Well, I was just showing Hannah around, but my shift ends in a few minutes. Want to take over, Evan?"

"Ethan," he corrects, his voice still quiet but sure.

"Yeah, right, of course." Patrick gives a wide grin. "Sorry, man." He then turns to look directly at me. He seems to be attempting a smolder with his dark eyes, and I have to admit it's kind of working. They are very nice eyes.

"*Hannah*, it was awesome meeting you. Looking forward to . . . getting to know you this summer."

I swear Ethan coughs behind us.

"Same here," I say, smiling at him.

Patrick gives me a quick wink before walking away. When I turn back to Ethan, he's standing with his thumbs tucked into the pockets of his jeans. Ethan has always been comfortable in silence, happy to stand by while Joey runs the show. With some people, silence is awkward, but I've known Ethan too long to feel anything but comfortable around him, even the new him with the muscles and the height and the haircut that makes the planes of his face, well, striking, to be honest.

Oy vey.

Striking?

What is wrong with me? Ethan is my *younger brother's* best friend.

I clear my throat and nod. "Hey, Ethan. How have you been?"

Good. Nice, normal conversation from wise older-sister figure.

Ethan glances behind us as Patrick leaves through the automatic doors. I notice his white skin is slightly tanner than last summer and wonder if he ever works on the mini-golf course with Brie.

○ ○ ○ **29** ○ ○ ○

When he turns back to me, he says, "Patrick's kind of a douche. Just so you know."

"He seems all right," I reply.

Ethan shrugs. "I guess we all have different definitions of 'all right.'"

I raise an eyebrow. Combative words from Ethan Alderman. The guy is about as aggressive as a Labrador retriever puppy.

"Noted," I say. "Don't worry. I can handle myself."

"I know," Ethan agrees, then asks, "When did you get back?"

I hesitate. Unfortunately, the question *When did you get back?* leads to things I don't want to talk about. Instead of answering, I haul the trash bag over my shoulder and ask, "Where do I dump this stuff?"

Ethan, bless him, accepts my evasion. "I'll show you."

We walk through the bowling alley in companionable silence. It's late afternoon now, and the crowd has shifted from senior citizen to preteen, sodas and soft pretzels and awkward groupings of people with giggles ricocheting all around.

We stop at another overflowing trash can. Ethan hoists out the heavy bag. Despite Patrick's compliment, my muscles aren't what they used to be. At Mountain Bliss, yoga for beginners kept me from regressing to a state of complete inactivity, but it didn't compare to hours of weightlifting in the gym, muscles burning as Brie kept a steady diet of Lizzo and Cardi B pumping from our speakers.

Before Ethan ties up the garbage, he pulls a few plastic bottles off the top and tosses them into a second bag. "Recycling," he explains. "Every little bit helps, right?"

I smile. "Definitely."

He replaces the liner. "We have to change these things every couple of hours. Humans are great at trashing up the planet."

"I should do more than use a reusable water bottle," I reply.

"Well there's plenty of opportunity at Bonanza. Detritus everywhere."

I laugh. "Detritus?"

Ethan's cheeks heat, his head ducking down. "My mom got me a word-of-the-day calendar for the SATs."

"Way to go, Judith."

Ethan and I hoist up our respective bags and walk toward the back entrance. "Are you going to enter the tournament?" he asks.

"What tournament?"

He raises an eyebrow. "Wow, I'm surprised you haven't heard of it yet. Joey never stops talking about it. Every year the employees put on this massive tournament called the Bonanza Olympics, and—"

I stiffen, anxiety suddenly pulsing through me. Ethan notices and stops talking.

My body flushes, embarrassed to be triggered by a single word.

It was probably silly even thinking I could make the Olympic team in the first place. That's what I tell myself. It was a young girl's fantasy, like how other people dream of their acceptance speech for best actress.

But—

It wasn't silly. Not really. I was good. I was *excellent*. The best my coach had seen in years, she said. "On my list," that scout from USC said. And, of course, the Olympics are in my genes. If I stayed on course, it was possible. I had a chance. More than a chance, and then—

"I'm sorry," Ethan says. His genuine tone cuts like a knife.

"Shut up," I reply, whipping out the words as a defense.

Ethan's eyes flash with hurt.

Panic builds in my throat. Quickly, I correct what I said. "No, not like that. I didn't mean you need to shut up. I mean shut up as in, you don't have to apologize. You didn't do anything. I'm sorry. Tell me more about the tournament, okay?"

To his credit, Ethan doesn't hesitate. As we walk, he launches into all the details. His voice is slow and calm, like the water that runs through the small creek in our backyard. I feel the tension release from my muscles as he tells me about all the competitions—mini golf, bowling, arcade games, laser tag, and so on. And how almost all the employees participate, some in just one category and others in all of them. And then at the end of summer, at the closing ceremonies, because apparently they have *closing ceremonies*, the one person with the most medals is deemed the Bonanza Champion and gets unlimited free concessions for the next year.

"Jesse Simons went through so many platters of free nachos that even the mention of artificial cheese makes her vomit now, so beware of that if you win," Ethan advises, opening the door to the back alley. The bright sun peeks through. He keeps the door open for me to step outside first, and as I do, I fully notice how tall he is now. Last year, we were about the same height. Maybe he had an inch on me. Now my eyeline lands right around his Adam's apple. I swallow hard, then avert my gaze to his silver mezuzah necklace.

"Um, who gave you the necklace?" I ask. "I can't remember."

Ethan follows me out into the alley. The sun is high in the sky, and as Ethan pulls open the top of the dumpster, a rancid smell fills the air. Gross.

"My grandmother," he answers. "For my bar mitzvah."

I remember her. An image of a slight woman in a shimmery gold suit crosses before my vision.

And then, an image of my own bubbie. Her eyes, smiling and crinkled at the edges; her hot-pink cane, special-ordered from a local artist; her kitchen, brimming with the scent of brisket, roasted potatoes, and onions. My step falters. I miss her, an unbearable amount. The thought of her absence makes my muscles ache.

I think we all get one person on this earth who truly understands us, one person who sees us fully as we are, our deepest dreams and greatest fears in plain sight. For me, that person was my bubbie. I had my soul mate for sixteen years. And then she was gone. And I know that no one will understand me like that ever again.

"Hannah?" Ethan asks.

His eyes are on me. I swallow hard, trying to force away the painful thoughts. "Yeah?"

"I seem to be saying a lot of wrong things today," he says.

I shake my head. "It's not you. It's me."

He smiles. It's a small smile, but it hits his eyes in a way that brightens his entire face. "You breaking up with me, Hannah Klein?"

Wait.

Was that—

Is Ethan flirting with me?

Obviously, the intense sunlight and rancid garbage smell is messing with my thoughts, because Ethan Alderman, my brother's best friend, the kid who spent an entire weekend with my brother re-creating the *Stranger Things* theme music using only a kazoo and kitchen utensils, certainly cannot be flirting with me. Absolutely not.

"Anyways." I heft up my garbage bag and toss it into the dumpster. "The tournament. Sounds, um, interesting I guess, but I'm just here to work. Get a paycheck and all that. I'm not signing up for any extracurriculars." I glance around. "This place has a light cult vibe, you know?"

Ethan laughs as he throws in his own bag of trash. "That's not an inaccurate description."

I gesture to the dumpster. "Can we close this thing now?"

Ethan's nose crinkles. "Yeah, trash duty is the worst. Well, after vomit duty."

"Yikes."

"Exactly."

Silence passes over us as Ethan closes the dumpster and we walk back toward the door. And in that silence, my thoughts turn inward again, and I think of my bubbie, of how desperately I wish I could have one more day with her, and I think of my ankle, of how I'll never play soccer again, and I think of Brie, of how my best friend is so physically close to me and yet we've never been further apart.

"I'll show you how to fix the pins when they get stuck, okay?" Ethan asks.

It's hard to imagine that these things will ever be okay. It's hard to imagine that I will ever be okay.

"Sure," I tell Ethan, and follow him back inside.

The air-conditioning blasts us, and I shiver.

Last Summer

Crickets chirp as I slide out of my car. Night presses in, dark and heavy. I open the back door for Figgy, and she hops out, tail wagging. After practice, I swung by home to pick her up. I let us into Bubbie's house with my spare key and call out, "Sorry! Practice went long!"

"You're shvitzing all over my home," Bubbie says as I walk into the kitchen. She's at the table, wearing her favorite pink silk bathrobe and gold-chain glasses. A mug of chamomile tea and today's crossword puzzle sit in front of her. "So. Practice went long?" she asks with a pointed look. "Or you made practice go long?"

Bubbie knows me better than anyone. "The latter," I admit.

I convinced the team to run an hour of extra drills after Coach left. My muscles feel like jelly.

Bubbie smiles with approval. "That's my girl." Figgy gives a tiny bark. "And my other girl. Come here, sweetie."

Figgy pads over, and Bubbie slips her a dog treat from god knows where. Figgy rubs against her knees, then settles by her feet.

"The game against Kensington is coming up," I say, sitting down at the table. My fingers twist together.

We play Kensington, our local rivals, every year in a summer scrimmage. It always sets a precedent for the year. Win the scrimmage, win the season.

"I believe in you," Bubbie says. "Hard work and talent. The perfect recipe."

My bubbie understands my Olympic dreams more than anyone because my bubbie was an Olympian. A cross-country skier.

I've made her tell me her Olympics stories so many times they practically feel like my own. As a little girl, I'd spend hours tracing my fingers over her bronze medal. It felt like a portal into another world. And there's a picture of her on the podium. It's grainy, obscured even more by the snow falling in big flakes that day. But Bubbie's smile shines through—radiant and proud.

Bubbie is a champion. One day, if I'm lucky, I'll have my own podium photo taken. And I'll put our pictures side by side on my mantel.

"Mamaleh." I look up and meet Bubbie's eyes. They're dark blue and can see right through me. "You're thinking too hard. Turn that brain off. Come, we'll make babka. You'll be my assistant."

I watch as she struggles out of her chair, shooing away my

offer of help. Bubbie has weakened from her battle with cancer. She hates that term, "battle."

"Something about a battle insinuates that it's a fair fight, and there's not one fair thing about cancer," she says. But she's a tough lady and has been battling nonetheless.

She's made of different stuff than the rest of us, the kind of stuff that wins Olympic medals and builds tidy real-estate empires when it wasn't so easy for a woman to even own her own house. If any eighty-year-old woman can kick cancer, it's her.

I grab the heavy mixing bowl and various ingredients from the cabinets. Together, we measure and mix. Her hands are bony, her skin soft and as thin as paper. She allows me to knead the dough on my own with no protest, which is unusual for her. Instead, she carefully lowers herself back into a chair, then slips Figgy another treat. My thoughts drift to the Kensington game again.

Once the babka is in the oven, we move to the living room and settle into the couch. I inhale the scent of her perfume. She has a whole tray of perfumes up in her bedroom. Glass bottles, some opaque, some shiny, some with tassels, and some with gold pumps. This one smells like spice, a mix of cloves and cinnamon.

I lean closer to Bubbie and say, "Tell me a story."

"What kind of story, mamaleh?" she asks.

"One of the old ones." I settle deeper into her, head tucked on her shoulder. "Of when you were a girl."

Chapter Four

I'M EXHAUSTED WHEN I get home from work. I used to have endurance. I used to run for hours. When I expended energy, it felt like I was creating *more* energy—a frenetic ball that built on itself over and over again.

But now it's like someone cut my power. And working at Bonanza is no joke. Six hours of hauling trash, wrangling kids, and scrubbing counters has left my body aching for bed.

I feel *old*.

Ethan continued my bowling alley training for another hour, but then I decided to try out one more station before the end of my shift, for a well-rounded education. And, well, because I was uncomfortable with the heat that crept to my cheeks every time Ethan gave me a sideways smile.

I went to the concession stands, figuring it was a safe

bet to stay clear of Brie since I'd be cordoned off into one small section of Bonanza. The staff in the kitchen was older, a middle-aged duo named Gary and Sherry. They told me they're *sick of showing youngsters the ropes and they're running the kitchen their way, so I'd better fall in line, ya hear?*

I didn't mind falling in line under Gary and Sherry. I passed the rest of the afternoon in the loud buzz of their chatter (topics ranging everywhere from politics to the best brand of kitty litter to gossip about other employees) and the most menial tasks in the kitchen that apparently *even a fresh-legged newbie like you can't screw up too bad,* which mostly meant refilling the condiment trays and wiping down the counters so often that the scent of bleach overpowered the scent of lukewarm corn dogs and greasy grilled cheese.

At the end of my shift, I swung by Pete's office once more as he'd requested, and he handed me a shift calendar for the next two weeks, of which I'd be working almost every day.

I slip out of my car now and wince as I land on my ankle. My parents are home. They're always home by five thirty, working true nine-to-five jobs with titles so vague I'm still not sure exactly what they do each day, something about accounts and accounts management. They met in college and married five months after graduation at Dad's parents' ranch home. There's this one photo with my grandfather's old chestnut mare nudging its nose into the remnants of the wedding cake and my parents laughing hysterically. Now, I barely recognize them in that picture—they seem so young and carefree, not at all stressed about the well-being of their seventeen-year-old daughter.

I sigh and head into the house. Figgy hears me and rushes over with a wagging tail. I missed her so much last year. I give her a tight hug and some good pats. Her scent unwinds the tension from my shoulders. "Sweet, gentle giant," I murmur into her fur. Another year at Mountain Bliss would mean another year without Figgy, and what's the point of existence without this fluffy angel?

My parents are waiting for me in the kitchen, our first family dinner in ages. Joey is still at work, but I'm expected to be at the table at six o'clock to eat Dad's famous chicken enchiladas and talk about my day. I do miss his enchiladas. The man can cook.

Mom's eyes light up when she sees me. My mom is beautiful. She's one of those people who makes other people stop in their tracks in the midst of their menial errands at the grocery store or the post office. She inherited Bubbie's dark blue eyes and thick auburn hair. And her huge smile is a copy of her father's smile. He passed away when I was little. It radiates warmth and makes you want to do favors for her. Like a Julia Roberts–level smile. Joey inherited that smile, and I think it's one of the reasons everyone loves him so much. It's impossible not to be drawn to them.

Mom knows she's pretty. Not in an obnoxious way. She just knows the effect she has on people. She watched Dad work up the nerve for two months to ask her out, watched his pencil tap his desk and his eyes flick over to—and then quickly away from—her, time and time again. After two months, she'd had enough. She stood right in front of his desk after class and stated, "We're going to dinner tomorrow night. And you're borrowing my class notes. I don't think you've paid attention to a single word the professor has said all semester."

She was right. And he was grateful—for the notes, but mostly for the date.

They've been together ever since.

Not that Dad is unattractive. He's tall and has eyes that crinkle when he laughs, and his voice has the pleasant tone of an NPR reporter.

"How was your first day?" Mom asks me now. "Did you work with Joey?"

"Uh, no, we actually didn't." I shrug. "He didn't start until later, and it's a big place."

Mom keeps looking at me. It takes me a second to realize I didn't answer her first question. "Um, my first day was fine. Good! The manager is . . . nice."

"There's my verbose daughter," Dad says. "The detail you gave . . . extraordinary . . . titillating!"

Joey might have gotten his smile from Mom, but he definitely got his penchant for turning everything into a joke from Dad. Still, I'm grateful to have the corny jokes. I knew things were bad last year when Dad stopped using humor to break the tension.

I give him a *ha-ha* smile and sit at the table. Dad takes the giant tray of enchiladas out of the oven. He has a bit of Jewish mother syndrome when it comes to feeding his family. More is just enough and less is unacceptable. The heavenly smell wafts toward me. My lunch today was a burnt grilled cheese and a bag of off-brand barbecue chips. The grilled cheese was free, a ruined customer order. The barbecue chips will dock seventy-five cents from my pay. "Don't you go ruining food on purpose," Gary said when he slid me the burnt sandwich. "We'll know, and we'll report you to Pete."

I don't really see Pete as a strict authoritarian figure, but I'm also not looking to get fired over a grilled cheese that tastes like plastic.

Dad places the enchiladas on the table. Figgy plops down next to my chair and is asleep in seconds, probably on her tenth nap of the day. Good life that dog leads. Usually Joey would sit on my right, and without him here, I feel like I'm in trouble. Well, I *am* in trouble. I suppose that's just my constant state of existence now. Guilt tugs at me. I hate everything I put my parents through. I wish I could make it all go away.

I pick up my fork. "Looks good," I say. "Really good. Thanks."

"So, tell us more about work," Mom prods.

Pre-injury, I never talked much at dinner. I didn't have to. My parents and Joey ran the show with fast-paced banter about their days. It was my job to laugh at appropriate moments, scarf down my food, and then collapse into bed.

But now, I'm center stage. Observed. It makes my skin itch.

"Well, my coworkers seem . . . nice." I think of Brie and how there's nothing nice about working with my ex–best friend. I think of Patrick and how my parents would certainly think there's nothing nice about the way he was eyeing me. "Um, I liked working at the bowling alley. It was cool."

"That's wonderful," Mom says. She gives a smile of encouragement, but I can see the strain tugging at the corner of her lips, the worry in her eyes. She glances at Dad. I can hear their unspoken words.

Do you think we brought her home too soon, David?

We won't know until we know, Sarah.

Dad clears his throat and turns back to me. His smile is strained as well. "Were you able to do your good deed today?"

My stomach knots. In the chaos of my first day at Bonanza, I didn't have time to think about my checklist.

Technically, my return home is temporary. I have to complete a list of tasks this summer, or it's straight back to Mountain Bliss. One of the top items is to perform a positive action every day, something to put a little good into the world.

I swirl enchilada sauce on my plate. "Um, I'm sorry. I forgot. But I'll do it tomorrow. I'll do two tomorrow. I promise."

"It's important," Mom says, her tone soft, hesitant. "Your dad and I are so happy to have you home. But we need to see you working on that list. We're here to help, if you want."

Guilt swirls through me. They shouldn't have to tiptoe around me like this. They shouldn't have to worry about me. I've added stress lines to their smooth skin.

"I'm on it." I nod. "Promise."

I glance at our fridge. The list is held up by a World of Coca-Cola magnet.

Mountain Bliss Home Rehabilitation:
1. Clean out all drug and alcohol paraphernalia
2. Perform one good deed per day
3. Repair mismanaged relationships
4. Find a passion that brings joy

Number three makes my eyes roll. "Mismanaged relationships" sure is an interesting way to describe absolutely annihilated friendships. It makes my falling-out with Brie sound like a tax form issue.

And number four, a passion that brings joy, is impossible. I *had* a passion, soccer, and that's gone now. Nothing can hold a candle to that joy—to the feeling of my cleats breaking fresh grass, my eyes searching for an opening, being completely in sync with my team, the perfect pass, the perfect score. Wins so sweet they tasted like honey on my tongue.

But I have to show my parents I'm making an effort so I can stay home. Maybe if I do enough positive actions and help out around the house, they'll overlook the rest.

"I'll do the dishes," I offer. "To make up for today."

Mom smiles. "That's wonderful."

"Thanks, sweetheart," Dad says.

I let out a tiny exhale of relief, but then Mom's expression grows anxious again. "And we just wanted to remind you . . . ," she says. "Bubbie's unveiling is coming up in a few weeks, so you'll need to request off work that day."

I swallow back a sick feeling in my throat. It can't be that soon. She was just here. I swear if I drove over to her house right now, she'd be there waiting for me with fresh-baked babka and a treat for Figgy.

But that's not true. Her house was emptied, then sold,

her most prized possessions sorted into her children's homes and storage.

It's a Jewish tradition to unveil the gravestone eleven months after the burial, which means my bubbie has been gone for almost a year.

She was just here.

"Okay." I swallow hard. "I'll, um, make sure I'm not working then."

Silence passes between us. I can tell Mom wants to say something more, and I can tell Dad is uncomfortable, his hands furling and unfurling his napkin. He breaks first and asks, "How are the enchiladas? Cooked enough? Want to make sure those chickens aren't still clucking!"

The joke isn't funny, but Mom and I laugh anyway.

I clean the dishes and then take a long, hot shower. Afterward, I pad barefoot and towel-clad into my room. At Mountain Bliss, I wore flip-flops in the communal showers to avoid foot fungus and then yanked on the bare minimum of clothes (underwear, oversize T-shirt) in the humid stall before walking to the room I shared with three other girls. I missed flopping onto clean sheets in only my towel, a simple, perfect pleasure. Soccer has made me comfortable with a certain level of nudity around girls, but those are girls I know well, not a rotating cast of delinquent teens, some staying no longer than three days before calling their parents in tears over the "harsh" conditions of Mountain Bliss, like our generic conditioner instead of their favorite salon brand.

Mountain Bliss wasn't cheap. Most of the girls came from wealthy families. My parents refused to tell me how much they spent, but I know the cost was way outside of their yearly budget. I need to complete that checklist so my parents have no need to send me back and waste more of their hard-earned money.

I glance at my phone. I still have a habit of checking for texts even though my social status has gone into remission. I'm surprised to find one message. It's from my teammate Elizabeth. The sight of her name makes my pulse race. It reads: Is it true you're back home?

I haven't talked to her since I left the hospital. My last message to her read: I don't know. Thanks for the flowers.

She sent more than a dozen messages after that. Other girls from the team have sent messages as well. In the beginning it was "I'm so sorry" and "How are you?" and then it was "Where are you?" and "I'm worried," and then it was a lot of nothing. Elizabeth tried the most before giving up in the face of my silence.

I couldn't reply. It was too painful thinking of them playing without me. My entire world was on that field. Those summer nights with my team were the best times of my life. I'll never have that again.

My heart squeezes as I stare at the text from Elizabeth.

Then my phone buzzes again. It's a new number: Hey newbie, how's your night going?

I narrow my eyes. Who could this be?

Another text comes in: Got your number from the employee list, it's Patrick Cho

My cheeks warm. Patrick, with his lean arms and easy smirk, was thinking about me enough to look up my number and text me.

Okay. So. My standards for effort might be pretty low. But it's nice to know that someone, anyone, is thinking of me in not a negative way, and it's nice that such a nice-looking boy is doing so, and it's especially nice that Patrick knows nothing about the last year of my life.

I ignore Elizabeth's message and text back instead.

Hey! Night is going well. How about yours?

Patrick: Would be better with you here

Okay, then, Patrick. Straight to the point.

Patrick: Want to hang out?

Me: Tonight?

Patrick: Yeah, people are chilling at Sophie's house. You meet her today?

Sophie must be another Bonanza employee. Before I can respond, Patrick texts again: Come on, join us, it'll be fun ☺

I chew on my lip. He really had to go and throw an emoji in there.

It *could* be fun. A group of people who know nothing about me. A cute boy who likes me enough to think about me when he's with that group of people. I could drink a beer and kiss him and forget for a few hours that my life isn't a complete mess.

But it's late. I can hear my parents' muffled voices in the hallway. No way would I be allowed to go out right now, and I'm not going to pull an old Hannah and slip out the window. I have to stay on the straight-and-narrow, and that means no sneaking out of the house to hang out with a boy I met mere hours ago.

I text back: Maybe another time. Have fun. See you at work!

Patrick sends a sad-face emoji, and we leave the conversation at that.

I finally get dressed, pulling on a pair of shorts and a plain T-shirt. My drawers are bare, all my soccer gear thrown out last year in a rage, shoved into garbage bags and left outside of Goodwill. I half-heartedly run a brush through my hair. I had a girl at Mountain Bliss hack the bulk of it off with a pair of kitchen scissors. She actually did a nice job. Wavy pieces fall just above my shoulders.

I turn to face my room, ready to cross item one off my checklist. I'm not expecting to find much paraphernalia, but as I go through my things, I discover a flask of honey whiskey and a loose joint in my old purse. And a few lighters in jeans pockets and one in my nightstand. And then an airplane bottle of vodka inside a jacket pocket, which reminds me I hid two joints under the soles of my sneakers in case we got pulled over. Plus a couple of loose pills someone passed me at a party that I never even considered taking—yet also never threw away.

At the end of it all, there's quite a collection spread out on my bed, much more than I thought. Especially considering all the easier-to-find items my parents already threw away. I chew the inside of my cheek.

I don't want to be that girl.

Am I that girl?

A knock on my door startles me. It opens before I have a chance to react, but I sag in relief when I see it's just my brother, Joey. His nest of golden-brown curls pops into my room.

He grins at me, still wearing his blue Bonanza T-shirt. "Hey, big sis."

"Hey, li'l bro."

Unlike with Ethan, I didn't go a whole year without seeing my brother. He drove up with my parents on family visitation weekends. It was weird at first, showing them around campus and introducing them to roommates I'd never talk to again. But Joey being Joey lightened the mood in an instant, playing tour guide like *he* was the one living at Mountain Bliss, showing us all around with made-up commentary about the accommodations and programming. It was comforting to know something had stayed the same, that he was at least the same brother I've always known.

"What time's your shift tomorrow?" he asks me now. I realize he's had a growth spurt, just an inch or so, but his face also looks older, his cheeks less red and round.

"Four," I answer.

"Nice, same." He nods. "Bet Pete did that on purpose. He's good with stuff like that. We can drive together."

"Cool." Silence beats between us for a few seconds, and that's when Joey's eyes slide to my bed. Unease washes over me as his expression wavers. He looks worried, maybe hurt, as well.

"I'm throwing it all away," I quickly say. "Just some dumb stuff from last summer."

"Right." Joey nods. "Cool."

He hesitates, as if he might leave. The loneliness hovering over me grows like a heavy weight. "How was work today?" I blurt out.

The beautiful thing about my brother is that he can talk for twenty minutes straight without a single contribution from anyone else. Some might also call that an annoying thing about my brother, but he's such a good storyteller, most people don't mind.

I relax as Joey enters my room. I sweep all the paraphernalia into my trash can and tie up the bag, and Joey hops onto my bed. I sit by my window, and we toss a hacky sack back and forth as he tells me about his day at Bonanza, which apparently involved *three* whirly-ball birthday parties.

But the climactic moment of the day happened in the arcade when someone finally scored the step-counter watch out of the claw machine. Apparently, it's worth all of twenty bucks, but people were trying to get it for weeks. "Pete might be a simple man," Joey says, "but he's got claw-machine skills. Positioned that step counter in the sweet spot. Looked getable but efforts were foiled for so many."

I laugh, but it's a bit weak. I'm exhausted from today, my mind weighed down with heavy thoughts.

"You know I hate a fake laugh," Joey says.

"It wasn't fake," I argue. He gives me a look. "Oh, whatever."

His smile slips, concern in his eyes. "Mom told me the unveiling is coming up." He pauses. "I miss Bubbie."

"Yeah." My muscles tighten. "Me too."

"Remember when she used to check us out of school early?" he asks. "When we were little? She'd take us for ice cream and—"

Something catches in my throat, and I look out my window into the night sky. Dark branches sway in the wind. Of course I remember. She'd always get caramel sauce on her ice cream and order extra cherries for us. We'd hold competitions to see who could finish eating first. Joey always got brain freeze.

Tears threaten, but I tense my jaw and force them away. I steady my voice and say, "I'm sorry, Joey. It's been a long day. I think I'm ready for bed."

I can feel him staring at me, but I keep my eyes on the window. He throws the hacky sack in the air once more and lets it land on the bed. "Okay," he says.

When he leaves my room, I feel more alone than ever. Before I can do something stupid, I grab the trash bag and toss it in the container outside.

Last Summer

I'm sweating like a pig when I walk into the house after practice. Joey and Ethan are sprawled out on the living room floor, playing video games. I'm pretty sure there's a picture of them as eight-year-olds in the exact same position.

They hit pause and both turn to look at me.

"Jeez, Hannah," Joey says. "Is it raining outside?"

"Ha-ha," I reply.

Ethan gives me a little *Oh, Joey* eye-roll. He's already in his pj's, blue-and-green flannel pants and a school shirt. "Good practice?" he asks.

I shrug. "Fine."

Truthfully, my muscles are tight with nerves. The Kensington game is fast approaching, and my team isn't pushing hard enough. I managed to wrangle half of them into staying late tonight. We ran sprints and went over plays for an extra hour until

Nina told me, "Girl, it's enough," and even Brie said, "When you feel like your legs are going to fall off, that's a sign you should stop."

I just want to be prepared. I want to win. But they're probably right. My muscles are completely fatigued, and my left ankle is throbbing, pushing too hard on an old injury. I need to ice it.

"I saw Bubbie today," Joey tells me. "We were supposed to go shopping, but she was too tired, so we watched a movie."

"Cool." I nod. "I'm gonna shower."

Twenty minutes later, I'm in clean pj's and scavenging through the kitchen for sustenance. I gather an impressive amount in my arms–two cold slices of Dad's homemade veggie pizza, a bag of carrot sticks, a container of hummus, a Snickers bar Mom tried to hide in the back of the pantry, and a family-size bag of Doritos–and then head into the living room, where Ethan and Joey are still playing their game and cursing at various volumes (Joey, loud, earth-shattering; Ethan, quiet, tense). The second I open the chip bag, they pause the game and turn to me, staring like they didn't eat half a pizza each earlier.

I laugh. "Fine, I'll share. Y'all are worse than the dog."

Figgy whines at that.

They both climb onto the couch, Joey close, holding out his hands and begging with Pixar-character eyes. Ethan sits farther away, scooched to the edge of the three-seater. "Thank you for the personal space," I tell him. "I'm assuming you would also like some chips."

He smiles, cheeks pink as he holds out his hands. "Yes, please."

"Look at his manners," I tell Joey. "You could learn a thing or two."

"Could you sound more like a Jewish mother?" Joey replies.

I swat him with a pillow. He steals the chip bag. Figgy jumps onto the couch.

With her help, it only takes us ten minutes to get through the entire bag, which might be a record. Then Joey and Ethan pressure me into playing their game, even though I'm exhausted, and even though I don't understand the appeal of shooting aliens with paintballs. But I agree to one round and suddenly it's two hours later, and the rest of the snacks have been eaten, and we're all laughing, slap-happy, and overtired as a purple alien corners Ethan and tickles his character health down.

"This game is so disturbing," I say, gasping for breath.

Joey is in hysterics. "Can you believe it's kid-friendly for lack of violence?"

"There is nothing nonviolent about tickling," Ethan says solemnly.

We all laugh even harder.

Chapter Five

"ALWAYS PARK NEAR the back," Joey tells me as we pull into the Bonanza parking lot. It's late afternoon, but the sun is still bright in the sky. "Pete likes to save the good spots for the customers."

I nod. "Makes sense."

Things feel tense between us after last night, but I'm sure they'll go back to normal soon. I've always had a good relationship with Joey. He's so easygoing, surely even I can't mess things up too badly.

As we get out of the car, I go to pull my hair into a ponytail, but then I remember it's too short now. I fluff it instead.

Joey notices and lowers his voice to a baritone. "Hey, lady, trying to look good for someone?"

I smile at him. "Just keeping up the high family standard. I wouldn't want to embarrass you."

Joey holds a hand to his chest. "Thank you, that's appreciated." He clears his throat, voice now tinged with nerves. "Did you, uh, meet Tony yesterday?"

I shake my head. "No, who's Tony?" The name conjures an image of a burly man in his forties who likes protein powder and muscle shirts.

When Joey doesn't respond immediately, as is his typical response time, I look over at him and—

Oy vey. He looks like a stars-in-his-eyes cartoon character. My brother has got it bad.

He sighs dreamily and says, "Tony is the love of my life."

"Joey . . . and *Tony*," I clarify. "Are we sure this isn't a self-obsessing crush?"

"Our rhyming names are fate, not self-obsession," Joey answers. "Other than both being gay, Tony and I are very different. He is tall, I am not. He is muscular, I am not." *Sounds like I was right about the protein powder.* "Also— and this is very important." Joey turns to me and puts his hands on my shoulders so we're standing still in the middle of the parking lot and his eyes are locked in determination on mine. "He is, *unspeakably*, hot."

I laugh. "Great. Well, I'm very happy for you and your crush."

"Hannah, it's more than a crush. It's a way of life."

I let him go on about Tony for the rest of the walk,

grateful Joey is being Joey, ever enthusiastic whether it's about a crush or about the best brand of breakfast cereal (Honey Bunches of Oats).

My brother came out to our family when he was in eighth grade. He rushed out the reveal in one quick sentence and then stepped back and nervously eyed us. It was the least verbose he's ever been in his life. I of course was happy for him, and my parents were as well, but I'm sure it wasn't easy. I'm sure it was probably one of the scariest things ever, and I hoped he felt how much I cared in the giant hug I tackled him with afterward.

Since then, he's had a string of crushes. And one kind-of boyfriend in the ninth grade. They went to one dinner and two movies and had three awkward kisses, and one day when I asked Joey what happened to Ian since I hadn't heard his name for a while, Joey simply replied, "We had irreconcilable differences," and left it at that.

Later, while Joey was busy trying to beat his newest video game, Ethan found me slathering an apple with chunky peanut butter in the kitchen and said, "They broke up over Marvel characters. I kid you not, Hannah, apparently Ian said his favorite character was Iron Man, and Joey said, 'It's like you're a stranger to me. It's like I never even knew you at all,' and that was the end of their relationship."

Which does track. Ethan swiped the peanut butter from

me and dug out a giant serving with a fresh spoon, and we ate in companionable silence.

"Hannah, are you even listening to me?" Joey asks now as we walk through the main doors to Bonanza. The freezing air blasts us. I'm glad I brought a sweater today. Between the germs and temperature changes, I'm definitely going to catch a summer cold.

"Um, mostly?" I respond. He rolls his eyes. "Where should I start today? Maybe I'll just do the concessions again. . . ."

Joey's face shifts into a look of horror. "No way. You cannot get pulled into that dull vortex of doom. Nothing interesting *ever* happens in the kitchen. Give the arcade a shot. Tony is there most days. You'll get to see perfection personified."

"Nothing interesting" sounds just fine to me, but I concede and take Joey's advice. At least the arcade isn't mini golf. The employee schedule is listed online, and Brie is working again today. I'm hoping she'll stay in the same place, and I'll do my part by avoiding that place. I can't believe the chaos here sorts itself out without Pete assigning employees to certain areas, but Ethan told me yesterday that everything just falls into place. "It's like that cult thing," he explained. "We slowly become one living, breathing organism, functioning together with alarming adeptness."

"Sounds like a horror film," I told him.

"Well . . ." He trailed off with a shrug.

Joey heads to whirly ball, which is his part of the functioning organism, one of the highest stress and highest density little-kid jobs. I head into the arcade, which is quite busy as we're already approaching evening.

"Hey, you. Want a tour?" someone asks.

I look up to find Patrick in front of me. He's just as good-looking today, possibly even more so. His soft hair is pushed back, and his eyes have mischief in them as they sweep over at me.

I meet his gaze. "I'd love a tour. You offering?"

"Absolutely." Patrick leads us forward with his hand. "After you. The wonders of the arcade await."

We thread through the aisles of music and flashing lights together. The arcade feels smaller now that I'm an adult. When I was a kid, it was an endless horizon of games as far as the eye could see. Now I notice the exit signs and carpet stains and how outdated some of the machines look. As we walk, I ask Patrick, "How was the party?"

"Eh." He shrugs. "It was more of a hang than a party. Just like a dozen of us. You know, the crew. Hey, Tony."

Tony. My ears perk up. This must be Joey's crush.

Said crush is bent behind the back of the *Pac-Man* machine, fiddling with the wiring. After a moment, he puts down his pair of pliers, stands, and focuses on us. *Okay, then.* Joey was right. Tony is *tall* and *muscled* and very,

very hot. Muscles and cheekbones and that indefinable X factor that makes your pulse race. His skin is dark tan, and he's wearing a white Bonanza shirt in a size too small, likely so it can hug his muscles. Tony is a teenager but looks like he could be modeling for Calvin Klein. I have to admit: Joey has good taste.

"Hannah, this is my younger brother, Tony. Tony, new hire Hannah."

"Brother?" I ask, but as soon as the word leaves my mouth, I can see the similarities. Tony has closely cut hair and approximately double the muscle mass of Patrick, but they have the same smile, same eyes, and even similar mannerisms.

"Hey." Tony nods at me.

"Hey," I reply. "I'm Joey's older sister."

I wait for Tony's expression to shift at the mention of my brother, hopefully to interest, but there's barely a faint flicker of recognition. Weird. Joey makes an impact on everyone. I'm sure he'd be making strides with his crush. Maybe he's spent too much time cordoned off in whirly ball?

"Cool, cool," Tony says. "Nice to meet you, Hannah."

He extends his oversize hand for a shake. It dwarfs mine in a comical way. Tony definitely ate his Wheaties growing up. "You too," I say.

Tony's eyes shift to Patrick and crinkle. "So, this the girl you were telling me about?"

Patrick coughs, cheeks reddening. I bite back a smile as he mutters, "Asshole." He quickly turns back to me and claps his hands together. "Introduction complete. Let's finish your tour. See ya, Tony."

Tony laughs and goes back to *Pac-Man*.

Patrick shows me more machines, how to fix the card readers when they aren't working, how to sanitize all the alarmingly sticky surfaces. The bulk of work at Bonanza seems to be sanitization. We talk about ourselves as well. Patrick tells me he's going to study history at a local college next year. When I ask why, he says because his parents want him to go to college, and "Old shit is cool, you know?"

I skirt around my own life, focusing on stories about Figgy or my brother. After an hour, Patrick's phone buzzes with a request for backup at the bowling alley. "Gotta go," he says. "Until we meet again, m'lady."

I laugh, and when he smiles back at me, there's a warm glow in my stomach. He is *really* cute.

Once he's gone, I get to work sanitizing. I wipe down machine after machine. The work is easy and blissfully routine. It numbs my thoughts and almost puts me in a trance. I could keep this up all afternoon, starting from the beginning again when I hit the last machine. *This* is the job I want. A literal rinse-and-repeat and nothing else. Maybe Bonanza will work out if I avoid the mini-golf course and sanitize arcade machines for the rest of my days.

But then, as I'm spraying down the glass surface of a Simpsons pinball machine, someone calls out, "Hannah? Is that you?"

My spine grows rigid. My chest tight, I turn to find three of my teammates circled around the high-tech *Mario Kart* machine.

No, not my teammates. Girls who *used* to be my teammates.

Carrie-Anne, Nina, and Elizabeth all stare at me with wide eyes, like they've seen Bigfoot or the Loch Ness Monster.

"Holy shit," Nina says. "That *is* you. Where the hell have you been?"

Nina was never one to beat around the bush.

I didn't tell anyone I was going to boarding school. Brie knew. In a way, she practically sent me there. But I guess she didn't fill in the rest of the team, out of guilt or lack of caring, I'm not sure.

So on the first day of junior year, when I wasn't at school, no one knew why. At first there were texts that came in bursts whenever I had a second of service at Mountain Bliss, and then when I ignored those texts, there was silence.

Except for Elizabeth. Sweet Elizabeth. I think of the text she sent last night as she steps forward with her sincere brown eyes. "So you *are* home," she says now. "My friend said they saw you here yesterday. We were all so worried. How are you?"

My cheeks are hot, my throat is tight, and my brain is screaming, *Run.* But I can't run. Literally can't. Not on my broken ankle. I swallow hard and tuck a strand of hair behind my ear. It immediately pops back out. "Um, I'm good. Just working."

"But where were you?" Nina asks again.

Carrie-Anne doesn't seem the least bit interested in this interaction. Her eyes stay locked on her phone, where she's scrolling through Instagram with one finger. We never really bonded.

"Um." I might as well rip off the Band-Aid. "I was at another school. Mountain Bliss."

Elizabeth's brow creases. "Why'd you go to another school?"

"Boarding school, right?" Nina asks. "I think that's where my cousin's friend went after she got caught huffing glue in the janitor's closet."

It's very possible Nina's cousin's friend lived in the room next to mine.

I nod. "Yeah, boarding school."

"You started hanging out with Shira and them last summer," Elizabeth says. There's a light note of condemnation in her voice, and Nina picks up on it too.

"Hey, Shira is cool," Nina says. "She always let me

borrow a pen when I forgot one in class. She's good people."

I feel like I should defend Shira too. Shira Chen, an old friend from my Hebrew school days, took me under her wing last summer when my whole world fell apart, when I alienated everyone else. But my tongue stays glued to the roof of my mouth. I just want this interaction to end.

"So are you home just for summer, or for good?" Carrie-Anne asks, glancing up from her phone only long enough to give me a judgmental look. Carrie-Anne's parents are rich. Carrie-Anne's house has a swimming pool and *acreage*, and she was given a brand-new Audi on her sixteenth birthday.

I straighten my shoulders and clench my hand around the bottle of generic industrial cleaner. "For good." I silently say, *I hope*.

"I'm glad," Elizabeth tells me. "How's the ankle? We really miss having you on the team. It's not the same without you."

Tears spring to my eyes with no warning. Embarrassment, then panic, floods my system. I try to take a calming breath, but it comes off more like a panicked intake. Nina's eyes grow concerned.

Damn it.

Frustration overwhelms me. Before me stand three completely healthy girls. They're conditioned, keeping their bodies trained over the long summer. This year they'll compete against the most skilled players in the country. In the next five years, some of them will try out for the Olympic team, some of them might *make* the Olympic team, the team I so desperately wanted to be on, the team I thought I was destined for, so I could stand on that podium just like my bubbie. So I could honor her memory.

These girls have everything, and they're staring at me with so much sympathy. I hate them for it. I know it's wrong, but in this moment, I hate them so desperately.

"The ankle is fine." I use all my will to keep my voice level. "I have to get back to work. Have a good summer, okay?"

Elizabeth looks wounded. Nina looks analyzing. And Carrie-Anne looks constipated. I turn around, wincing at the awkward pressure it puts on my ankle, and then rush for the nearest exit, bursting out of the dark arcade and into the blaring sunlight. I'm breathing too hard, panic flailing against my chest. My vision goes loopy, like when I step off a roller coaster. It's possible I might pass out.

My mind swims for a solution, for a way out, for *relief*, and suddenly I'm pulling out my phone to text Shira. We haven't communicated all year. As soon as I wasn't available to party, I was off her radar. Our friendship was mutually temporary, and she floated out of my life as easily as she floated into it. But I know if I text her, she'll respond with an idea for tonight. I'll go. I'll drink a few beers, maybe invite Patrick along, and—

"Are you okay?"

I snap up from my phone.

Brie is in front of me. She's wearing different earrings today, little silver dangling ones that catch the fading sunlight. She manages to look both concerned and exhausted by my presence.

"Yeah." I shove my phone into my pocket. It's only now I realize I've wandered out toward the path to mini golf, the one place I was determined to stay away from. "Fine."

Brie's expression flickers, and I see so much in her eyes—hurt, anger, sadness. After a long moment, she says, "You should drink some cold water. It's hot out here."

The comment stuns me. An unexpected wave of gratitude washes over me. I forgot what it was like to have Brie looking out for me. I forgot how nice it is.

"Yeah. I will, thanks."

She looks at me a moment longer, and I think she might say something else. And when she doesn't, *I* feel the instinct to say something else, to reach out to her.

But the distance between us is impossibly vast.

Brie nods, then walks away, and I head back inside alone.

Chapter Six

"BAD DAY?" Daisey asks.

She's caught me red-eyed in the bathroom. I splash a little more cold water on my face, then dry it off with the bottom of my shirt to save a paper towel.

Daisey is wearing an orange Bonanza shirt with the sleeves pushed up again. Her eyes, swept with dark shadow and liner, emit a balance of interest and nonjudgment.

"I've had better days." I pause. "But I've also had much worse days."

The perspective helps a little and eases tension from my shoulders.

"Rough," Daisey says. She jumps up on the bathroom counter and angles toward the mirror, pulling out a tube of matte lipstick and applying it with two easy strokes. "Hey, you should hang with us tonight. After we close."

"Oh, thanks. I can't, though—"

"C'mon," she cuts me off. "It'll be fun. Much better than sulking alone, I promise. Plus, Owen's dad is actually going to take care of his son for the night, so I'm all free. And we're just hanging out here. Join us. At least for a little."

Daisey bats her eyes at me, and I give her a small smile.

I was planning to binge reality TV and white cheddar popcorn after work, but I'm not sure even *90 Day Fiancé* can distract me from my thoughts today. I'm also technically grounded, but maybe since the hangout is happening here . . .

"Um, maybe," I tell Daisey.

"Gimme your phone," she says. I hand it over, and she puts in her number. "Just text me if you decide to come. I'll send you the details. Low commitment, promise." She passes my phone back. "Hope your day gets a little bit better, newbie."

"Thanks, Daisey."

She swipes on one more layer of lipstick before leaving the bathroom, and then I'm alone again.

I don't *want* to be alone tonight. I don't want to sit in my room and think about all the things I'm not doing and all the people I'm not with. And Daisey seems cool. And nice. And responsible! I mean, she has a kid! It's not like I'm texting Shira to get drunk. This is different. This is a responsible social interaction.

And that's what I text my parents—that my new coworker invited me to hang out at Bonanza after close and that she has a kid and is very mature and that I'll be home before midnight if it's all right with them. There's about sixty seconds of gray text bubble from my mom before the response comes through: Okay, sweetie. We're glad you're making friends. Let's make it before 10:30. I feel the tiniest shred of endorphins as I head back to work.

The bowling alley seems like a safe spot to land for the rest of my shift. The double doors whoosh open and reveal the loud sounds of clattering balls and pins. It's chaos this evening, almost every lane booked. Through that chaos, my eyes land on Ethan.

He's on lane nine, futzing with the ball return machine as two stressed parents and a half-dozen little kids gather around him. Ethan is calm as he adjusts the machine, his hands steady and capable even as the parents watch with anxious eyes.

He gets the machine working again. A bright pink ball pops up, and the parents both sag in relief as the kids grab for it.

Ethan maneuvers away from the family and looks up, immediately catching my eye, almost like he could sense my gaze. His smile is instant. Ethan has always smiled at me. Why wouldn't he? But something about his smile is different now. For some reason, his soft, easy grin makes my stomach flip.

He walks toward me, scratching the back of his neck. He's wearing worn jeans and a sky-blue Bonanza shirt. His eyes look lighter, like they've been dyed by days in the sun. "Hey, Hannah," he says.

I clear my throat. "Hey, yourself."

"How's your second day going?" he asks.

I think of my teammates. I think of Brie. Then I lie. "Going great."

Ethan raises an eyebrow, lie caught with ease.

"Okay, whatever. Not great." I laugh. "How's *your* day?"

He laughs too. "Fine, about the same as always. It's nice you're working here now, though."

I nudge him playfully. "I'm sure you say that to all your best friends' sisters."

"Yup." He grins. "All one of my best friends."

His eyes stay on mine a second too long. There's a warmth in them that feels reserved for only a few select people in his life. Heat crawls across my neck.

"Did someone say 'best friend'?" a voice asks.

I jump like I've been caught doing something wrong, then turn to find my brother next to us.

Joey looks even *more* energized than this morning, like he siphoned the energy off two dozen kids and is ready to stay up all night. Maybe he got into the ice cream cake.

"Look at us!" Joey says. He slings his arms around both of our shoulders and brings us in for a squeeze. The hug is borderline sweaty, and Joey is wedged between us, but I still feel thrown off at the close contact with Ethan. He smells different. Fresh. *Manly.*

Thankfully, Joey releases us quickly and says, "So cool we're all working here now. We should tell Mom and Dad to quit their jobs and work here too. It can be a family affair. We'll be like one of those reality TV shows you watch, Hannah. Drama at every corner."

I laugh. "I hate to break it to you, Joey, but I don't think David and Sarah Klein are going to make entertaining television for anyone. They're way too *pleasant.*"

"Ugh. True," Joey replies. "They can keep their boring jobs. Still fun to have you here. What's everyone doing after work? We should hang."

"I think we already are?" I ask. "I told Daisey I'd hang out with everyone after close."

Joey freezes. *"Daisey Liu?"*

"Yeah . . . ," I reply slowly. "Why? She seems cool."

"She *is* cool," Joey says. His eyes are wide as he runs a hand through his hair. "She asked you to hang out with . . . *everyone?*"

"Yes. What is—"

"Cool, we'll come with you!" Joey cuts me off. He

throws an arm around my shoulder. "It'll be fun. The three of us hanging out again!"

Ethan looks mildly sick. Something very strange is going on here.

"Um, sure," I say. "Sounds good."

"Great! So we'll meet after work. Ethan, you can sleep over after. See y'all later!"

And then my brother speeds off.

"Hmph," Ethan says.

"What was all that about?" I ask. "Joey was acting odd. I mean, odd for Joey."

"You got an invite from the 'cool crowd,'" Ethan explains, putting air quotes around the last two words.

"The cool crowd?" I look after my brother's retreating shadow. I can't remember a single time in my life I've had a higher social status than Joey. Not that I'm an outcast, but Joey is Mr. Popular at school, friends with everyone, while I'm a jock, relegated to my jock circle. Or, I was a jock. I guess now I don't know what I am.

"There's a *cool crowd* at Bonanza?" I ask.

"Yeah." Ethan nods. "It's like high school."

"We're *in* high school."

He laughs. "Almost everyone here is nice. But there's still a 'cool crowd,' and we're not in it."

"But everyone loves Joey." I pause. "I mean, you're great, too."

Ethan smiles, hard. "Thank you, Hannah."

I roll my eyes, smiling back at him. "You're very welcome."

"Look," Ethan explains. "We were young when we started working here. Most of the cool kids are older. It's natural to not welcome us with open arms. You can't blame them for not wanting to be friends with sixteen-year-olds."

I think of all my college parties I attended at sixteen. No one seemed to have a problem with my young age then. Sure says something about our world—something gross and sexist. "Maybe we shouldn't go tonight . . . ," I say. "Doesn't sound like these people are good for Joey."

"Oh, no." Ethan shakes his head. "We *have* to go now. Joey will flip if we don't. This is his chance."

I sigh and glance around the bowling alley. "Is there any chance of this ending well?"

Ethan laughs, his eyes lighting up and easing my stress. "Certainly not, Hannah. Certainly not."

"Sweetheart, grab me that green ball," a woman tells me as I walk by.

I turn around to find a group of elderly women in matching blue silk bowling shirts. The words "Golden Oldies" are scrawled in gold glitter across the backs. The woman who asked for the ball has white skin and permed blond curls. An Asian woman with deep brown skin and large silver earrings asks for a plate of cheese fries while I'm at it. "Here," she says, shoving a five-dollar bill into my hand.

"Um—" I start to say.

"Add in a Fresca for me," another woman says, more cash in hand.

"And a pair of shoes in size eight, please," yet another woman adds. Her hot-pink socks remind me of Bubbie.

"Um," I begin again.

My brain whirs. Bonanza is a self-serve bowling alley. But these women don't seem like they'll take no for an answer. Whatever. Maybe I can count this as a good deed for the day since it's not technically my job. I'm being nice. Or, being too scared to say no to them.

I put on a smile and ask them to repeat their orders again. Then I type it all up in my phone and scurry to grab everything.

It takes me a few trips. I've seen Patrick cradle four bowling balls at once, but I'm not looking to break my toes in addition to my ankle. As I finish the final task, a bit breathless, I ask, "Anything else?"

"Yes," the original woman says, voice stern. "Your name?"

My stomach drops.

Crap. Am I in trouble? For what?

"Um, Hannah," I reply. "I'm Hannah Klein."

"Well." The woman extends a perfectly manicured hand.

"It's lovely to meet you, Hannah Klein." She has a Southern drawl. I shake her hand, and the skin is smooth as butter. "Always nice to see a bright new face at Bonanza. I'm Madeline, and this is Ginger, Vanessa, Tashia, Bella, and Adele."

"It's nice to meet you all," I say. "I should probably get back to—"

"We're here three days a week," Madeline says, cutting me off. "So you be sure to come and say hi, all right now?"

Her tone is filled with spice, and her smile is warm. She's like a gingersnap cookie. And just like that, I'm won over.

And although Madeline looks nothing like my bubbie, I can't help but be reminded of her, a confident woman who can command a room. It makes me feel a little more balanced being in a presence like that again.

"All right now," I agree, noticing the smallest hint of a Southern twang echoed in my own voice, something I've never had before. I swear Adele smirks at this. "Just let me know if y'all need anything else." Adele's smirk widens.

My cheeks reddening, I wave goodbye and head back to work.

The rest of the day zips by. I even manage to work in another "good deed" when I pass by a food court vomit situation and offer to clean it up. The relief in Gary's and Sherry's eyes is immeasurable. And then, I went above and beyond by getting the kid some damp napkins, ginger ale, and crackers. I told Garry and Sherry to deduct the $2.50 from my paycheck, but I think they let it slide. It felt kind of nice when the parents thanked me so much.

After my shift, I meet Joey and Ethan in the parking lot. We close at nine on weeknights, which means the sun has just set, dark pinks and purples still on the horizon. The air is fragrant, almost sweet, with the threat of rain later in the evening. I grab a thicker hoodie from the back of the car and pull it on over my Bonanza shirt. I'm going to have an entire wardrobe in my trunk by the end of summer, just like I used to with my soccer gear.

Ethan rolls his neck a couple of times while Joey again asks, "So where exactly are we going?"

I texted Daisey earlier and told her I was in. She replied, Perfect! We're hanging at the graveyard. Just take a right behind the go-kart course and walk five minutes down the gravel path. You might need a phone flashlight. It's kind of dark.

Yes, she said the graveyard.

I definitely thought this hangout was *at* Bonanza, not *near* Bonanza, and wonder if I should text my parents with the correction. Also, I don't want to hang out with the dead. The last time I was at a cemetery, it was for Bubbie's funeral. I was saying the Mourner's Kaddish. I was covering her casket with dirt. It's not something I want to think about tonight.

But with Joey practically jumping in excitement, there's no getting out of this. I share the instructions with the boys and then say, "All right. So, off we go."

"To our inevitable deaths," Ethan adds quietly, and I laugh.

Joey, for once, is silent. He keeps fidgeting with the hem of his shirt. My heart tugs for him. This isn't the Joey I know. "Do you think anyone changed into regular clothes?" he asks. "Should we put on regular clothes?"

I shrug. "I just have this hoodie."

"I don't think it matters," Ethan says nicely. He gives Joey a gentle squeeze on the shoulder. "Don't overthink it, friend."

Watching Joey think at all is strange. He was set into motion from the day of his birth and hasn't looked back since. His life motto is basically: *Do first. Ignore consequences later.*

I eye my brother and try to assess what else has changed. How much did I miss in the year I was gone? Or, maybe, was he always more sensitive than I thought, and I was too caught up in my own stuff to notice?

I twist my fingers together as I walk over to the go-kart course. The floodlights are still on, bathing the area in large swaths of artificial light. Maybe I should try working here tomorrow. It's set apart from the rest of the megaplex. I could stay out of Brie's way. I hope she's not here tonight.

We find the path, our tennis shoes crunching the gravel as we walk. Ethan swipes on his phone flashlight, and I do as well. The lights intermingle in front of us, guiding our way as the go-karts recede and darkness folds in. A bit of wind picks up and rustles the tree branches. Crickets chirp in the dark grass.

"So," I whisper. "I'd love to not get murdered tonight."

"Same. Agreed." Ethan nods. "Would love to not get murdered."

We glance at each other and giggle. Something flutters in my stomach.

"I hear them!" Joey shouts, then freezes, realizing he shouted. "Do you think they heard that?"

"Probably," I say.

"No," Ethan replies at the same time.

I shoot him a sheepish look and mouth, *Oops.* Then I stride forward. "C'mon, we can't stay out late, so might as well make the most of it."

I feel a bit of my old confidence return as I take the lead. My ankle makes me wince as I pick up my pace, but I tamp down the pain with gritted teeth and emerge into a clearing—into the graveyard.

"Whoa," I say.

"Whoa," Ethan agrees.

Joey comes up last behind us but with the same thought: *"Whoa."*

Last Summer

My dress doesn't fit. No one told me I need a black dress in my closet in case there's a funeral. Apparently, it's something you're just supposed to know. The only black dress I own is from my eighth-grade dance, shoved in the back behind winter coats. It's too short, too tight. Even with the scratchy pantyhose under it and cardigan over it, I feel exposed, disrespectful.

And it's hot out, sweat already dampening my skin at ten in the morning.

I force myself to stop fidgeting as the rabbi speaks about my bubbie. Her casket is right in front of me. I can't believe her casket is right in front of me. I can't believe she's gone. Last week we were making babka, and then three days ago she was in the hospital for a "small procedure," and now she's gone.

She didn't tell us how bad it was, Dad said. She wanted to enjoy her time with us, or maybe she didn't want to admit it to herself. I don't know. I guess I'll never know.

Mom is crying. She holds a tissue in one hand and Dad's arm in the other. Joey's eyes are trained on the ground. He's crying too.

The surgery was too much for her, the doctors said. She insisted on having it anyway, they said. She never woke up from it. We didn't get to say goodbye.

A hand takes mine. It's Brie. She gives me a light squeeze and a small smile. She smells like fresh flowers. It's nice she's here. We have practice today. I never miss practice. But now I am and so is Brie. And then I'm going to miss an entire week because we have to sit shiva. And then I'll be playing the game against Kensington with rusty skills.

I shouldn't think about the game right now. Bubbie would want me to do well, but this is her funeral. I shouldn't be thinking about missed drills at her funeral. I can't believe I'm at her funeral.

She won't be in the stands to cheer me on. She has the loudest whistle of anyone I've ever met, a fire-alarm whistle. She'd want me to win. I should win for her.

"We now rise for the Mourner's Kaddish," the rabbi says.

Everyone stands. There are a lot of people. "A nice turnout," one aunt whispered, loud enough for three rows of people to hear. The rabbi gave a good speech, too, all about her life, her Olympic victory, her business, and her beautiful family.

"Yitgadal v'yitkadash sh'meih raba," we pray.

The words are familiar, ones I've said for distant relatives, victims of the Tree of Life shooting, and even for Ruth Bader Ginsburg.

"*B'alma di v'ra chiruteih v'yamlich malchuteih.*"

I've never said them for someone like my bubbie, though.

"*B'chayeichon uvyomeichon, uvchayei d'chol beit Yisrael.*"

I've never said them for someone who passed away and took a piece of me with her.

Chapter Seven

I'M RELIEVED TO discover the graveyard is not an *actual* graveyard. It's a Bonanza graveyard, a burial ground of outdated and broken items, a football field's worth of rusted go-karts, busted arcade machines, cracked bowling pins, and ramshackle tables and chairs, an archaeological dig of decades of megaplex family-friendly fun.

A single floodlight illuminates the area. I can see now that someone ran an extension cord all the way down the gravel path to set it up. There are about twenty employees here, spread out among broken furniture and small bonfires. It's like I've stepped into another world. A magical garbage *Alice in Wonderland* world.

Daisey spots me as we walk into the floodlight's reach. She jumps up from her chair to come say hello. I spot Patrick and Tony standing by a metal trash-can fire. Patrick lifts a hand and winks at me. I can feel Joey's nerves jangling. In another direction, my own heart skips as I notice Brie hanging with a small group of friends. They're gathered around another fire, lounged out on reclaimed furniture from Bonanza's heyday in the eighties. I swear she looks up, catches a glimpse of me, and averts her eyes. Not that I can blame her. I do the same thing.

"Hey, newbie," Daisey says, drawing my attention as she approaches. "Welcome! This is your brother, right? Joey. And Ethan! Glad you guys made it."

"Thanks!" Joey tugs on his Bonanza shirt. I hope he's relieved to see that everyone else is still in their work clothes as well. "We're happy to be here. Very cool place. Lots of trash, but cool trash. Not boring trash. This is classy trash. It's—"

Ethan elbows Joey in the side to get him to stop talking. Daisey is unfazed, smiling brightly.

"Thanks for the invite," I say. "This place is cool."

"Of course!" She winks at Joey. "And yes, definitely classy trash. Only the best for Bonanza employees. C'mon. I'll give you the tour."

Daisey guides us around the graveyard. Items are grouped together by decade. Moving from section to section is like a real-life time machine, the history of Bonanza splayed out in broken machinery and outdated furniture. Someone split the power cord so that letters of an old

Bonanza sign are lit up, with only the *O* and second *N* missing. When we approach Brie's section, nerves pinch my spine, and I almost laugh as Daisey begins introductions. "Hannah, this is Lanie, Zoya, Brie, and Anthony."

I was just introduced to my own best friend. Well, my own ex–best friend. Ethan and Joey of course know of our relationship, and how there no longer seems to be one, and it feels all the more awkward to have them witness this moment.

"Hey," I cough out, waving at the group.

The three unknowing employees cheerfully say hello. When my eyes find Brie's, I'm surprised to discover she seems to be holding back laughter as well. It's a bittersweet moment, that despite everything, we still find the same things funny. She gives me a quick nod before we move on with the tour.

My nerves are jangling by the time it's all over. I bite my lip, wondering how I'm going to survive a summer here with Brie at every turn, a stark reminder of what I lost. I'm grateful for the distraction when Patrick shouts my name. "Hannah!" he calls, waving me over. He has a dark flannel open over his work shirt now and a gray beanie on his head.

I wave back before turning to my group.

Daisey's smile is gleeful and all-knowing. "He's a nice guy, mostly harmless. Enjoy." She then nods at us all. "I'll see y'all around!"

As she returns to a cluster of friends, I glance at Joey

and Ethan. Both wear odd expressions, Ethan's closed off and Joey's too eager. "So." I clear my throat. "I'm gonna go say hi. You guys want to come with me?" "*Yes*," Joey answers, practically before I can finish the question. This is of course because Tony is standing right next to Patrick. "Ethan?"

He shakes his head. "I'm good, thanks."

A weird feeling pinches my spine. The floodlight and fire cast strange shadows, Ethan's cheekbones pronounced in their scant light. He looks . . . *older*. I swallow hard, my feet glued to the ground. But Joey is tugging at my arm, and it doesn't make sense to stay here when I just said I'm leaving, so I give Ethan an awkward half wave and say, "Um, see you soon, then."

He nods back.

I bite my nail as Joey and I walk toward Patrick and his brother. I glance back to find Ethan settling onto an old bench, paint chipped and wood battered. There are people in conversation around him. He gives them a quick acknowledgment, then pulls a sketchbook and pencil out of his bag. His brow automatically vexes with concentration. Ethan has always loved drawing. He calls what he does "doodling," but I've thumbed through his stuff, and it's much more than that. There's something human about his cartoon characters, simple lines bringing a depth of emotion to the page.

I asked him to draw me once when we were in middle

school and I was going through a phase of complete self-obsession. It was a two-month grace period between my preteen acne and my teen acne, and my body had gone through all sorts of growth spurts, and when I looked in the mirror, I imagined myself to be the secret love and obsession of every cute boy at school.

Ethan said no. He said he doesn't draw people he knows. It'd be like kissing his sister. And I said, "You don't have a sister," and he said, "That doesn't matter," and then my mom said dinner was ready, and I sullenly pushed my pasta around my plate for the entire meal and locked myself in my bedroom after.

I cringe as the intense feelings of angst rush back to me now. I took that rejection so personally. Ethan really doesn't draw anyone he knows, doesn't draw realistic portraits at all. I glance back once more as he focuses on his sketchbook. The concentration brings a smile to my lips and tugs my stomach. God, I miss that feeling, being entirely focused on the thing I love so deeply.

I take a breath and turn back ahead.

Patrick's eyes glint as we approach. "Hey, *you*," he says, voice seeming smoother and lower out here at night. Maybe he's dropping it on purpose, which is kind of a cute thought. It's endearing to see beneath his cool-kid exterior.

"Hey, *you*," I echo with a smile. "You know my brother, Joey, right?"

"Right." He nods. "Joey. How's it going?" Patrick holds out his hand for a fist bump, and Joey jumps forward and knocks fists with only a smidge of awkwardness.

Then Joey turns to Tony, who is currently burning a bundle of different items, from twigs to chip bags to receipts. He cut off the sleeves of his Bonanza T-shirt, turning it into a muscle tank. "Hey, Tony!" Joey says. "How's it going? Good night? Nice fire y'all have got. Great burn. Tons of heat."

Tony raises an eyebrow in response. My shoulders stiffen. I can feel the awkwardness rolling off Joey in waves, and it's my impulse to protect him. I want to tell Joey to forget about Tony, that it's not worth putting himself through this for someone who has no interest in him. But I know that won't work. I know Joey is in too deep. And, to be fair, Tony *is* obscenely attractive. It's honestly ridiculous. So I understand if Joey can't see the trash personality through the jawline.

So instead of giving in to my urge to pull Joey away, I lighten my voice into a tease and ask, "Anyone want to play Never Have I Ever?"

I have no desire to play Never Have I Ever, but my brother needs a wing-woman.

Patrick shrugs and says, "Sure. I'm in."

I smile at him, and he must slip up because instead of his standard smirk or smolder, he gives me a goofy grin back. It's cute, really cute.

Tony puts a chip bag in the fire. Black smoke billows up. I wonder how much Pete knows about these graveyard hangs, especially the pyrotechnics part.

"Sure, whatever," Tony says. "Let's get some other people."

Joey's face lights up. I knock into his shoulder, and he beams at me.

Tony leads us over to where Ethan is sitting, since the most people are gathered there and there's plenty of seating. With a sweeping glance around the graveyard, I notice Brie has departed. I can't help but wonder if my presence had anything to do with it. Or worse, the thought that I didn't affect her at all, that I no longer take up any of her mental space. Our friendship is over, but the thought of that door truly being shut forever makes my chest hurt.

Tony rounds up the troops, and almost everyone agrees to play. I half expect Ethan to get up and leave, but when I sit down next to him, he stays put. Patrick then squeezes onto the bench as well, and suddenly I'm pressed between two boys. Patrick knocks into my shoulder with a smile. Then Ethan shifts to put his sketchbook away, and as his arm presses against mine, my skin buzzes.

I look down, pulse racing.

What is going on?

"Who's starting?" Daisey asks. She runs a hand through her short hair. Her makeup is more dramatic than earlier today, one step from late-night punk show. She pulls off the look with ease.

There's about a dozen of us gathered, everyone but a few guys smoking cigarettes farther out in the field. Gross. Only a couple of people are drinking. The rest are holding concession sodas or water bottles. A six-pack sits on a table with three of the beers still left. If I asked for one, they would probably say yes. I could crack the tab and take a sip, and it would smooth out the jagged edges of my thoughts, make the night glossy and warm. I could forget about Brie, about last summer, about all that I've lost.

I push away the temptation and concentrate on the faces around me. I recognize a few but can't place their names. Bonanza is a big place. I'm sure it'll take weeks to meet everyone, and by then there will be new hires.

Yet there's an incredible ease to the way everyone interacts—natural, like they've known each other forever, like mopping up vomit and sweat bonds you in some deep, indescribable way. A yearning feeling twists through me, sharp and painful, as I'm reminded of the team I used to share that feeling with.

"I'll go first," a guy with a forest-green Bonanza shirt says. He has dark brown skin and a row of earrings to rival Daisey's. "Never have I ever . . . gotten a speeding ticket."

A few people drink. Daisey goes next. "Never have I ever clocked in late to work."

Everyone drinks but me. Including Ethan and Joey. A bunch of people laugh and call Daisey a Goody Two-shoes. She shrugs and says, "If you want to hate on me for getting a full paycheck, that's your business."

"Okay, okay, my turn," Patrick says. "Hmm." He strokes his chin in thought, then turns to me, his smile glinting. "Never have I ever gone *skinny-dipping*."

I give him a cool smile back before drinking from my reusable water bottle. Daytona with the team. The pool was closed after hours, which only encouraged us more.

His eyes widen in interest. "I'm going to need details on that."

"Absolutely not," I reply, my smile warming.

"I'll go next," Ethan interrupts us, clearing his throat and sitting forward. He has a reusable water bottle too, a green one with a Squirtle sticker that Joey bought him as a birthday present one year. Ethan stares at Patrick for one long moment before saying, "Never have I ever cheated on someone."

Tension pulses between them, thick in the air. My muscles tighten as Patrick rolls his eyes at Ethan. "We weren't official, man. Anyways, you'd have to date someone to cheat on someone, so you wouldn't know anything about it."

"I had a girlfriend last year and managed not to be a scumbag, thanks," Ethan cuts back.

I take a tight breath. This is . . . uncomfortable. Patrick's clear annoyance and Ethan's tamped-down bite. My eyes search for Joey across the circle, but he's too busy staring at Tony to take in what's happening over here. I catch sight of the beers again. Condensation drips as they sweat in the night air.

I turn away, biting my lip. Why are Ethan and Patrick fighting? It couldn't . . . does it have anything to do with me?

No, that is some twisted self-obsessed thought. Obviously, they just dislike each other and are having a pissing contest because boys are ridiculous. I have nothing to do with it.

But also, what's this about Ethan having a girlfriend? Ethan is *Ethan*. He doesn't date.

Except, I guess he does now. Ethan is no longer a little kid who considers gushers and Doritos a well-rounded lunch. He's older. He's grown up enough to be someone *dateable*.

I glance at him, at his face cast in shadows, at his large hands covered in ink. Ethan is only one year younger than me. A gap that once seemed like a vast chasm is now the same gap between Patrick and myself. My pulse races, the sounds around me tinny in my ears.

"I got one," Tony suddenly says. I hunch my shoulders and decidedly keep my eyes away from both Ethan and

Patrick. "Never have I ever had sex at Bonanza."

"Guess jerking off doesn't count," Daisey teases him.

Tony shoots her the bird and a smile. A real keeper my brother has chosen.

Some people laugh, while others say, "Gross."

Then, to the surprise of us all, Daisey takes a casual sip of her drink, the only one to do so. "What?" She shrugs. "Sometimes the itch demands to be scratched."

"Where?" a girl asks.

"Yeah, tell us," another guy adds.

"Please, I'm not trying to blow up my spot." Daisey shakes her head. "Y'all will never get it out of me."

The game devolves into jokes and laughter. Ethan and Patrick ease up at my sides and participate as well. The conversation shifts as someone else admits they didn't have sex, but they might have gotten into a similar activity during cosmic bowling when they were supposed to be resetting the pins. Then people start trading stories about the many, many Bonanza rules they've broken over time, from sneaking in friends to play for free, which everyone does; to sneaking concession food, which is a high-stakes heist thanks to Sherry and Gary; to messing with the go-karts so they can drive faster than normal. That was Tony and Patrick, of course.

"Sounds awesome," Joey says, his eyes wide.

"Join us next time," Tony tells him. Joey looks like he

won the lottery, while Tony is already in a new conversation. And I realize in that moment, Tony isn't mean—he's just oblivious of Joey's adoration. With his looks, Tony has probably walked through life with a trail of admirers, to the point where he's likely anesthetized to all compliments, come-ons, and lingering looks. He's not dismissive so much as oversaturated.

Eventually, people disperse. Ethan pulls his sketchbook back out, and I'm about to ask what he's drawing when Patrick grabs my hand gently and pulls me up from the bench. It gives me a head rush, and I blink, my nerves jumping when I realize how close we're standing now. He smells like smoke and Bonanza's citrus cleaner. We're about the same height, which means his lips are *right there*.

Patrick nods, hand still in mine, and we walk a few feet away. I feel some eyes on us, and I wonder what everyone thinks of me, the new girl.

I look up at Patrick. His smile is shy, sweet, and it makes my stomach flip.

"What are you doing after this?" he asks.

I laugh. "What am I doing *after* the after-party?"

Patrick laughs too. "This is no party. And I think you know that."

"Oh yeah?" I cross my arms. "You think I'm a party girl."

"I think you can hold your own," he replies, then nods

toward his brother. "Tony and I are hanging out with some friends downtown. They go to ME Tech, have their own place. Join us. Your little bro can come too."

I didn't like the way Patrick and Ethan fought tonight, but I do like the way my skin tingles when Patrick's thumb traces my palm. His eyes drop to my neck, where I've pushed my hair behind my ear, and I imagine him kissing me there. I think it'd feel quite nice.

But it's late, and I don't plan to break curfew. Plus, I'm tired. It's been a long day, and my comforter is calling my name. "Maybe another time," I tell Patrick, then squeeze his hand. "I've got the day shift tomorrow."

"Me too." Patrick ducks his head. "I'll see you then, Hannah."

I nod and give his hand one more squeeze. When I walk back to the circle of people, Ethan is immersed in his drawing. We have to leave soon, but we still have a few more minutes. I sit next to him and say, "Let me see."

Chapter Eight

WE GET HOME right before curfew. In the parking lot, it was like a cloud of stress overtook Ethan. Joey pulled him aside while I waited at the car. I couldn't hear what was said, but after, Ethan seemed noticeably more relaxed, and I caught Joey saying, "You know you're always welcome."

Back home, I pass my parents' room. They're pretending to be asleep, but their lamp is still on, shining light under the crack of the door. I give a quick knock and say, "We're home, good night."

It's strange to no longer have their trust. I'm not sure I'll ever get it back. If there's anything I've learned this year, it's that not all broken things can be fixed.

Joey heads to his room, probably to play video games. Ethan goes to the bathroom for a shower. And I walk into the kitchen for a snack. My appetite disappeared at the end of last summer and struggled to reappear at Mountain Bliss, but Bonanza has certainly kick-started it again. The job isn't the same level of exertion as soccer, but standing on your feet all day is no easy task, and my hunger has come back with a vengeance.

I pull out a random assortment of items from the pantry and fridge—pretzels, M&Ms, baby carrots, celery, cheese sticks, and guacamole. When I close the door, my Mountain Bliss checklist stares right at me. My eyes linger on steps three and four, my body tensing. I have time. I'll figure something out.

I sit at the table and eat while scrolling TikTok. A few minutes later, I jump when Ethan says, "Hey."

He's standing at the entrance to the kitchen. "Sorry." He holds his hands up. "Startled you?"

"Since when are your footsteps as silent as mice?" I ask.

He laughs. My pulse ticks as I take him in. He's wearing sweatpants and a T-shirt, and his hair is wet from the shower, a few drops trickling down his neck. He looks good. Really good. And he's in my kitchen at night, a place he's been a million times, but he's never been in my kitchen at night when he looks this good. My throat feels dry as he takes the seat next to mine and smiles and asks, "Want to share?"

My tongue sticks to the roof of my mouth. "Sure," I somehow manage to say. "You don't want to play video games with Joey?"

Ethan sighs. "Joey isn't playing video games. He's watching Korean horror films."

"*What?*" I ask.

"Tony *loves* Korean horror films," Ethan clarifies.

"Ah," I say, understanding. "But Joey hates scary movies. *Toy Story* gave him nightmares."

"I mean, to be fair, that movie is kind of creepy."

"True." I shake my head. "This is going to be bad."

"Real bad," Ethan agrees. He reaches across the table for a handful of pretzels and begins to dip them in the guac. "No double-dipping," I warn.

"I know." He laughs, his eyes glinting. "You've always been a bit of a germ freak."

"Have not."

He raises an eyebrow. "Remember in fifth grade when you went through that Clorox phase? You carried wipes with you everywhere. You tried to Clorox *me* once."

"That's because you were all dirty from running around in the mud."

For some entirely unknown reason, my cheeks flush when I say "dirty."

Ethan seems thrown off as well. He looks down as he pops a pretzel into his mouth. Then, after a few moments of crunching, he says, "It was weird last year . . . you being gone."

I toy with my M&Ms, sorting them by color. "Yeah?"

"The house felt different without you." He pauses, swirling another pretzel into the guac. "I'm glad you're back now."

I twist my fingers together as bad feelings swarm. I think of steps three and four on the checklist. Of how impossible they are. Of how I might not be home for good.

I don't want to think about that. So, I change the subject. "How was *your* year? Did you say you had a *girlfriend*?" I try to ask it in a teasing way, like the older sister of his best friend would, but the question comes out awkward.

"Uh, yeah." Ethan shifts in his chair. He sorts his own pile of M&Ms, sending me a quick smile. "Wendy Phelps. My grade. She works on the school newspaper. I started drawing comics for them, and we just—clicked, or whatever."

"Nice." I nod. "Cool." My body feels weirdly tense hearing him talk about another girl. I tell myself it's just exhaustion from the long day. "So, uh, why'd you break up?" The question slips out of its own accord.

Ethan slowly raises his shoulders and then lowers them again, like it's an impossible question to answer. "I guess we stopped clicking. We're still friends, though. I'm doing the comic again next year."

I feel more questions bubble on the tip of my tongue, like how serious were they and what did he like about her and did he walk her to class and did they kiss, but—

Those would be very strange questions to ask my younger brother's best friend.

I glance up at Ethan—at his dark lashes, his full lips, his fingers smudged with ink.

Then I grab a carrot and crunch into it as loud as possible. "That's cool about the comics," I say. "Can I see them?"

"Yeah?" The brightness in his voice warms me, eases some of my nerves. "I think some of the old papers are in Joey's room. . . . I can go get them?"

"Sure. I'll be here. There are plenty more M&Ms to get through."

As I wait, the nerves return. My foot taps the ground. I feel ridiculous being nervous around a boy I've known my entire life, a boy who spends more time at my house than his own.

But I *do* feel nervous—and excited, a weird fluttering going through me.

This is bad. Very bad. I might need to seek professional help.

And then Ethan is back, papers in hand. He joins me at the table once more, and I relax. It's strange how the same person who makes my pulse jump can also calm it.

Ethan spreads the newspapers out in front of me. I feel a tiny lurch seeing my school name scrawled across the top. Returning to school next year, *if I return*, will be uncomfortable at best. I'll feel out of place. My teammates are no longer my friends, and I never made more than surface-level connections with anyone else. I want to be home, but the thought of the school year starting makes my skin itch.

Ethan's eyes are on me. I bite back the sudden urge to snap, "What?"

Instead, I unclench my jaw and look through his comics. They're different from what I saw in his sketchbook earlier tonight, finished products, cleaner lines, simple and fun. Ethan narrates as I shift through them, always talking down his skill: "Ah, not my best work" and "This one isn't that great."

Even though he brought them for me to see, he tries to pull them away before I can get a good look. Finally, I slap my hand down over his own. His skin is warm, soft, and my own skin buzzes in response. I take a quick breath, then tug my hand and the newspaper away. "Come on," I say. "Let me see."

"Fine," Ethan relents, sitting back in his chair, arms crossed and shoulders slouched in resignation. His cheeks are faintly pink.

His art has improved over the last year. It's more distinct, like I could pick his style out of a lineup of fifty others. The comic panel in front of me is an ingeniously subtle dig at our Spanish teacher, who is white and has never stepped foot outside of Georgia, yet pronounces everything in a thick Mexican accent. "Oh my god." I laugh. "I can't believe they let you get away with this. Also, they really need to fire her."

"Turns out you can't get fired for microaggressions if you're white and have tenure," Ethan says.

"Can you really call that accent a *micro* anything?"

Ethan laughs and shakes his head. "Definitely not."

Then he shows me another comic and another, all which he says "aren't his best work" or that he "wishes he'd had more time," but I love every single one. Most make me laugh, but one about two gerbils having crushes on each other makes me swoon. I knew Ethan was a talented artist. He *sees* the world in a way I don't. He sees *people* in a way I don't.

Maybe I should be paying more attention.

I look up at him. "These are amazing, Ethan. Really. You could publish them in a book one day."

He shakes his head. "They're just doodles."

"Call them whatever you want. They're awesome."

His cheeks grow red. When he says "Thanks," the word is so soft I can barely hear it. He shifts in his seat and starts organizing everything into a neat pile. "You know, they need more people on staff at the paper. If you're looking for something to do next year. Like a passion. I saw the list on the fridge. You could do interviews, or cover sports. . . ."

I tense at his words, and the little bubble of warmth

in my stomach suddenly goes cold. Because the tone in Ethan's voice has changed, and I realize something awful: he pities me.

He knows I lost the one thing, the only thing, I was good at, and now he's trying to find me some kind of hobby handout just like how Joey landed me a job. But finding a new passion isn't something I can just check off the list. It's not something I can do, or that Ethan can do for me. I can't replace the thing that meant the most to me like it's changing a pair of socks.

Ethan continues, "I can't imagine how hard it's been for you. Is there anything I can do to help?"

He's looking at me with so much sincerity, it makes me want to scream.

"It's fine." My voice is tense. I grab another handful of M&Ms even though my throat is too tight to eat them.

"Sorry, I was just—"

"What were you and Joey talking about earlier?" I ask, cutting him off. "In the parking lot."

Ethan freezes, and I see his own walls stack up. "Nothing. Just . . . nothing."

"Yeah. Okay." I nod. "So how about you don't pry into my business, and I won't pry into yours?"

"I wasn't prying." His expression looks pained. "I was just trying to—"

"Trying to what?" I ask, my tone sharp. "Fix me?"

"Hannah."

The hurt in his voice folds my stomach in on itself. I hate myself for it. He needs to stop looking at me like that. Like I'm some wounded, rabid animal.

I stand up from the table. "I'll see you tomorrow, okay?"

I retreat to my room, leaving the mess of food for him to clean up, because why not add fuel to my bad-person fire?

I try to latch onto my anger as I walk because it's preferable to any other feeling. I don't need Ethan prying. I don't need Ethan, or anyone, trying to fix something that can't be fixed. I just need to be left alone and to get through this summer in whatever way I can.

When I make it to the room, I close the door and turn the lock, even though no one else is awake to bother me. I slide down against the door, sitting on the wooden floor, my feet pressed into old slats. Our house, beneath its comforts, shows its age in its worn floorboards. At night, anything can cause them to creak: a hard blast from the AC, the scattering legs of a bug escaping the summer heat. The floors were always an obstacle whenever I snuck out last year, like a house full of trip wires. Usually the easiest route was avoiding them altogether and slipping right out my bedroom window. Later on, I stopped caring if my parents heard. I'd stride across the groaning floor and open the front door like it was the middle of the afternoon.

I miss that freedom—the freedom of not caring.

The house is silent now. I should go to sleep. Or go apologize to Ethan. The guilt of snapping at him makes my skin crawl. But as I stand up, my foot presses down on the creakiest floorboard of all.

I forgot about that one.

The one that moves.

As a child, it was my treasure trove. I filled it with glitter pens and My Little Pony figurines and a deck of playing cards my parents brought back from their Vegas trip. I filled it with scraps of paper—notes Brie and I passed in class; fortune-cookie slips with lottery numbers on the back; bracelets from soccer tournaments.

I scootch forward and lift up the wooden slat now, checking behind me first to make sure the door is definitely locked.

Buried beneath are all my childhood things. On top are all my things I stashed away a year ago. When I cleaned my room, I forgot about my favorite hiding spot.

There's a fifth of flavored vodka, still half-full. Two lighters, one hot pink, another tie-dye swirled. An Altoids tin.

I grab the tin and open it to find three joints inside. The smell is faded yet distinct, sending me back to long, humid nights, smiles flickering in the dark, illuminated only by the spark of a lighter. My head fizzing pleasantly. The faucet of thoughts shut off.

I pick up one of the joints, feeling the dried paper between my fingers. It's old, but I'm sure it'd still do the trick.

Suddenly, my heart is pounding in my ears.

I'm *tempted*. More than tempted. I could turn off my lights and open my window and take a few hits and *relax*. I could forget about the checklist. About Brie. About snapping at Ethan. About pleasing everyone and getting better.

I swallow hard, my throat thick.

It'd be so easy to light this thing up.

In the hallway, the bathroom door opens. I startle, dropping the joint back into the tin. My body tenses as the door clicks closed. Ethan must be brushing his teeth before bed.

I look down at the tin. The temptation has now dissipated, but my heart still drums heavily.

I should throw this stuff away so it doesn't happen again.

But instead I put everything back where I found it and replace the floorboard.

It's a windy night, and as I sleep, the house creaks.

Last Summer

Anticipation knots my stomach as the Kensington team files onto the field. My eyes lock onto a few players in particular–

Tina Yu, their all-star forward with more career goals than anyone in the state.

Annabeth Carleton, their formidable goalie, who makes physics-defying saves.

And, of course, Lily Thompson, their defensive powerhouse, who kept me from scoring last year.

When Lily sees me, she gives a little wave and a smile. I smile back.

I will demolish her into dust.

"Easy there, girl," Nina tells me, her hand on my shoulder. "We can't beat them if you bite their heads off first."

"I'm good, I'm good," I say, shrugging off her hand and turning back to my team.

Nina laughs. "Sure you are."

In truth, my body is wound tight. Shiva for my bubbie, only seven days long, seemed to stretch on for a month, a constant parade of casseroles and prayer and kind words from distant relatives and friends, a continuous loop of missing my bubbie so deeply I could feel the loss in my bones.

The second shiva ended, I ran sprints and drills until my lungs burned and sweat poured down my back. Back at practice with my team, I felt awkward on the field, out of sync with everyone else. I pushed everyone to extend practice. The extra time helped ease me back into our rhythm, but I still feel unprepared. And now, instead of excitement when I look into the stands, I'm heartbroken Bubbie isn't here to watch, heartbroken she'll never call me mamaleh again. The pain slices so deep, I can barely breathe.

I have to win. It's what she would want. I have to do this for her, for us. I'll win the game, impress the scouts, secure my spot on a D1 team, and then make the Olympic team. And one day I'll put my podium picture on the mantel right next to Bubbie's. I'll make her proud.

Ten minutes later, we're out on the field. Adrenaline pulses through the air. The sun is high in the sky, beating down on us with vicious intensity. A bead of sweat drips down my temple, but I don't move to wipe it away. I just focus on Lily. Tension between the two teams grows heavy. My muscles beg for action as I dig a heel into the fresh-cut grass. I've always been an impatient girl.

And then the whistle blows. And the world launches into motion.

I imagine it looks beautiful, like a synchronized ballet, every action with an equal reaction. I lean left, and Lily mirrors me. Carrie-Anne angles right and is mirrored as well. It's a beautiful symphony, except the only sounds are shouts and grunts and calls of "Open!"

The competition between our teams is dead even. No one keeps possession for long. My pulse races faster with each passing minute, but my focus and determination grow stronger as well. I glance into the stands, and for a second, I see my bubbie there, whistling with two fingers.

I can do this. I can win for her.

I bear down and search for an opening. There's always an opening, and the trick is whether you can find it in time. I inhale sharply and scan, my heartbeat thudding in my ears as the symphony plays on without me, and then–

And then I see it.

Like a glimpse into the future, the play opens up in front of me. Lily has fallen back to block Carrie-Anne, but Brie hasn't made the pass yet, and then I'm sprinting forward to an empty spot, and no one has eyes on me. Except Brie. She sees me, and Lily is too far away, and the pass gets made, and I have the ball in my possession, and I'm sprinting down the field, Lily now on me with ferocious speed.

I hope the scouts are watching.

My heart pounds, loud and drumming, and my stomach jumps up into my throat. This is it. A shot on goal. I can score. I can win. The memory of my bubbie's whistle sings out over the field.

I bear down with even more determination than before, but Lily is right there behind me, gaining ground every second. And my muscles are screaming, and I should have fit in more sprints, and I should have trained harder, but I didn't have the time, and then Lily's foot is striking out for the ball, and–

The sound that escapes my mouth is unintelligible.

The pain that explodes in my ankle and shoots up my spine is impossible to process.

I collapse to the ground and shake, the pain so bad that my teeth ache. I'm writhing in the grass as the sound of the crack echoes in my ears.

Lily struck for the ball and hit my bad ankle instead.

I'm vaguely aware of the action stopping, of people gathering around me, of Coach Peterson rushing to my side. "This isn't real, this isn't real, this isn't real," I whisper as she gets to her knees, her green eyes dark with worry.

"Hannah, it's going to be okay. We've got you."

Her calm voice offers no reassurances. I continue the same chant. "This isn't real, this isn't real, this isn't real."

I inhale as she touches my ankle. The sharp crack continues its echo.

Chapter Nine

IT'S EARLY, barely nine on a Saturday, and I've been tossing and turning since seven. The shower helps chase away some of the sleep from my eyes, but I'm feeling tired as I stand in front of my mirror. My jean shorts are loose, thanks to my shrunken thigh muscles, and my skin is the palest it's been since I was a baby. I hardly recognize myself.

I look away, then without the mirror, put on mascara and tinted lip balm and spray a mist from Bath & Body Works, one Brie left in the bathroom. I grab my phone as I head out of my room.

"Good morning, sweetheart," my dad greets me as I enter the kitchen. "Hungry?"

It takes a lot of willpower not to groan in response. I was counting on having breakfast alone, bathing in my bad mood in peace. Last night still has my shoulders tense, the fight with Ethan, the paraphernalia stashed in my room. Guilt swirls in my stomach as I watch Dad move around the kitchen. He thinks I've already thrown it all out, that I've been a good girl, that I'm following all the rules. I didn't light that joint last night, but I didn't throw it away, either.

"Um, sure," I tell Dad. "I could eat."

No wasn't really an option because Dad has already cooked stacks of waffles *and* pancakes, plus chopped up a bowl of fruit salad the size of his head. My parents usually sleep in on the weekends, crawling out of bed around ten for coffee, bagels, and lox. I don't know why he's up so early. Ethan has a later shift, and Joey doesn't work today, so they're still fast asleep.

I grab a plate and say, "It looks good. Thanks." I stack my plate with a generous portion, then search for the syrup. There's none on the table, so I walk over to the fridge, where of course I see the Mountain Bliss checklist.

Dad must catch me staring. "How's that all going?" he asks, voice tentative. "Need any help with it?"

My conversation with Ethan from last night rattles around in my brain again. My fingers clutch the fridge door tightly. I just want to be left alone. Unobserved.

I open the door and pretend to hunt for the maple syrup, even though I see the bottle right away. "Um . . ." I rummage a bit longer before grabbing the bottle and heading to the table. "I'm okay. . . ."

"How's the passion one going?" Dad asks.

"Um, I don't know." My throat feels like it's closing up. Anger nips at my heels. I wish people would stop pushing me. "I mean, I can't just get a new passion. But I'm going to work really hard at my job, and I've been doing a lot of good deeds. I'm doing well, yeah?"

I force a lot of brightness into my voice for that and hope Dad will give me a pat on the back. But instead he clears his throat, shuffles the food on his plate. "Hannah." My stomach clenches. "Your mom and I don't want to hang over your head all summer, but we're serious about that list. We need to follow the guidelines. Finish the list and stay home. Don't finish, and—"

"That's not fair!"

I shrink back after my exclamation, tears threatening to well. Dad blinks at me. I attempt to take a steadying breath. "Um, sorry. I mean I don't have control over finding a passion. It doesn't feel fair."

I used to follow all the rules; Dad used to look at me with nothing but wonder in his eyes. Now he looks at me with sympathy, worry, maybe even disappointment.

"I know it's hard, sweetheart," Dad says slowly. "And you're right. Passion does have a lot of weight to it. Let's call it a hobby, all right? You've just got to try a few things. We don't want you to feel so adrift again. Is there anything that interests you? I can take you golfing with me one weekend."

I make a face. "No thanks."

"What about yard-sale flipping?" he asks.

My parents love picking through yard sales and thrift stores. Every now and then they'll buy something and clean it up to its former glory or turn it into something new and inventive.

"I don't know. I'm not sure shopping counts as a passion."

I hunch over my food. I'm not *trying* to be difficult, but his suggestions are stressing me out. I already found my passion, and it was the best thing in the world. I'm never going to find that again, and I don't understand why everyone can't just accept that.

"What about puzzles?" Dad asks. "Your mom just started a thousand-piece one. She could use a helper."

All the guilt and stress come to a head. It's clear he's not going to let up on this. Maybe the best way to be left alone is to show that I'm trying.

"Sure," I say, unclenching my jaw. "I'll give it a shot."

Hannah Klein, puzzle master. *Yeah right.*

When I get to work, I find Tony in the arcade. His muscles are on full display, shirtsleeves cut off and a bandana tied around his right bicep. The muscle flexes as he twists to fix one of the race-car machines. "Hey, Tony," I say, stopping a foot behind him. I need a distraction today, and I have the perfect plan.

Tony looks at me with a slow blink. I think it takes a second for him to recognize me. If I had to guess, Tony doesn't have the strongest short-term memory in the world. Eventually, he nods and asks, "What's up, Hailey?"

Hannah, obviously, but close enough. I tuck a strand of hair behind my ear. "Where's your brother?"

"Bowling alley," he answers, spreading out his arms. "It's his domain."

"Cool, thanks."

I make my way to the bowling alley. It's quiet this morning, just a few of our senior teams taking up lanes on the far left. I search for the Golden Oldies, but they aren't here. Then I turn to the front counter and find Patrick there with another employee. I haven't worked with him before. He has freckled white skin and short-cut blond hair. Patrick finishes ringing up a customer, and then he sees me and smiles. His hair is rumpled today, like he woke up just in time for his shift.

I smile back at him, maintaining steady eye contact. His eyes grow intrigued.

"Good morning, Hannah," he says.

"Morning, Patrick." I tilt my head. "Can you show me where we keep the trash bags? I forgot."

I did not forget. And Patrick knows this.

His smile widens. "Absolutely. Nick, you're on register."

"Uh, okay," Nick says, eyes flicking back and forth between the two of us like he's missing something. Which he definitely is.

"Thanks, Nick," I say. Then I turn and head to the supply closet that Patrick is supposed to be leading me to. Patrick follows behind. I can feel his eyes on me. The back of my neck heats as my pulse starts to race.

Stupid. I know this is stupid. But I'm reveling in the adrenaline pulsing through my veins, and I like the way my stomach flipped when Patrick looked at me in pleasant surprise. And I like that I can focus on those feelings and leave no room for other, stressful thoughts.

I open the door to the closet and step inside. Patrick walks in behind me and goes to flick on the light, but I grab his hand and say, "Don't."

I feel him take a slight inhale as he closes the door. And then, slowly, he backs me against it, hands cautious and soft. "Is this okay?" he asks.

I reach up in the dark, and I kiss him. "Yes."

He kisses me back, and immediately I feel a spark of excitement. My toes curl; hairs rise on my arms.

It turns out sober kissing is quite nice. Better than tipsy kissing, because I can feel everything. Patrick's hands explore slowly, sweeping across my neck, then my back, then to the sides of my legs, right beneath the hem of my shorts. He makes a soft little noise when he hits bare skin, and I pull him closer, body flushing.

"You smell nice," he murmurs into my neck, kissing me there.

I pull my hands through his hair and inhale. He smells nice too, fresh shampoo and only the faintest whiff of Bonanza's chemical cleaner. I try to capture his bottom lip as his arms draw me closer. My brain fizzes. All other thoughts slip away as his hands wander farther, now slipping under my shirt to touch my bare back.

"Still okay?" he asks, kissing my cheek, then my lips, then my cheek again.

His fingers are warm against my skin, and I go to tell him yes, to let every anxiety disappear under his touch, but then suddenly the door I'm pressed against falls open, and I stumble, and Nick is standing there with a goofy smile.

My stomach drops. I cannot imagine what Patrick and I look like in this moment.

Actually, I can, because I can see Patrick, and his lips are red, and his hair is a mess. And I'm not going to look down, but if I did look down, I'm pretty sure I'd see tenting in his pants. In this moment, I'm very grateful not to have a certain body part.

"Nice." Nick's smile skeeves me out. "A little morning delight, huh?"

My discomfort turns to anger, as my hands fist by my sides.

"Dude, go away," Patrick tells him.

Not the strongest defense of my honor, but he tried.

Nick's smile only widens, so I say, "Seriously. Fuck off."

The hard edge to my voice must work. Nick plays it off with a shrug but turns and walks away. Now alone with Patrick again, I feel the tiniest hint of awkwardness. I clear my throat, then adjust my shirt before looking up at him. I catch a glimpse behind his cool exterior. He looks *soft*, and it makes me smile.

"That was a nice surprise," he says. His cheeks even seem red. "What brought that on?"

"Just seemed like it'd be fun." I pause. "And it was."

"I agree." Patrick smiles. "There's a party tonight. My friend's apartment. He's a sophomore in college."

I raise my eyebrow. "Is that an invitation?"

"It is. We could have some more fun."

I bite my lip. I'm tempted to say yes. Kissing Patrick is fun. Much more fun than getting interrogated in my own kitchen. Maybe I could go for just an hour or two. Tell my parents I'm hanging out at work again. I wouldn't drink. I would just—

My phone buzzes. Three times in a row. I slip it out of my pocket to find all-caps texts from Pete. The messages read:

WHIRLY BALL EMERGENCY
IMMEDIATE REQUEST FOR HELP
NOW!

I show Patrick the texts and say, "I'm gonna go help. Thanks for the, uh, kissing. I'll see you later."

"Anytime, Hannah." He salutes me. "Anytime."

There are kids *everywhere*. There is screaming *everywhere*. There is cake *everywhere*.

It's possible I'm breaking out into hives just from the sight.

Pete looks on the verge of tears as he tries to calm the parents. Two older employees and Daisey are multitasking, trying to clean up while keeping the kids from wreaking additional havoc or sneaking out.

When Daisey spots me, she practically sags in relief. "Oh, thank god, backup."

"What happened?" I ask, grabbing a towel. The birthday boy, dressed in a Spider-Man outfit and princess crown, stands on a table and ups his cries to full-on wails.

Daisey takes a giant breath, then says, "Two of the whirly-ball cars broke." She kneels on the floor, scrubbing the carpet with full force. "Which happens all the time. It's usually an easy fix, but not today. So the kids got upset. We offered to move the party to the arcade, but the parents didn't want that because they don't believe in *screen time* for their children, so I suggested that we have cake and sing 'Happy Birthday' first, and then hopefully the cars would be fixed by the time that was done, which seemed to appease everyone. But *then*—"

Daisey takes another big gulp of air and sprays the floor with more solution. I bend down to help her scrub. "I lit the candles on the cake, but one of the kids was having a tantrum because they still wanted to play, so they ran up and banged the *lit* cake off the table, and that"—Daisey points to a scorch mark on the ground—"set the carpet on fire. Just a little. But you know, fire, kids. Parents were not happy. I put it out with my boot and then the extinguisher just to be safe, but by then everyone was crying and screaming, and the cake was of course ruined, and I almost had my very first panic attack. Fun times. That's about when Pete showed up."

She looks around the room, then back to me with exhausted eyes. "So, yeah, that's what happened. How's your morning?"

"Whoa." Gingerly, I extend a hand forward and pat her shoulder. "That's a lot. What can I do to help?"

Daisey sighs and looks around the disaster zone. "Anything you can do to keep these kids occupied would be amazing."

"Okay, no problem," I say. But internally, I feel a hint of unease. If Joey were here, everything would be fine. He's great with kids. He's creative. He's *fun*. But I'm not good at this stuff. I only ever had one skill.

"I want my caaaaake!" the birthday boy screeches, directly into my eardrum. "This is the worst birthday ever! I hate you all! Cake, cake, cake!"

My pulse rises along with his voice. Daisey's stress lines are growing and Pete is melting down. I need to do something. This is my job. I should be able to do this.

"CAAAAAKE!"

I want cake too, kid.

Wait a second. . . .

Cake.

An idea sparks. Maybe it could work.

Bonanza doesn't make cakes, so I can't just grab a new one, but I have another idea. The thing about kids and cake is, what they really want is *sugar*. And there are plenty of sugary food items at Bonanza. "I have an idea," I tell Daisey as I stand up. "Hold the fort down a little longer?"

"Please be quick," Daisey pleads.

"Promise."

I turn from the room and start to jog, but that makes my ankle twinge. Ugh. I kind of want to punch a wall. Instead, I speed-walk to the EZ Eats concession stand. Once there, I find Gary and Sherry arguing over the best episode of *Battlestar Galactica*.

"Hey, y'all!" I interrupt them.

They look at me with immediate suspicion. Sherry speaks first. "What is it?"

"I need a favor," I reply. "Please."

Fifteen minutes later, I return to whirly ball, my arms stacked with treats. Gary and Sherry were not happy about my kitchen takeover, but they know the true horror of a kid's birthday party meltdown, so they begrudgingly let me root around, while eyeing me with suspicion the entire time. I'm now carrying a tray of Rice Krispies treats covered with marshmallow fluff, a platter of brownies, three soft cookies with a side of fudge dipping sauce, and a menagerie of ice cream treats.

The whirly-ball room feels even more chaotic when I return. Additional employees have shown up to help. Tony is here, working on the broken bumper cars with Pete, and—

My shoulders stiffen at the sight of Ethan. His eyes catch mine for just a second before his attention is drawn away. Something flips inside me as I watch him. He's now on soothe-the-parents duty and seems to be doing a much better job of it than Pete, his posture calm and relaxed. I swallow hard, then turn away and head over to Daisey.

Her eyes widen at the sight of everything in my hands. "Whoa." She blinks. "Planning to sugar-coma the kids into submission?"

I laugh. "Sort of."

Then I hesitate. What if it's a bad idea? Did I just waste time and money? What if—

"Go on . . . ," Daisey prods.

I pile all the food onto the table. "Well, um, I thought we could do a cake walk. Just, er, minus actual cake. We used to do them in elementary school. An activity plus sugar. Guaranteed fun. Right?"

I look up and wait for Daisey to give me a weird look. But she doesn't—she just smiles, her eyes brightening. "*Perfect* idea! I'll set up the music and you confirm with the parents!"

"Cool," I say. "Great." I try to keep my voice casual as relief floods through me. "Awesome."

Ethan is still with the parents, and despite his adult-soothing smile, I can see the fatigue in his eyes. I have a feeling I'm not the only one who slept poorly. Nerves beat through me as I walk over and introduce the cake-walk idea to the parents. Ethan's gaze decidedly lands everywhere but on me as I speak.

"Sounds great!" the dad says. "Is there gluten in the food? We had a gluten-free cake." He glares over at Daisey, like it's her fault. "Before it was destroyed."

I push back the urge to shoot him my own death glare. "Um, yes," I reply. "There's definitely gluten."

That's when the mom lets out a giant sigh and says,

"Jesus Christ, Nathan! Let the damn kids have gluten. It's not like they're allergic!"

I stifle my laughter. My eyes instinctively catch Ethan's, and he's biting back a laugh too. As we step away from the parents, some of the tension melts between us. Ethan's even looking at me now. Well, my feet. But close enough.

"Need help setting up?" he asks, his head ducked.

"Yes, please," I say, grateful he raised a white flag. "And, well, I'm sorry." I rush out the words quickly. "About last night."

"I know." He looks up, and this time his eyes meet mine. His smile is soft. "We're all good, Hannah."

I feel lighter as we set up the cake walk, then google the rules for the cake walk, not that the kids really care if we're following proper cake-walk protocol. I head over to the birthday boy, who has now gone from wailing to sniffling with the occasional hiccup, and inform him of the new plan.

"So we get cake?" he asks.

"Better than cake; you get a whole bunch of different desserts! Look!"

His eyes light up, and he says, "Okay! I want to go first!"

Going first isn't really how a cake walk works, but I tell him sure. It only takes a few minutes to round up the rest of the kids because sugar is a compelling force, and then Daisey gets the music playing and off we go. My adrenaline is still racing as I emcee the event, teasing the kids and trying to keep them as entertained as possible. Other than a scuffle over who really won the oatmeal pie bowl (mashed oatmeal pies with whipped cream and chocolate syrup on top), the event runs smoothly, and the parents look beyond relieved.

And just as we're starting to run low on desserts, Tony walks into the main room and announces, "All fixed," in a cool tone. He twirls his screwdriver, then slides it into his back pocket.

"Thank god," Daisey groans.

Tony walks over to us and smirks at me. "I heard *someone* started their morning off well."

My cheeks heat. "Excuse me?" I ask, even though I know exactly what he's talking about by the look he's giving me. Annoyance rattles through me. It's not like I told Patrick to keep our make-out session between just us, but it seems like a dick move to go and immediately brag about it.

"What's going on here?" Daisey looks back and forth between us.

I'm acutely aware of Ethan in the background, who can overhear every word as he hands out ice-cream sandwiches.

"Newbie and Patrick went at it in the storage closet this morning," Tony says.

I feel Ethan freeze in my peripheral vision. My pulse races, anger blurring my vision. What right does Tony have to announce that to everyone? And it sounds like an insinuation that we did something more. What did Patrick tell him?

"We didn't *go at it*," I say, my voice hard. "We made out. Not that it's anyone's business. Did Patrick say we did something else?"

"Huh?" Tony shakes his head. "Nah. Patrick didn't say anything. It was that kid Nick. He's telling everyone."

"Oh." I feel a small press of relief. I'm not happy about being Bonanza gossip, but at least Patrick wasn't being a tool. Now I feel bad that I blamed him.

"Heading back to the arcade," Tony says. He lifts up two fingers. "See ya."

As he leaves, I stand there quiet and confused. Daisey takes my hand and gives it a little squeeze. "Bit of advice, Hannah girl. Number-one thing to know about this place is nothing stays secret. Gossip spreads like wildfire. People get bored out of their minds and would spread gossip to a brick wall if that were the only option."

"Great, wonderful," I mutter.

"Yup," Daisey says. "Super fun. But, so hey, was Patrick any good?" She nudges me. "He's too young for me, but he's a cute match for you."

I still feel uncomfortable. And acutely aware Ethan overheard all that. But Daisey's smile relaxes my shoulders, and I tell her, "The kissing with the cute boy was not bad."

She winks. "What a roundabout way to say you liked it."

I laugh.

Daisey wraps an arm around my shoulder. "Come on, let's get these kids playing whirly ball."

We go back to work, but amid the chaos, I can't help but notice that Ethan leaves without saying goodbye.

Last Summer

There are too many machines around me. The beeps are loud, grating. I want to smash them. But my body feels weighted down—with drugs, pain, and fear.

Joey and Dad sit in the two chairs. Mom paces a tiny circuit in front of my bed, three steps forward and three back.

It all feels incredibly strange. I've never been the patient before. My trips to the hospital were all for Bubbie. The last time, she didn't come home. I didn't even see her before the procedure. She told me it was minor, not to rearrange my day for it. So, I went to practice.

By the time I showed up to give my bubbie a kiss in her recovery room, the doctors were saying she wouldn't wake up.

My doctor enters the room. His name tag reads DR. WESTMAN. He looks young for a doctor, barely older than my cousin Eliza in college. "Hannah," he says. "I'm afraid I have bad news." I wish the doctor were a woman, only because I'd feel more comfortable.

Mom speaks for me, which is good, because my throat feels swollen shut. "What do you mean?" she asks. "How bad?"

I glance out the window. How much time has passed since the game? The sun is still out, but it's fallen low in the sky. Golden hour. That's what they call it. When everything looks more beautiful.

Dr. Westman turns on a monitor and taps a few things on his tablet and suddenly we're looking at the scan of my ankle, which seems to have more breaks than should be mathematically possible. My heart plummets.

Beneath the haze of drugs, I'm acutely aware of my ankle throbbing beneath me, but I'm too scared to look down and see the real thing.

"Unfortunately," Dr. Westman says, pointing at the screen, "since the joint was already severely weakened from previous injuries, the damage was far easier to inflict. And the damage is . . ." He pauses, his face shifting, like suddenly he realizes he's talking to a person and not writing notes up in a case file. He turns to me, and his voice softens as he says, "Hannah, I don't believe you'll play soccer again. Not at your level, at any rate. The damage is—well, it's catastrophic."

My stomach heaves. There's an empty bin beside my bed. I grab it and vomit. I think Dad gasps.

I wipe my mouth. Then I tell the doctor, "You're wrong." I turn to my parents. "He's wrong, right? He's just one doctor. We'll get an expert. . . . We'll get . . ."

"I'm actually an orthopedic attending specializing in sports medicine," Dr. Westman replies.

"You didn't just 'But actually' my sister," Joey snarls.

I look over to my brother with a wave of gratitude.

Dr. Westman hesitates, then allows, "Of course, I encourage second opinions. Recoveries are different for everyone, and we can get you into the best physical therapy available. . . ."

He continues speaking, but I don't hear him. It's like my brain shuts down and refuses to take in additional information. Because this can't be real. This isn't real. My soccer career isn't done. I'm an athlete. I'm going to the Olympics, just like my bubbie.

It's everything I've ever worked toward. It can't just be over.

I turn toward the window. The sun has dropped lower in the sky, its final tendrils of light snaking into the room.

Chapter Ten

"HOW MANY TICKETS for the koala bear?" a kid asks, a stick of Laffy Taffy in one hand and a paper bag of popcorn in the other.

It's a panda bear, not a koala, but it doesn't matter because the three-foot stuffed animal is way out of his league. "Three thousand," I reply.

He pouts. "I only have eighty-seven."

"Do you like fidget toys?" I ask, guiding him over to the section employees have lovingly labeled "vacuum fodder." I pull out a selection of spinning tops, finger traps, and stress balls, and let him pick out one of each even though his tickets don't quite cover it. Hey, his teacher is in charge of math lessons, not me.

As soon as he skips away, another kid approaches, and another. It's a busy Saturday night at Bonanza. I've been working the prize counter at the arcade for the past week. It's a good spot. Air-conditioned. Easy. I like the bowling alley, as well. The Golden Oldies are a hoot. But Ethan is there most days, and most days, I don't want to deal with the strange feeling in my stomach when I'm around him.

"Hey, Mario master!" a voice calls out as I finish up another prize exchange.

I look up to find my brother approaching. He's wearing light-wash denim jeans and a neon-green Bonanza shirt with the sleeves rolled up. Very eighties chic. His eyes are bright and full of their never-ending energy.

"Very funny," I reply.

In an effort to make Dad happy, I've been trying new hobbies all week. Puzzling with Mom did not go well. It took me thirty minutes to find one piece, and by the end of the night I had a neck crick that wouldn't leave me alone for days. Then there was gardening on Tuesday with Dad. It was nice being outside, warm sun on my skin, fingers in fresh soil. But since the garden is his pride and joy, Dad's rare type-A tendencies came out, and under his watch I felt like I was performing heart surgery instead of planting tulips. Not relaxing. And then there were video games on Thursday with Joey. He introduced me to "the easiest Mario game." I cursed every time I died, which was often. Eventually Joey took the controllers away from me because I was jamming the buttons so hard he was scared they would break.

The new hobbies aren't working. Trying to force a new passion is like trying to grow a plant in a desert. It won't work. And if somehow it does work, it's going to come out all sharp and prickly and no one will want to be around it. My only hope is to find a hobby I can fake well enough to make my parents happy. Maybe I'll try meditation next. I just have to sit there, right?

I bite the inside of my cheek as Joey circles the counter.

"Mind if I help for a bit? I *love* the prize counter."

"Have at it," I reply.

He snakes his hand into the candy stockpile, pulling out two pink Starbursts. "Don't tell Pete," he whispers, sliding me one.

We help customers for the next half hour. Joey is great at the job. No matter the number of tickets, each kid walks away like they've won the lottery. He's a veritable Willy Wonka, without all the toxicity. Pete is lucky to have him as an employee.

"*So,*" Joey says, jumping up to sit on the counter since there's a lull in traffic. His legs knock against the glass case as he peers down at me like a teacher. I feel like I'm about to have a discussion about my report card.

"*Yes?*" I ask.

"I could use your help with something," he says. "Don't say no."

I laugh. "You'll have to give me a little more information before I can commit to that."

He sighs heavily. *"Fine."* Then he straightens his back and says, "The Olympics are starting next week, and we're a little hard-up on volunteers. Particularly for—"

A buzzing starts in my ears at the word "Olympics."

Why do they have to call it that? Why can't it be a tournament? The Bonanza Games? The Anything Other Than Olympics.

It's just a word. I know it's just a word, and it's silly to get upset over a word. But I can't help how it triggers this gut reaction. My body tenses. Throat tightens. Fingers dig into my sides.

"So what do you think?" Joey asks. "Four shifts would be ideal, but anything would help. Please, dear sister!"

I blink at him. I have no idea what he just asked me to do, but I do know my answer.

"Sorry, can't."

My jaw stiffens as he continues his plea. He's so upbeat. I begrudge him for it. I begrudge him for being carefree. For being happy.

Anxiety builds as I tell him no and no once more. I'm going to snap if he asks me again. My eyes blur with annoyance. Why can't my family just leave me be? Why isn't working and coming home on time and being a "good girl" enough?

"I have to go," I cut Joey off. "You've got the counter covered?"

He blinks. And in that moment, my brother looks younger. Like the kid I used to split my Popsicles with on hot summer days. "Well, yeah," he says. "Sure, but—"

"Great. Bye, then."

I rush away from the counter, pulling out my phone as I walk and sending a quick text to someone who won't make me talk.

Where are you?

Patrick responds instantly: Pete's office, filling out paper-work

I send my reply just as fast: Are you alone?

"Pete's dealing with a go-kart emergency," Patrick tells me as I walk into the office. "Just left. Should be gone for a while."

My heart beats wildly in my chest as I take in Patrick, his tousled hair and easy smile. He's lounging comfortably on his chair, his long limbs splayed out like he owns the place. Perfect-distraction Patrick. Since our time in the supply closet last week, we've found a few more moments to be together. A quick kiss in the shoe-cleaning room, a make-out session against a brick wall when he "walked me to my car" to grab my sweater, a heated moment behind the bowling lanes when we were supposed to be fixing jammed pins.

His lips are exceptional. Soft and dedicated. They skirt across my skin, always exploring, always wanting. His fingers twist through the loops on my jean shorts; his hands push back my hair to reveal my neck. And best of all, when I kiss him, all other thoughts go away. I don't think about puzzles with Mom or gardening with Dad. I don't think about soccer or Bubbie or being sent back to Mountain Bliss. I just think of how his lips feel against mine. Kissing is a skill, and Patrick is an expert.

I click the door shut behind me.

Patrick raises an eyebrow as I approach. He's wearing black jeans today and a white Bonanza shirt over his lean torso. His tattoos peek out of the sleeves.

"What's this one for?" I ask, sitting down next to him in one of the hardback office chairs. My thighs stick to the tacky faux-leather seat as I lean forward to trace a floral design on his arm.

"I just thought it was pretty," he replies.

"And this one?" I ask, rolling up his sleeve to reveal a small row of moon shapes, crescent and gibbous and full. His skin prickles under my touch.

"I like the moon more than the sun," he replies. "You can look right at it."

He's looking right at me, want in his eyes. I feel warmth in my belly as he leans forward, his lips pressing a soft kiss to my jaw. There's a yearning in me. A yearning for him, but truthfully, a deeper yearning to shut everything else out. He can give that to me.

"Is that paperwork important?" I ask, glancing at the desk.

His voice is low, graveled. "Couldn't give a shit about it."

And then I kiss him, hard.

His hands pull for me, and I push off my chair, dropping all pretense as I move forward onto his lap. He lets out a soft groan in my ear as I settle onto him, legs straddling his waist, feet skimming the floor. It feels exciting and new and dangerous.

"This okay?" I ask.

"Don't you dare get up," he replies, wrapping his arms tight around me so my chest pulls flush with his own.

And then his lips are everywhere, searching my skin like I'm hiding something. My body flushes, and my thoughts grow fuzzy until they fade altogether, until all I know is warmth and want and need. I can feel him beneath me, and it makes a whimper build in the back of my throat. Now *this* should be my new hobby.

And then I hear a walkie-talkie.

It beeps loudly in the hallway, a voice coming in over the static. "Pete, we need . . ."

Pete!

Terrified, I jump off Patrick, my heart pounding in my ears. I barely have time to smooth out my clothing before

Pete pushes open his office door and strides into the room. I feel the guilt written all over my red face. I'm shaking. What the hell was I thinking? Hooking up in my boss's office? Regret washes over me, making my stomach turn.

Pete isn't looking at me, thank god. Or at Patrick. He's looking at his walkie-talkie and replying to the person there, while biting into one of his peanut-butter protein bars. If my heart pounds any harder, I might pass out.

I pray for more time for my skin to cool down.

Then Patrick, calm and collected, says, "Hey, Boss, just finishing up that paperwork."

Pete looks up with a slow blink, just realizing we're both in the office. "Great, good." He nods at Patrick. Then glances at me. "What can I help you with, Hannah?"

Thank god my brain throws me a lifeline. "Oh, um, I just wanted to ask for another work shirt. I only have three, and with all my shifts . . ."

"Of course," Pete replies. "Pick one out from the supply closet."

I'm aware of every slight movement as I walk over to the closet and pull a shirt at random off the shelf. I don't even check to see if it's my size. I make a beeline for the door. As I'm about to walk out, Patrick puts his pen down and says, "All done!"

"Great," Pete replies, settling into his chair.

I rush out the door as quickly as possible, Patrick following behind me as I speed-walk down the hall. As we turn a corner into an empty corridor, he tugs my hand to stop us. And then he starts laughing. "Well, shit, that was close." He leans back against the wall and runs a hand through his hair. "You like a bit of danger, huh?"

"No." My throat is tight. And I think I want to throw up. An uncomfortable combination. "No, that was—that was bad. That was really stupid. We could have gotten fired."

Patrick shrugs. "Eh, I doubt it. And if so, whatever. It's just a job."

I shake my head, guilt swarming my thoughts. Since I've gotten home, I've been failing at everything. Except this job. And now I've put that at risk. I'm so angry at myself. I'm so angry at *everything*.

"It's more than just a job for me," I tell Patrick.

He tilts his head. "What do you mean?"

And so I tell him all about last year. That I injured my ankle, went off the rails ("I knew you were a party girl," he interrupts), and then my parents sent me to boarding school.

"If I don't stay in line this summer, I'm getting sent right back," I say. "I'm sorry. I shouldn't have started that in Pete's office. I could've gotten us both in trouble."

Patrick presses forward off the wall and throws an arm around my shoulder, pulling me into him. He smells of men's deodorant with a faint addition of bowling-alley funk. "Don't stress, Klein. It was no big deal. It's okay to have a little fun."

"It *was* a big deal," I insist. "I was straddling you in our manager's office. I don't know what I was thinking."

"Well, I liked it."

I roll my eyes. "I'm well aware of that."

He smiles. "Why don't you come out with me after work? My friend is throwing a party at his place. Low-key, promise. We can have a drink, let off some steam." He laughs. "Get away from this place."

I shake my head, irritation seeping into my voice. "I just told you. I can't do that kind of stuff."

Patrick shrugs. "You're a teenager. It's normal to go to parties. You parents know that."

"Stop, okay?" I snap. "I told you I can't, and I need you to leave it alone."

His face shifts, regret in his expression. "You're right. I'm sorry. My bad, for real." He smiles, a hesitant one, and holds out a hand. "Truce?"

Jumping at the chance to be done with this conversation, I shake his hand. "Sure, truce."

I'm spiraling as I walk to the bowling alley. If we'd been caught . . . I can't imagine the disappointment on my parents' faces. Not that kissing someone is wrong, but in my manager's office while on the clock? Definitely wrong. Dark feelings make my breath tight. I wish I had someone to talk to. I wish I had Brie. Or Bubbie. My heart clenches at the thought of her, at the thought of her kindness, her spot-on advice, the simple warmth of her hand on mine. Her absence aches.

It feels like there's not a single safe space in the whole of Bonanza. Joey might still be at the prize counter. Brie is always at mini golf. Patrick just told me he's heading off to help Tony with the go-karts. And Ethan—

Sure enough, I walk through the alley doors and see him at the front counter, ringing up a group of teenagers. It strikes me just how tall he's gotten, towering over the coworker next to him. I chew the inside of my cheek as I turn away. Maybe I can make an escape to the shoe closet and spend the last two hours of my shift polishing in solitude.

As I head that way, I spot the Golden Oldies on lane twelve. They're here late. It's eight on a Saturday night. Despite my mood, a smile tugs at my lips as I walk over to them. They've got balloons at their lane (not allowed), and a pitcher of margaritas (we do not sell pitchers of margaritas), and they're all wearing pink party hats.

"Hey, y'all!" I chirp brightly as I approach.

"Darling!" Madeline greets me, throwing her hands up into the air. "Come give me a hug!"

Her blond hair is teased into a large pouf, and her gold

earrings glimmer under the bowling alley lights. She looks like a Pink Lady from *Grease* with her hot-pink jacket and black pumps (also not allowed at the bowling lanes). As she pulls me in for a hug, I catch a scent of her spiced perfume, which reminds me so sharply of Bubbie, tears prick at my eyes.

I wipe them away quickly as I step back and greet the entire crew. "What are y'all celebrating?" I ask.

"My birthday!" Vanessa trills, standing up and then giving me a curtsy. She's wearing a fake tiara and has a corsage pinned to her Golden Oldies jacket.

"Happy birthday!" I tell her. "How old are you?"

"I'll answer that over my dead body," she replies, smiling with dangerous sweetness. I laugh as she ushers me forward to sit down with them.

Ginger offers me a margarita, and Tashia chastises her. "Our Hannah here is on the clock! And not of legal age!"

They offer me birthday cake instead, and I agree to a slice of "Coconut Delight." Adele tells me it's her secret recipe, passed down from her own mother. Bella laughs and says, "Sweetheart, we all know that's a Sara Lee."

I pepper the ladies with questions, as I've learned their favorite subject is themselves, as it should be. Perhaps I can count my birthday cheer as my good deed for the day. I could certainly use the cosmic brownie points after snapping at Joey and my disastrous decision-making with Patrick.

After about ten minutes, I try to segue to my exit, telling them I'm on shift and need to go back to work, but they won't hear it. "Having a young face like yours around makes us all feel our youth again," Madeline says. "Be a doll and stay a while longer."

"Ooh!" Ginger trills. "And I smell another young whippersnapper coming this way. Ethan! Ethan, darling! Come on over and say hello."

My shoulders tense. Ethan is approaching, and my back is to him. My pulse feels thready. Things have been off between us for the last week. I thought we raised a white flag at whirly ball, but we've settled into silence instead of peace. All our interactions have been as distant as a hotel concierge with a guest.

I turn around to face him now, forcing a smile onto my face. "Hello, Ethan."

I cringe at how robotic the words sound.

He nods. "Hannah. How are you?"

"Good, good." I nod as well.

Thank god for the Golden Oldies, who usher Ethan forward, plying him with a slice of cake and talking his ear off.

I glance at him covertly. His hair is beginning to grow out again. And the brown strands are threaded with blond highlights from shifts under the blistering Georgia sun. His hands draw my notice as well. Long fingers, always covered in spots of ink. He's wearing his favorite sneakers, worn and comfortable. His left foot taps the ground, a nervous tic. Just as I'm about to draw my eyes away, Ethan looks up at me.

My breath catches in my throat. For a moment, I feel like he can see me exactly as I am, my every thought transparent. My mind tells me to run.

I stand up. "Um, I've got to go."

The Golden Oldies immediately try to change my mind. Ethan stays quiet.

"I'm sorry," I say, placing the plate down, cake slice only half-eaten. "I've really got to work."

This at least is true. I've spent the last hour of my shift making out with Patrick and attending an old woman's birthday party. Certainly not the job I was hired for.

"I'll see y'all later!" I say. "Happy birthday, Vanessa!"

I hurry away toward my original plan, the shoe closet. I turn the knob and slip inside. It's cool and dim in here. I shut the door, hoping to shut everything and everyone else out with it.

Last Summer

Physical therapy was a disaster. My therapist, Ainsley, wore an aggressively high ponytail and was all sunshine and rainbows when she told me that with enough hard work, I might be able to jog again. *Jog*. Like that was good news. Like jogging is a fantastic consolation prize for my entire soccer career going up in flames, for my entire *life* going up in flames.

I might have gotten angry—at her, at everything—and told her exactly where she could shove her shiny attitude. I might have also told her that her scrubs were ugly. It wasn't my best moment.

Now I've been in bed for a week, staring at a water stain on my ceiling, ignoring calls and texts, ignoring my parents' pleas to return to rehab. I've refused to go anywhere or see anyone. It's been five days of staring at the spot on my ceiling, five days of not actually watching Netflix, five days of thinking about my team on the field without me. The only person I've allowed around is Figgy, and she's not even a person, she's a dog. But then Brie texted about Cody, and I knew I couldn't ignore her.

She's over here now, sitting at the foot of my bed and crying.

"I didn't see it coming." Brie sniffles. "I thought he loved me."

Cody loved himself, I want to say.

I can't believe she's crying this much over him. It's not like Cody is god's gift to women. He's boring, basic. He thinks drinking protein milkshakes is a personality trait. Good riddance, I say.

But Brie liked him. Loved him, I guess. They were together five months.

And I hate seeing my best friend upset.

"Here." My nightstand is strewn with items—tissues, water, ibuprofen. I grab a box of tissues and toss them to Brie. She catches them with ease. Brie and I don't fumble.

"Thanks," she says, wiping her eyes.

"Can I help?" I ask.

I feel bad she's upset, but it's also frustrating. She's torn up over a boy, when her best friend just lost her grandmother and then crushed her ankle and dreams along with it. The two things don't compare, and I'm struggling to muster up the appropriate empathy.

"I don't know." She sighs. "I lost my virginity to him. Not 'lost' it, because losing your virginity is a patriarchal concept and not something you can lose. I'm a feminist. That's not even it. But you know, I was intimate with him. I trusted him. And then a month later he breaks up with me."

"I'm sure the two events are unconnected," I tell her.

"What?" Her voice comes out confused.

"The sex and the breaking up," I clarify. "Unrelated, probably."

Her brow furrows. "That's not really the point. And kind of a mean thing to say."

"Oh." I pause. "Sorry."

Silence beats between us, heavy and taut. When Brie looks at me, it takes my breath away a little—there's confusion in her eyes, like she doesn't even recognize me. She opens her mouth, then closes it, then opens it again to ask, "How's your ankle?"

"What's that supposed to mean?" I snap.

Brie gives me that look again, like I'm an alien that's replaced her best friend. "I mean, how's your ankle feel? I'm asking how you feel. Because I care."

That's a whole lot of passive-aggression stuffed into one sentence. My phone buzzes beside me. I should put it on silent. Almost every text is from a teammate "checking in." I suppose they're doing it to be nice, but the reminder that I'm broken just makes me angry.

"The ankle is shit," I say, glancing at my phone. Not a teammate. It's a text from Shira. I look back up at Brie. "Can you go home?" I ask. "Sorry, I'm tired."

Her expression flickers—frustration, anger, hurt.

Guilt eats at me, but I say nothing as she packs up and leaves.

Chapter Eleven

THE NEXT WEEK flies by in a blur of kid wrangling, Golden Oldies catering, and every-surface sanitizing. I'm slowly growing used to the chaotic rhythm of Bonanza and letting myself be hypnotized by its patterns instead of worrying about that checklist and things unspoken with Brie—and with Ethan. Each employee in this strange petri dish seems more eccentric than the last, but most of them are also nice and funny, in their own ways, and get along like they were custom-cut for each other. It's easy enough to fall into a being a cog in this chaos machine.

Between the nonstop work, Patrick and I have found more moments to spend together. Although I turned down his offer of attending a party, I've spent a couple of after-work evenings with Patrick and crew at the graveyard, his arm slung around my shoulder, his fingers tracing patterns on my thighs.

The incident in Pete's office still makes my stomach tense every time I think about it, but not enough to part ways with Patrick. It's not like it was his idea. And so far, Patrick continues to be a wonderfully effective distraction.

"Come on, stay," Patrick says now. He nudges my foot with his own. His Vans are solid black, but Daisey rimmed the edges in silver Sharpie a few shifts ago.

I look up at him with a tiny yawn. It's the end of my shift. I'm exhausted, and I have no desire to stay for the opening ceremonies of the Bonanza Olympics. I have no desire to have anything to do with the Bonanza Olympics, as I made perfectly clear to my brother last week.

Patrick's hand is on the small of my back, warming the skin through my T-shirt. It makes my spine tingle pleasantly. "I'm tired," I tell him. "I just worked all day."

I should be focused on the checklist instead of toeing the line with Patrick. But I *hate* that list. I feel like a failure every time I pass it in the kitchen.

And I *like* kissing Patrick. I like the way his hands settle on my hips. And the way his lips smile against mine. And I like that kissing Patrick comes with snacks. He stops by his favorite Korean bakery whenever he has a hangover and now picks up something for me as well, sweet breads filled with custards and creams, powdered sugar that melts on my tongue.

It's easy with him, even if we don't have much common

ground. Our conversations never find footholds outside of Bonanza life. We've already run the gamut of family talk. His mom is an ER nurse, and his dad is a paramedic. They're both too busy to control Patrick's late-night activities, and when they do have the time to discipline, it's always Tony who's in more need of reprimanding.

"There's a party after," he tells me now. "A friend's place. By Callaway Lake. His parents let him use the house. Should be pretty damn nice."

I eye him with a raised brow.

He raises his hands. "Not an invite. I know, no parties. Was just letting you know what I'd be up to."

"*Mm-hmm*," I say. "Sure."

Patrick is a good guy. Not perfect, but I'm sure as hell not perfect either.

I turn to take in the scene around us. The crowd has continued to expand as everyone finishes their shifts. The concession area overflows with Bonanza employees, a sea of different-colored T-shirts and hairstyles. Shouts and laughter boom out and echo across the room. Everyone seems in high spirits, a buoyant energy radiating through the air. Even Gary and Sherry are here, passing out red plastic baskets of popcorn for everyone to share.

"I can't believe Pete allows this." I shake my head. "We are definitely breaking fire codes."

"It's a Bonanza institution," Patrick explains. "It's been

around way longer than Pete. The owner likes it, thinks it helps with company morale." He takes a half step toward me, nudges my shoulder. He smells like boy, bar soap, and laundry detergent, a light sheen of sweat from a day of work. "*Stay.* Just for the opening ceremonies. Your brother is the host, after all. Please."

He puts his hands together and smiles. It's nice that he wants me to stay. And I do feel bad about shutting Joey down last week. I'm not going to volunteer, but I suppose I could at least support him on opening night.

"Okay," I relent, smiling back. "I'll stay."

Patrick's smile widens, eyes brightening, and it immediately makes me feel good about my choice.

And then someone shouts out, "Saltine challenge!" and there's a massive cheer through the crowd.

"What challenge?" I ask Patrick as people rush forward to sit at one of the tables.

"Saltine challenge!" he replies, grabbing my hand. "C'mon on. Let's do it!"

I shake my head. "Um, no. I'm good."

"Your loss." He shrugs. "Hope you'll watch me dominate, though."

There seriously must be something in the water here, grown adults playing around like little kids. I watch as Patrick and six other people line up next to each other at one of the tables. While shaking his head, Gary hands out saltine crackers to each person. Sighing, Sherry provides cups of water—"For the losers who can't handle it," she says. "Now don't you dare cough cracker dust all over my tables."

"Ever try this before?" someone asks me.

I spin to find Nate Howell next to me. I met Nate last week, and we worked the prize counter together two days in a row. He's my brother's age, has dark brown skin, and is sweet and soft-spoken. His voice is so pleasant he could run an ASMR channel on YouTube. Nate is definitely one of the few introverted Bonanza employees, and it was a welcome reprieve working with him.

I laugh. "Try what, exactly?"

"Saltine cracker challenge," Nate explains, adjusting his slim glasses. "Eat six crackers in sixty seconds with no water. It's virtually impossible. Your mouth turns to sawdust."

My eyebrows crease. "And *why* do people do this?"

"The addiction of competing, I suppose." He shrugs. "This always happens around the Olympics. Everything gets turned into a competition. How many golf balls can you hold at once? How many bowling balls can you hold at once? How many video games can you play with your eyes closed? How fast you can sprint from the go-kart tracks to the concession stand? The list goes on. And on." Nate pauses. "And on."

I laugh. "You're funny."

"Thanks," Nate replies. "You're funny too. And quieter than your brother, which is nice."

"Well, that's an easy benchmark." I grin, then tilt my head. "So, what? Not a fan of Joey?"

"He's *fine*," Nate says, glancing over at him. Joey is pulling on a *tuxedo jacket*. I notice Ethan is with him, setting up the microphone. "Cute, I'll admit. But louder than a teacher with a bullhorn on a field trip."

I laugh. "You're not wrong, but you get used to it. You might even start liking it."

"Mm-hmm," Nate says. "We'll see about that."

We turn our attention back to the saltine table as the competition begins. Daisey holds her phone over her head and shouts, "One! Two! Three!" and a buzzer blares from her phone, then everyone begins to shove saltine crackers into their mouths.

There are different strategies—some people, like Patrick, shove in all six at once and get to chewing. Others try one or two at a time, feeding them into their mouths like dollars into a vending machine. I watch panic in their eyes grow as Daisey shouts, "Thirty seconds!"

One person instinctively reaches for their water, then snaps their hand away at the last second. Another, to Sherry's horror, is coughing up cracker dust all over the carpet. Patrick is in full concentration mode, his eyes on the table in front of him, chewing forcefully like the crackers have turned to concrete in his mouth.

"Is it really that difficult?" I whisper to Nate.

He grins. "Why? Want to try it?"

"*No.*"

Yes. Maybe. I don't know. It kind of *does* seem fun, in the most ridiculous way possible.

Oy vey. What is this place doing to me?

"Ten seconds!" Daisey screams.

Half the people have tapped out now, chugging water or gagging into a paper towel. I lean forward, my eyes on Patrick and the girl next to him, who just cleared her mouth and only has one cracker left.

Daisey begins the final countdown: "Five, four, three—"

"Done!" Patrick shouts, holding his hands up and mouth wide in victory. "Done! Done!"

Silence overcomes the crowd. Daisey walks over, inspects his cavernous mouth, and then agrees, "Patrick Cho is our winner!"

I find myself cheering and clapping wildly. He looks up at me with a grin and quickly returns to my side, chugging a cup of water before saying, "Told you I was good at that."

"What a great skill set to have," I joke.

"I'll see you later," Nate says, giving me a nod before heading back into the crowd.

"Bye!" I chirp, then glance around the room. It seems like the entire staff is here now, even those who didn't work today. Out of the corner of my eye, I spot Brie with a couple of people. My breath catches. After a few initial run-ins, I've managed to avoid her for weeks now, and it throws me off-balance to see her. She's wearing a mint-green Bonanza shirt and matching Adidas and is in a half circle of friends, chatting and laughing.

My stomach twists as I look back at Patrick. I nod along as he talks about some new band he's into. The excitement of the saltine cracker challenge fades, and my anxiety kicks into gear. I want to leave.

My brother's voice cuts through the crowd. I look and find Joey *standing* on the EZ Eats concession counter. Ethan sits next to him, adjusting the sound on the speakers. Gary and Sherry gasp. Everyone else laughs.

"Attention, all!" Joey shouts. My brother has a loud voice, but he doesn't quite capture the raucous crowd's notice. "Attention!" he tries again.

I sigh and decide to help him out. I put two fingers between my lips and whistle, hard. It's a piercing whistle that cuts through the entire room. Dead silence beats after. A few people glance at me with raised eyebrows, including Patrick. I shrug, smiling smugly.

Bubbie taught me how to whistle like that. She said it's important for women to make noise. *Don't let anyone tell you it's unladylike. You make all the noise you want, you hear me, mamaleh?*

I could always hear her whistle at my games, louder than anyone else in the crowd. It made me feel special, loved. It made me play harder—for her and myself. It made me want to take up space and claim what I deserved. I cross my arms, heart squeezing at her absence, and try to take a steadying breath.

"Attention, Bonanza employees," Joey says, now commanding the room. He looks like the Joey I've always known, comfortable and confident. His energy lights him up from the inside out, and I can see the enjoyment written across his face.

"We welcome you tonight to the opening ceremony of the Bonanza Olympics," Joey continues. "This time-honored event has occurred every summer for twenty, yes *twenty*, years. And this summer we will honor that anniversary by putting together the very best Bonanza Olympics yet! I'd now like to introduce last year's Grand Supreme winner to say a few words."

Suddenly, a girl wearing an American flag one-piece spandex suit with a Bonanza logo inscribed on the front runs to the counter, a blue cape billowing behind her. Yes, a cape. My laugh surprises me—it's big and sudden. But it's an incredible sight.

"Who is that?" I ask, glancing back at Patrick.

The girl has dark curly hair and medium-brown skin. I think she works at the go-kart track, so I haven't met her yet.

"Sophie Flores," Patrick tells me. "She won the Grand Supreme title last year—earned the most medals during the Olympics. Kicked my ass in mini golf. The girl has skills. Many skills." I raise an eyebrow, and he laughs. "Nah, not like that. She's twenty-three. Also exclusively into other chicks. Why? You jealous?"

"No," I say. I like Patrick, and I don't exactly want him making out with every girl in the place, but I'm not at a point of possession with him.

"Thank you for that wonderful introduction, Joey," Sophie says, now standing on the concession counter right next to him. I think Gary and Sherry might pass out. "I believe I can speak for all of us when I say we know you'll make the games special this year." She then turns to the crowd. "It is my honor to be the reigning Bonanza Olympics Grand Supreme champion. It is a title and a duty I do not carry lightly, and I have been grateful to represent our humble play-nation for this past year. As is my right, I will try to defend my claim this year, though we all know only the great Betty Richter won the Grand Supreme title twice. Still, I will try my valiant best to keep my crown. Though if I fail, I will gladly hand over the title to my worthy opponent, whoever she, he, or they may be!"

Sophie hands the microphone back to Joey, takes a bow, and then jumps off the counter with grace, her cape billowing behind her. I feel a strange tug from her speech, and I realize it's the long-buried desire to compete.

The feeling stuns me, a spark I thought was long flamed out.

"Thank you, Sophie," Joey says. "We will now light the ceremonial torch and sing the national anthem to open the games. Sherry?"

Sherry tamps down her frustration and looks impressively regal and serene as she lights a tall candlestick wrapped in a thick sheath of aluminum foil. Daisey turns on music. The song sounds vaguely familiar, and I realize it's the *Bonanza* theme song that used to play on the local commercials when I was a kid. Suddenly, with zero shame or embarrassment, everyone around me begins to belt out the tune.

"Oh, how we love Bonanza!
It's the very best of times!"

I glance at Patrick and find him singing at the top of his lungs.

"Seriously?" I ask.

"Yes!" he says. "Sing!"

He joins back in with the crowd while I shake my head. I swear, these employees have all been brainwashed.

"We love to run and play here!
We love to skip and jump and climb!

Oh, how we love Bonanza!
It's the best place in all the land!
We want to spend all day here,
Oh, that would be so grand!"

"And again!" Daisey shouts as the music loops. The employees sing even louder this time, and okay, I have to admit, it's kind of catchy. That's the point of jingles, after all. I don't quite sing, but I find myself smiling and mouthing some of the words. This is silly. Ridiculous. And, well, kind of *fun*.

I'm scanning the crowd and spot Brie again. She's swaying arm in arm with Sophie Flores. She looks so happy. Suddenly, she glances up, and her eyes catch mine, and I feel a spark of hope that—

She looks away, like she never saw me to begin with.

A lump forms in my throat, fast and hard. Next to me, Patrick is still singing at full blast, even waving his arms in the air. I slip away from him and the rest of the crowd. I've been distracting myself with work and with Patrick, ignoring everything I lost. This joy, this camaraderie that other people have, it's not for me anymore. I don't get to be part of that.

The doors are heavy, and as soon as I close them, the cheerful song disappears.

"Thanks for this," I say as Shira hops out of her car to open the door for me. She's wearing a pair of wide-legged jeans and a cream tube top. I hobble into the front seat, awkwardly stuffing my crutches in the back. It's a luxury car, with buttery leather seats and an engine you can barely hear running.

"My pleasure," Shira replies. "Going to parties alone is a drag."

I've known Shira Chen since toddler days. Our families belong to the same synagogue, and we attended its preschool program together. We bonded over finger paint. My artistic talents stopped there, but Shira has continued to create—and curate. She's always talking about a new talented friend, from musicians to papier-mâché artists. We've always gotten along, but our paths diverged as I got wrapped up in soccer and Shira got wrapped up in partying with older friends. She's invited me to parties a few times, but tonight, when she texted and asked how I was feeling after my injury, I ignored the question and asked what she was up to instead. And now we're on the way to my first college party.

"You'll have a great time," Shira promises me as she backs out of my driveway, silver bangle bracelets glinting in the setting sun. As my house fades from view, I feel a tug of guilt. I kicked Brie out just hours ago, mumbled some half excuse to my parents about where I was going, and have been dodging physical therapy for a week. I should be trying to pull the threads of my life back together, but all I want to do is escape—and Shira can provide that for me.

Thirty minutes later, we pull into an apartment complex near the downtown perimeter. Music pounds through open windows. We get out of the car, and Shira pulls a flask from her purse. She twirls open the cap deftly with one hand, then takes a swig and smiles. "Don't worry. I'll Uber us home. Here."

I hesitate when she shoves the flask in my direction. I've had alcohol before, plenty of times, actually. It comes with the territory of being Jewish. Sips of wine on Shabbat; many sips of wine on Passover. But kosher wine at my parents' house is different from liquor from a flask.

"Don't worry," Shira tells me again. "I know a ton of people inside. It is a"—she puts on a PSA voice—"safe environment. And that whiskey tastes like honey. It's not too bad."

The thing is, I don't need much convincing.

This is why I texted Shira back.

I need someone to help me let go.

"Okay," I say, and lift the flask to my lips.

She's wrong. The whiskey is bad. It burns.

But it also makes my stomach feel warm, so I take another small swig, and another.

"Pretty good, huh?" Shira asks. I shrug, and she laughs as she says, "It tastes better with each sip. Promise."

Shira makes a lot of promises. But I have a feeling she's pretty good at holding up her end of the bargain. I take one last sip and pass the flask back to her. Then she sweeps her arm forward and ushers me toward the party.

Hours later, I find myself talking to a boy.

I like his name: Alexi.

He's Russian. His thick accent wraps around consonants and makes them sound much better than boring American accents. His hair is sandy blond, and his eyes are blue, and they track me across the room as I go to grab another beer. I don't particularly like beer, but Shira told me that since I'm new to drinking, I shouldn't have too much liquor.

"Only take from my flask," she said. "And if you want to drink more than that, have a beer. It'll help you pace yourself, and no one can put anything in a closed bottle."

She must mean drugs. I thought she knew these people, but I guess that doesn't count for much.

I return to the couch, awkward with my beer and crutches. I yearn for the agility I've always had. Alexi's eyes stay on me, and a smile flits to his lips. "What happened?" he asks, gesturing to my ankle.

"Shark attack," I reply.

"Liar." His smile widens. "What really happened?"

"Trapeze accident."

He laughs, short and hard. "Mysterious lady. All right, that's fine. I like that." He scoots closer to me on the couch. We aren't touching, but we could be if either of us leaned a fraction of an inch closer.

The apartment is packed. There must be at least thirty people crammed into this small space. The furniture is sleek but shitty quality, probably from IKEA or something. The music is loud, bass throbbing in my ears. There's a cloud of smoke from people taking bong hits in the back room. Shira offered me a joint a while ago. I've never smoked pot before. I couldn't before. They drug test us on the team. But I'm not on the team now. That's all over. So I took a hit. And another. And then one more.

"Are you in college, mystery girl?" Alexi asks.

"Soon," I respond, even though I still have two years of high school, even though I'm not sure about college anymore, about anything anymore. My fight with Brie surfaces with a sharp sting. I push it away, swigging my beer.

"Your eyes are glassy," Alexi tells me.

"Your eyes are blue," I reply.

And then I close the fraction of an inch between us, and I kiss him. His lips are soft and taste like the cigarette he smoked earlier. He kisses me back with slowness and ease, like he knew this was going to happen and has no fear of me pulling away. I meld into him, into the warm haze washing over me, into the dimming of my thoughts. He wraps a hand gently around the nape of my neck and rests his fingers there. I curl my toes and feel grateful.

Chapter Twelve

CRICKETS ARE CHIRPING when I park my car in the driveway. It's late, almost ten o'clock. I step outside and wrap my arms around my waist. I breathe in the sweet night air and attempt to relax, but my muscles only tense in the open space. I blink up at the stars, wondering if I'll always feel like this now, wound tight as a coil.

When I step inside the house, my parents call out. They're in the living room, watching TV, cuddled up on the couch with Figgy snoring soundly at their feet. "Just you?" Mom asks when she sees me.

"Yeah, the boys will be back soon," I explain. "Opening ceremonies."

My parents know all about the Bonanza Olympics because it's Joey's favorite topic. "You didn't want to stay?" Dad asks. "I thought it sounded fun!"

I bite my cheek. It was fun, for other people.

"I'm just tired," I say. "Long day."

"Come." Mom pats the spot on the couch next to her. "Sit with us."

I want to escape to my room, but their concerned faces move me toward the couch. I don't want them to worry they made the wrong choice by bringing me home. I walk over and give snoozing Figgy a few pats before settling on the couch, watching with my parents as a grandmother hunts for the perfect retirement beach home.

I miss Bubbie. I miss my friends. I miss . . .

I miss feeling happy. Because beneath all the distractions with work and Patrick, I'm not happy. Not in the least.

Figgy whines for more attention. I run my fingers through her fur. As the show cuts to commercial, my parents chat about their days, pepper me with questions about mine, remind me again of Bubbie's upcoming unveiling. I try my best to be engaged, but my gaze keeps drifting out the window, searching the darkened night sky.

After two episodes of *House Hunters*, I tell my parents good night, then brush my teeth and retreat to my room. Bubbie's unveiling is in just a few days. The knowledge tears at me slowly, strip by strip. I curl up with my laptop and queue reality TV, trying to drown out my own thoughts. Close to midnight, Joey and Ethan get home. My stomach tightens. My lights are off, but I'm still nervous Joey might knock on my door and ask why I left early. I close my laptop very carefully so even it won't make light.

Their voices fade. There's ten minutes of the bathroom door opening and closing. And then I finally settle down into my pillows. Exhaustion takes over, and I sleep.

I dream of Bubbie. We're out on her back porch, Figgy at our feet, glass-bottle Cokes in our hands. Fireflies blink in the night. Branches rustle softly in the wind. Bubbie regales me with stories from her youth about girls with wild hair and men with electric smiles. Her voice washes over me like the coolest balm on the hottest night.

She's so real. She's right there. And I'm *happy*.

But then, I wake up, head throbbing.

Bubbie has been gone for almost a year now.

And I realize that at a certain point, she will be out of my life longer than she was ever in it.

That thought stabs like a fresh wound.

My legs shake with the pent-up energy of a benched athlete. I feel like I'm about to scratch off my own skin.

"Argh!" I say the feeling out loud. Then I kick off my covers and thump my feet onto my mattress, wincing from my ankle. "Damn it," I whisper, the words tight in my swollen throat.

Sighing, I get out of bed, carefully, and crack open my bedroom door. The house is so quiet I can hear the kitchen clock tick. My feet remember which floorboards to avoid. I pad down the hallway, into the living room, then the kitchen. My checklist stares at me in the moonlight. I fight the urge to rip it off and throw it away.

Instead, I pull open our sliding glass door and step into the backyard. While our front yard is picture-perfect, thanks to Dad's meticulous work, our gardening back here is haphazard and inconsistent at best. The flowers we planted one spring were abandoned and have started to grow wild. A creek trickles in the back.

I like how untamed it all feels. I've played on perfectly groomed fields my entire life. Our yard here is so desperately different that I can still enjoy it.

My bare feet press into the damp grass. It's still warm out, even in the middle of the night, but the grass is cool under my feet. I wander back to our old tree swing and sit on the wobbly bench. My dad built it when I was seven. Back then, my feet dangled high in the air, but now my toes brush against the ground. Night folds around me. The wind blows gently as crickets play their chorus. I feel a bit calmer, like I finally can breathe.

Then the sliding glass door opens. I startle in surprise, my heart jumping, and squint my eyes to see in the dark. My pulse thuds as a tall form takes shape. But as the shape comes into focus, my fear is replaced with a different type of anxiety.

It's Ethan.

Our hotel-concierge relationship has continued for the past week. When we're both at the alley, I often spend my shift dragging my eyes away from him, biting back the urge to ask what's wrong. Because maybe nothing is wrong. Maybe he's just my brother's best friend and this has *always* been our relationship. Maybe there's something seriously disturbed about my fixation.

A few nights ago, Joey, Ethan, and I were all so exhausted after double shifts that we didn't even make it to bed. We passed straight out on the living room couches. Sometime in the middle of the night, I rolled over and saw Ethan across from me, snoring softly, body curled around a pillow, hair falling into his eyes. My stomach fluttered so much I thought someone might be able to hear it. I turned my red cheeks into my pillow and forced myself back to sleep.

Now, my pulse thrums in my ears as he approaches. He's wearing gray sweatpants and a plain white T-shirt. His hair is rumpled, like he was tossing and turning. He offers me a small smile as he nears, and even though things have grown strange between us, I still feel myself relax at his presence.

"Evening," I say.

He laughs. I think it takes us both by surprise. Warmth blooms inside me, a smile drawing to my lips.

"Evening." His voice is graveled with sleep. "Can I join you?"

I nod and scoot over so there's room for him on the swing. His legs are so long now that they plant firmly on the ground. He rocks us back in forth at a slow pace.

Ethan looks different in the moonlight. Older. Almost like I'm catching a glimpse of him ten years from now. I can kind of see him like that, Ethan in his late twenties, with more stubble and the full height of his puppy-dog feet; more stylish clothes; slim pants and knit sweaters. I bet he'll carry a messenger bag stuffed with papers, and he'll still have ink on his fingers, just like he does now.

The wind picks up, and I shiver. I wrap my arms around myself, suddenly aware I'm only wearing an old sleep shirt, an oversize one down to mid-thigh, and no bra. My skin prickles at Ethan's nearness.

"You're up late," he says softly, glancing at me.

"Couldn't sleep." I clear my throat. "You too?"

Ethan shrugs. "Kind of. Uh, had a bad dream."

"Oh, I'm sorry. I thought those got better."

His eyes shift to the house, unfocused. I have an impulse to reach out and grab his hand, but I don't dare move.

"They kind of did." He looks back at me, and again I'm aware of the heat of his thigh. My breath tightens. "They're not as bad as when I was little. And I don't have to wake anyone up anymore." He gives me a soft smile. "I can make my own chocolate milk now."

Ethan had nightmares often as a little kid. Sometimes

they'd be so bad he'd wake up crying. Joey would get one of my parents, and they'd bring Ethan to the kitchen and give him a giant glass of chocolate milk. Sometimes Joey and I would ask for milk too, and all three of us would sit at the table together, sipping our drinks at midnight.

"What are the nightmares about?" I ask.

"They're not really nightmares. They're—"

He quiets, looks back down at his feet, then starts to swing us again, concentrated, slow and steady. I'm not sure if I should say something else, ask another question or—

"My parents fight a lot," he answers suddenly, eyes still trained on the ground. My back stiffens as he continues. "When we were twelve, Joey asked if I even had a bed at home, because I was sleeping at your house so much. He was kidding but also not kidding. He knew something was off. And so I told him that I liked his house better because it's quiet. Well, Joey isn't quiet. But he's the good kind of loud. My parents are the bad kind."

Silence stretches taut between us. I want to say something. My heart is beating hard, pressing against my chest with solid thuds. It feels impossible to form words. I didn't know. *How did I not know?*

I never questioned why Ethan slept over so often. I figured we had a better TV and Figgy and good snacks, and those were enough reasons. I didn't know his parents fought.

I didn't know they fought so much it gave him bad dreams.

"I'm sorry," I say, but the words aren't enough. I curl my fingers around the ledge of the swing, tightening them until my skin turns white. "Do my parents know?"

"Yeah." He clears his throat. "They know enough. We talked about it a few times when I was younger. They checked in with my parents, too, made sure it wasn't . . . Um. Look, it's not like they're abusive, right? They don't yell at *me*. They don't physically fight. They don't even threaten each other. They just argue, all the time. It never stops. I don't know why they're still together. It's like they're stuck on a loop and can't escape." He swallows hard, Adam's apple bobbing. "So I escape. Here."

My heart lurches. Again, I want to reach for his hand, and this time I have to physically clench my fist to stop. "I'm sorry." My voice is barely a whisper. "I didn't know. I'm *sorry* I didn't know."

All these years. All these nights with Ethan around.

How self-centered did I have to be to not know?

"It's not your fault," Ethan tells me. "Besides, everyone has problems. It's not a big deal."

This irritates me, like sand between my toes. It *is* a big deal. He deserves to feel comfortable in his own home. It's unfair. And he deserves better.

It can't be good, keeping this pain so close to his chest, letting that anger and frustration coil inside. He's so calm on the outside, yet there's a storm growing. I know the feeling well.

I'm about to push more, when Ethan turns his attention to me. His brown eyes are darker at night, and I feel sheer under his gaze. "So why are you up this late?"

"You know." I clear my throat. "Stuff."

He laughs, hard, eyes sparking. "Oh, c'mon. I shared."

I smile but stay quiet.

After a few moments, he tries again. "You left the opening ceremonies early. Why?"

It's my instinct to brush him off, to shrug and change the subject. But he's right—he did share. He told me about his parents. And the crickets are getting louder now. And my skin is starting to itch again, and if it's not healthy for Ethan to keep his problems all coiled inside, then it's also not healthy for me to do the same.

So I say, "I was sad."

Those three simple words form a hard lump in my throat. I look up at the sky, stars muted behind thin clouds. "I felt happy for a second. And then—it's like, being happy for a second made me sad. Because I'm *not* happy. It was a fake feeling." I try to force some lightness into my tone, but my voice cracks. "I guess I'm sort of broken."

Ethan looks at me then, so softly it takes my breath away. My heart catches in my throat when he says, "You're not broken, Hannah."

It's too much. This moment is too much.

I'm not sure if I want to take his hand or run away.

I fight both urges as I point at my ankle. "I'm literally broken, Ethan."

He won't let me off the hook. He nudges my leg with his own. "You know what I mean. You're not broken. You're . . . processing. You lost your bubbie. You lost soccer. It's okay to feel sad, to feel happy, to have complicated feelings. We all do. Except for, like, psychopaths. Or is it sociopaths? Anyways, you're not one of those, so that's a good thing. *Then* I'd be worried."

I crack the smallest smile. "It's funny to hear you talk so much."

"C'mon." He raises an eyebrow at me. "I *talk*."

I laugh. "You do not. You stand next to Joey and do look-to-the-camera like Jim on *The Office* while *he* talks."

"Fine," Ethan says. "Maybe you're right."

"Or maybe you've changed." I tilt my head. "I was gone an entire year. How strange is that?"

"Very strange." Ethan begins to rock us back and forth again. "A year is a long time at our age. That's like . . . one-sixteenth of your life?"

I grin. "One-seventeenth. I'm older than you."

He rolls his eyes. "Right, right. But I'm taller."

"Only now," I say. "I used to tower over you guys in middle school. Joey hated it."

"Nah, he didn't mind too much. He liked having a cool older sister."

I shake my head. "Joey did *not* think I was cool."

"Yeah he did," Ethan insists, turning toward me more. His eyes seem brighter now. "You were totally your own person in middle school while the rest of us were anxiety-ridden pimple-covered messes."

"Hey, I had pimples too."

"Okay, okay, so you had pimples. But still, compared to the rest of us in middle school, you had it together. You were confident. No one has confidence in middle school. Not even the teachers."

I laugh again. Hard. He's funny. Ethan is *funny*.

He continues, "Middle school is just one giant hormone-induced nightmare. But you had it together."

"Yeah. Well, I had a purpose then. Now—now I'm a mess." It's scary to say those words out loud, to say the truth out loud. "I guess I'm rocking middle-school vibes at seventeen."

Ethan laughs. "At least the pimples are gone."

I shake my head. "You're wrong." I lean forward and point to my chin, where a whitehead popped up earlier today. "Look at this nasty dude."

Ethan looks, then waves me off. "Please, that's nothing. I have you beat."

I scan his face, which is somehow free of all acne. "Yeah, right."

But now Ethan is standing up. And now Ethan is taking off his shirt. And, um, *wow, okay*. My mouth goes kind of dry because Ethan without a shirt is hot. Stupid hot. *How in the hell—*

Moonlight ghosts off his abs. Because he has *abs*. Not bodybuilder ones, but enough that I could solidly trace four of them with my fingers. And there's a dusting of light hair that didn't use to be there, leading down to the band of his sweatpants, and this observation makes my skin heat quickly.

Younger brother's best friend.

What is happening to me?

Thankfully, Ethan doesn't notice my internal spiral because he's turning around and pointing awkwardly to his shoulder blades. "Look at that guy," he says. "He's like a freaking mountain. Basically planted a flag on my back and claimed the land as his own."

I stand up to inspect, but stay at a distance. There is indeed a large underground pimple on Ethan's right shoulder. But my gaze only stays there a second before traveling down the rest of his back to where his waist tapers and . . .

I clear my throat. "Yup. That's a giant pimple. You win."

He turns back to me with a smile. "Told you so. Victory is mine." He slips his shirt back on, then returns to the swing, his weight thudding down. I sit as well, a little closer to the end this time. We swing for a bit in silence. It's nice out here with him. I'm not ready to go inside yet. As I think of something else to ask him, my mind strays back to tonight's opening ceremony. "So," I say. "Are you going to compete in any of the games?"

"For the Olympics?" he asks.

I nod.

"Maybe," he says. "I'm decent at mini golf. I think there might be a graph somewhere, lack of athletic ability correlating with solid mini-golf skills."

"Nah," I say. "Because I'm athletic and great at mini golf."

Ethan laughs. "Lack of confidence, huh?"

I shrug. "*Was* athletic. I guess."

Silence presses in again. I can tell he wants to say something else, is weighing out how I'll respond. Finally he asks, "You really won't be able to play soccer again?"

I want to brush him off, to even leave and head back into the house. But he doesn't deserve that. It's just a question. I should be able to answer a question.

"No," I breathe out the word. "Not professionally, at least." I look down at my ankle. "And I haven't really been keeping up with my physical therapy." My throat tightens. "It's hard. It hurts, and it's just like, what's the point, you know?"

"I'm sorry," Ethan tells me. "Maybe—sorry, not to give suggestions, but have you tried bowling?"

This takes me by surprise, and I laugh. *"Bowling?"*

He laughs too, his voice brightening. "Yes, seriously. It'll put a lot less pressure on your ankle than running, but you can still get some movement in. I like bowling. I go before work sometimes."

"Bowling," I repeat. "Like the ultimate retiree sport, bowling?"

"It's quiet in the mornings. Makes the crashing pins much more satisfying." He knocks into my shoulder. "Come with me. Tomorrow morning."

"It *is* tomorrow morning."

His smile grows warmer. "Okay, we'll go to sleep now and then go bowl *later* this morning. Before work. Sound good?"

"Sounds like I'll be getting about four hours of sleep."

Bowling. It sounds so boring. It sounds so safe. It sounds like an activity my parents would actually approve of. Which I guess is a good thing. Bowling won't be my new passion, but it's certainly closer to completing my checklist than making out with Patrick in Pete's office. It's a step in the right direction. A step I've been ignoring for weeks now.

"Okay." I nod. "Bowling. I'm in."

Chapter Thirteen

IT'S QUIET, CREEPY, and possibly even perverse to be at Bonanza before open.

Ethan slips the key back into his pocket as we walk through the empty bowling alley. It's dark in here, with only scraps of light from the slim windows and emergency exit signs illuminating the way.

"How'd you get a key?" I ask Ethan.

His features are half-visible in the dim light. "I asked Pete months ago if I could come in early on weekends and bowl. He said as long as I do the opener shift after, that's fine. They have trouble getting staff in first thing in the morning."

"Makes sense."

I follow Ethan behind the front counter and then into the small office, where he flips on two of about twenty switches on the electrical panel. Outside the door, lights come on over the far two left lanes. Ethan opens a metal box and flips another switch, and I hear the mechanical whirring of the ball return start up. He leaves the rest of the lights and the TVs off.

"It's nice like this, right?" he asks as we walk back into the main alley. "Relaxing."

Relaxing, not creepy.

I sweep my eyes across the alley with that in mind. And it is nice, having so much space to ourselves. It's almost magical that a place this loud is now quiet enough to hear a needle drop.

"C'mon." Ethan nods toward the far lane. "What size ball?"

He picks a navy-blue twelve-pounder. I choose a ten-pounder. It's black with sparkling purple swirls that make it look like a galaxy. The ball feels heavier than I'd like to admit, my muscles atrophied after a year away from the weight room. Ethan runs to grab us shoes while I sit idly at my lane. Nerves thrum through me—from Ethan, from bowling, I'm not sure. There's no reason to be nervous. This is a little morning exercise with a guy I've known my whole life. I take a quick breath, then stretch out my legs, pulling on the taut muscles out of habit. The familiar movements relax me, and when Ethan returns with our shoes, I give him a small smile.

"Ready?" he asks.

He looks relaxed himself, though a little tired, faint circles under his eyes. My heart twists as I wonder how many mornings he's escaped from his home to here.

I nod. "Ready."

He grins at me. "Need any tips?"

"*No.*"

Ethan laughs. "Just offering. It's been a while."

It *has* been a while. I used to bowl as a kid until soccer occupied every free second of my life. Still, I'm sure it'll be like riding a bike. "I remember the fundamentals," I tell Ethan. "Throw ball, knock down pins."

"Yup." Ethan nods, his smile growing. "You sound totally good to go."

I huff at him, then tug on my bowling shoes, knotting the laces with fury. "Just for that, I'm going to have to kick your ass."

"Good luck with that," he teases.

I growl. "I'm starting now."

His grin is planted firm. "Sounds good."

Our conversation fades as we focus on our lanes. The room quiets, save for the crashing of pins and whirring of the ball return. I *am* rusty. Each unfamiliar movement strains my muscles in a new way; the tightening of my calves, the tug of my biceps. And especially the twist of my ankle, reminding me of the injury there. But Ethan is right—it's not too painful. It's the good kind of discomfort, the kind that lets me know the joint needs this movement to heal. Bowling won't become a new passion, but it's nice to use my body, to soak up this calm atmosphere. I like it here.

I like it here with Ethan.

He's good at bowling, his score quickly outstripping mine. His form is solid, hands steady. When he bends to pick up his ball from the return, I can't help but notice the strength of his forearms, the muscles flexing and pulling taut. I swallow dryly and turn back to my own lane.

I fall into the reverie of competition. I'm not going to beat Ethan today, so I play against myself, working for each frame to be better than the last, examining angles I can try when the pins are split this way or that. It's a much more complicated sport than I gave it credit for, and my mind revels in trying to untangle its intricacies.

After I nail a second spare, I turn to find Ethan grinning at me. "Nice," he says. "You're good."

"You're better," I concede.

His smile crinkles the edges of his eyes. "I have a feeling if we give it a few more mornings, that will change." He glances at his phone. "We've got to open now, but we can play again tomorrow if you want," Ethan offers.

"Open?" I pull out my own phone to check the time. "Holy crap."

An hour passed, just like that. Suddenly, I'm much

more aware of my exerted muscles, of the thumping in my chest and adrenaline pulsing in my veins.

Ethan laughs at my surprise. "Tomorrow?" he asks.

His eyes are trained on me, warm and bright. Something flips in my stomach, and I have to look down at my laced bowling shoes as I agree. "Tomorrow."

Joey meets us at the alley right as we finish opening duties. He passes out three breakfast sandwiches with a giant yawn. "Y'all know normal teenagers do this thing called sleeping. You should try it sometime."

"Hmm." I unwrap my sandwich. "Never heard of it. Have you heard of it, Ethan?"

He's already chewing. "Not in the least bit a familiar concept."

Even though I only scraped together a few hours of sleep last night, I realize I feel more awake now than I have in a long time. The crashing of the pins echoes in my ears, and my fingers itch to play again, to do better than last time.

Joey looks back and forth between the two of us, suspicion in his eyes. "So are you guys, like, friends now? Is that what's happening here?"

Friends. *Yes.* That's what's going on between Ethan and me. We're becoming friends. That's all. I am Ethan's friend, and Ethan has nice forearms. A normal friend thought.

"Yup." I nod. "Friends."

"Gross." Joey scrunches his nose.

"You'll survive," Ethan says, casually slinging an arm around my shoulder. The weight is heavy, and I find myself wanting to lean in closer to its warmth. *Why does he* smell *so good?* I'm pretty sure we're all using the same shampoo at home.

I hold my shoulders rigid as heat crawls across my neck.

Joey eyes us. "*O*-kay, then."

Ethan's arm drops from my shoulder as casually as it went up. He shoots me a quick smile, and I think I manage to smile back normally.

"Prize counter?" Joey asks me.

"Sure," I agree.

But at that moment, my phone goes off with a text from Pete:

Mini-golf tournament today! Ten staff members required. The following report to the course now . . .

I forgot that was today, a charity tournament to raise money for the children's hospital. I scroll through the list, spotting my name first and then Brie's immediately after. I'm tempted to ask one of the boys to take my place. But I know this tournament is important, and I don't want to put more stress on Pete's plate.

"I should go, you guys . . . ," I say, showing the text.

"Sound good." Ethan nods. "See you later, Hannah."

Joey calls out loudly as I walk away, "Save the children!"

We're wearing the same color shirt. I *know* it irritates Brie, because it irritates me. If I had a spare, I'd change out of my aqua shirt right now and into anything else. Burnt orange. Mustard yellow. *Anything*. There seems to be an endless range of colors in the Bonanza T-shirt line, and yet here Brie and I are in the same exact hue. Her eyes skirt over me as I fold into the group of gathered employees.

I take a short breath, my stomach tensing. She was my best friend, so I can still pick up on any slight shift in her mood. I can still read the hurt behind her cool expression. Best friends aren't supposed to hurt each other. They're supposed to help each other even if the rest of the world is against them.

I'm relieved when Nate walks up to the course. He's wearing khaki shorts and a red Bonanza shirt. I move to the side with him and push some energy into my voice. "Hey, Nate! How are you?"

"I'm well, thank you for asking." He adjusts his glasses, then nods at his phone. "I was hoping to finish this up before the tournament, though."

"Finish what up?"

He shows me his screen. "It's kind of dorky, but here." There's a crossword puzzle on his phone, most of the answers already filled in. "I've been doing them since

I was a kid. I started on the *New York Times* ones a couple years ago. I'm stuck today. But it's fun to try."

I've never done a crossword puzzle in my life. Bubbie loves them. *Loved* them. A pencil in one hand and a glass of iced tea in the other. Sometimes Mom does them on vacations as well, in a little paperback book, but she always ends up falling asleep on the beach before she gets too far.

"I don't think that's dorky," I say. "I'd be terrible at it, though. I'm not exactly a genius."

"Uh-uh," Nate says, wagging his finger. "You fixed the card reader at the prize counter. That's *very* smart."

I laugh. It's a random compliment, but it makes me feel nice anyway. "Thanks."

"Besides," he continues, "the crossword is as much about practice as it is about being smart. No one is good at first. My mom has been doing them forever now. She's so good she does the Sunday one in the real paper and in *pen*."

I nod in admiration. "Your mom sounds badass."

"She totally is." Nate smiles. "Anyways, want to help me? I'm stuck on some of these clues. I'm never good at the geography and sports stuff."

Even though I'm not a trivia whiz with sports, soccer has bled into other interests. My family likes watching basketball, and Joey is hard-core into tennis. My teammates love football—in a bitter, "it gets too much attention and funding" kind of way. Maybe I know enough to help with a clue or two.

"Sure." I shrug. "I'll give it a shot."

As we huddle over his phone together, a wave of gratitude washes over me. Nate is an awesome coworker. We try to fill in answers on the crossword until the tournament starts. I help him solve two clues, and we high-five each time like we're good friends.

Pete assigns Brie and me to the same station. Perfect.

I gave him a tight smile, and Brie does as well. Neither of us is going to argue about it. Bonanza hosts this charity tournament every year. No matter how uncomfortable I feel, I know raising money for the children's hospital is more important than my feelings about getting matched up with my ex–best friend.

We head off in silence to our station. In our matching aqua shirts. We're posted at the final hole of the course, where we'll snap pictures and hand out frosted lemonades. Now, one might say to Pete, why do we need to stand here when the tournament just started and no one will be at our hole for at least forty-five minutes? But one does not get to question Pete today, so here we are, in the hot sun, just the two of us, holding Polaroid cameras and standing with the freezer cart between us.

I'm glad this isn't uncomfortable at all.

The early-morning heat isn't helping. It's going to crack ninety by noon. I've been getting away with murder soaking up air-conditioning at the prize counter and bowling alley.

I glance at Brie out of the corner of my eye. Her box braids are pulled into a low ponytail, and I'm pretty sure I can smell a whiff of Coconut Beach Dream, her favorite scent. I wish she were scrolling on her phone. But she's not—she's staring straight ahead, which makes the silence between us beat louder.

I clear my throat.

Shift on my feet.

Tug at my shirt.

Brie shoots a look at me.

I hold up my hands. "Sorry."

"It's fine." She pauses. "You were always fidgety."

She's right. I frustrated most of my elementary school teachers to no end. My favorite teacher, though, Mr. Schwartz of the fourth grade, let me stand up in class whenever I wanted.

We revert back to silence. I hate it. We cannot stand like this for forty-five minutes. Brie and I might not be friends anymore, but I'm sure we can at least manage polite conversation to pass the time.

"So." I turn to her. "How are Lucy and Riley?"

For a millisecond, I think Brie won't respond, but then

she turns to me as well and says, "They're good. In summer day camp. Having the time of their lives."

"Cool." I nod. "Sounds fun."

Brie yawns, then stretches one arm across her chest, twisting her body. Her muscles are more toned than last year. I wonder what she's added to her routine. "Yeah, the girls love camp," she continues. "You can barely drag Lucy out of the pool, and Riley refuses to step away from the craft table. She made me this." Brie shows me her wrist. Next to her team bracelet is a pink-and-black lanyard.

I smile at it, my heart giving a small lurch. I love Brie's sisters. I can't believe I missed an entire year of their lives.

"Cute," I manage to say. "I'm glad they're doing well."

I can't think of anything else to add. There's a giant elephant standing between us, and talking around it is more draining than the punishing sun overhead. Sweat beads down my neck as the midday sun rises into the sky. I lean against the freezer cart, desperate for something cold. Something . . . refreshing.

I look back down the mini-golf course. It's still entirely empty. I can't even hear people from here. I bet the tournament got a late start and it'll be ages before we're snapping pictures and handing out treats.

Treats.

I glance back at the freezer cart, then very slowly, with

only two fingers, slide the top open. Cool air blasts me. I practically groan in relief, then look down at a full stock of frozen lemonade cups. My eyes widen like Joey in Game-Stop.

My hand reaches for a lemonade of its own volition. And then I notice another hand is reaching in as well. A hand adorned with two bracelets.

I look up at Brie. She smiles, a tiny smile, but it's there all the same. "I won't tell if you won't," she says.

I smile back at her. "You've got a deal."

We eat a frozen lemonade cup each . . . and then split a third one. It's not our fault. The tournament participants take *so long*. And it's *so hot* out. We are blameless.

And because we're blameless, we stash the empty cups at the bottom of the trash can, covering them with all sorts of other debris so that no one will notice. We rub our hands with a hefty serving of hand sanitizer after. Conversation never picks up, but we scroll our phones in somewhat comfortable silence.

Finally, golfers make it to the last hole. We snap to attention and put on our bright Bonanza smiles, congratulating and thanking the participants, taking photos of each group. The crowd is older than Bonanza's usual clientele, but I suppose that's because not many young people have money for philanthropy.

Some of the couples have brought along teenage children who couldn't seem more annoyed to be here. They remind me of some of the rich kids at Mountain Bliss. Their eyes graze right over us, even when we're speaking to them. And they act like it's the worst punishment on earth to spend their morning here.

Which kind of really pisses me off, considering this event is to support a lifesaving children's hospital.

Brie senses my growing frustration, because when there's a break in the flow of people, she leans in to me and says, "Easy there, tiger."

I let out a surprised laugh, my shoulders relaxing. "Thanks," I tell her.

"Hannah?" a voice interrupts us. "Hey, Brie."

I look up, startled to find Elizabeth Mehta standing in front of us with both of her parents. They all wear matching outfits, khaki shorts and polos. Her hair is pulled back in a sleek ponytail. A white visor shades her eyes from the sun. Heat claws at my cheeks as I think of our encounter in the arcade and her unanswered texts on my phone.

"Um-m," I say, brain stuttering.

There's hurt in her eyes. I should've responded, even with something short.

My pulse races. I feel kind of queasy, the sun and sugar catching up to me fast.

Brie steps forward. She gives Elizabeth a tight hug, then

shakes hands with her parents. "So nice to see you guys! Is this your first year in the tournament?"

Elizabeth's mom waves her hand. "Oh, no, we play every year. Haven't gotten any better at golf, though, have we?"

"Very off-brand for rich people," Elizabeth jokes.

Her parents hush her. "That's not polite," her dad says.

She shrugs. "I thought it was funny."

It *was* funny. Elizabeth *is* funny. She might be one of the quietest girls on the team, but she'd always break us into laughter with her sharp wit. One time, at a team sleepover, she had me laughing so hard my sides still hurt the next day.

"Anyways." Brie claps her hands together. "Sorry to rush y'all, but I see another group right behind you. Time for the family picture! If you'll just step over here . . ."

We snap their picture and hand out their frozen lemonades, then wave goodbye. The entire time, my tongue feels glued to the roof of my mouth. I want so badly to say something, but feel immobilized.

"See you at practice," Brie tells Elizabeth as she leaves. I know the words weren't said to hurt me, but they cut like glass.

After they depart, Brie turns to me. I can feel the held-back judgment. Yes, Hannah ruined another friendship. Par for the course. *On* a golf course.

"Please, don't," I say.

She holds up a hand with the tiniest of smiles. "Wasn't gonna." Her smile fades into contemplation as she says, "Lucy and Riley are coming by tomorrow morning. We're going to play in the arcade, maybe go bowling. You should swing by if you want. They'd love to see you."

I'm surprised by the invitation. An olive branch, even though it's just for the girls' benefit. More interaction with Brie is a stressful prospect, but I do miss her sisters. And it was nice of her to invite me, for whatever reason.

"Okay," I say slowly, like I'm testing out the word. "Sure, sounds good. Thanks."

We snap pictures for the rest of the day, and as morning bleeds into afternoon, we steal another lemonade cup each.

"Just you?" Mom asks when I walk into the living room. She's sitting on the couch and watching Food Network. Figgy's on the couch with her, her giant fluffy head on Mom's lap.

"The boys are working doubles," I answer, then flop onto the couch. Ethan is going to be exhausted by the end of the day. Working a double is no joke, especially on limited sleep. Figgy looks up at me with her gentle, sleepy eyes and gives my leg a slobbery kiss. "Thanks, Fig."

I'm worn-out. Barely any sleep last night, then direct sunlight all day. Even during our long summer practices, we'd take breaks every two hours to cool down and hydrate. My pale skin is going to be tinged red tomorrow, despite my countless sunscreen applications.

"Want to watch with us?" Mom asks, like Figgy is also tuned in to the show.

"Okay," I agree, settling deeper into the couch. I pet Figgy's furry butt, and she wiggles closer to me in contentment. Giant fluffy goofball.

"How was work today?" Mom asks, looking over at me. She has on a pair of teal reading glasses, and I notice light circles under her eyes. There seem to be a lot of restless people in this house.

"Good." I nod. "We had the charity tournament for the children's hospital, so that was cool. I, uh, worked with Brie."

I half mumble, half whisper those last words, but my mom's crystal clear hearing catches them.

"Really?" she asks, her curiosity turned to a ten even though I know she's trying to hold back. "How was that? I invited them to the unveiling. Your bubbie loved Brie and her family."

"Oh, okay," I say.

I didn't know they were invited. Brie's family was at the funeral, of course. They brought a giant platter of fruit during shiva, enough to serve fifty people. But an unveiling is a much smaller gathering.

"You two were always attached at the hip," Mom adds.

I nod, my throat tight. "I know."

She's looking at me, testing out words in her head. I know what's coming next. "You know, the checklist, sweetheart—there's that item about repairing relationships." She looks down and pets Figgy. What a good dog, our Switzerland. "I think you would feel so much better if you could patch things up with Brie."

There's a lump in my throat, hard and swollen. Until this past year, I didn't know a life without Brie. She was always there, with me, for me. My broken ankle isn't the only thing that has left me unbalanced. "I'm going to see her tomorrow," I say. "Her sisters are coming to play games at Bonanza."

"That sounds nice," Mom replies, and I'm relieved she leaves the conversation at that.

And maybe, somehow, it will be nice. Today went okay, after all, better than I expected. Maybe I can mend things with Brie. At least a little. I wouldn't mind easing some of the tension Mom carries in her shoulders.

"This contestant sure is lacking in the brain cells department," Mom says, glancing at the TV as three chefs cook chicken parmigiana.

"Not sure he even has a brain cells department," I reply.

Mom laughs. Figgy nuzzles in closer, and we all finish the episode together.

Last Summer

Tonight's party is different. For one thing, it's outdoors. At first, this unsettles me. Outdoors should equate to on the field, practicing with my team under the floodlights, sweat dripping down our necks, muscles burning with exertion. Every day now I watch my thighs shrink from disuse. It's unsettling. I don't recognize myself. So even though the summer's heat lingers far into the night, I cover up with jeans and sweatshirts.

"Like it?" Shira asks.

"Different vibe," I reply.

I've been going to parties with Shira for the past few weeks now, ever since I kicked Brie out. All variations on a theme. Keggers at crappy apartments filled with secondhand smoke and secondhand furniture. Bottles of wine in mini mansions, the parents on vacation. Once a dim club, where Shira used a smile and a name instead of an ID. They all served the same purpose, a few drinks dulling my thoughts, unclenching my muscles.

Tonight's party does feel different, though.

As we trudge deeper in the woods, the trees open up into a grove. There's a bonfire, and the music is soft and acoustic. The crowd seems less desperate, more comfortable. I turn to Shira and smile. She's wearing a long black netted skirt and a lavender tank. Her hair is braided back into a crown, and the small birthstone pendant her parents gifted her for her bat mitzvah hangs around her neck.

"The secret is that I actually like these people," Shira tells me with a grin. "They're artists—they draw, they compose, they write." Her eyes glow in the firelight. "They create beautiful things."

"How'd you meet them?"

"It's like a daisy chain, you know? One links to the next. I meet Rafael, who paints, and he introduces me to his friend Heather, who sculpts, and she introduces me to her girlfriend Sara, who writes plays. It just goes on and on like that. It's wonderful. Come, now."

Shira leads me into the party and introduces me to her friends. I like them all. I like listening to them talk about their projects and ideas and how they started creating. It gives this slight stirring in my stomach, this excitement, and somehow I manage to feel happy for them, happy that they still have the thing in their life that makes their heart swell.

I scan the crowd for cute boys. Alexi, the Russian foreign-exchange student, was the first. Then there was Matt. Basic Matt.

He brought me a Smirnoff Ice and told me about his plan to major in accounting, and then we made out for ten minutes until it was his turn to play beer pong. Then Parth, then Daniel. A string of lips between changing songs and sips of liquor.

My parents aren't happy about the parties, aren't happy I keep pushing curfew later while refusing to attend therapy, physical or mental. They think I need to talk to someone–of course they do. Two nights ago, I stumbled through the door with alcohol still strong on my breath, and for the first time in my life, my dad was silent. I went to my room and slept until two in the afternoon. "Next time you're grounded," Dad said when he saw me in the kitchen. There were bags under his eyes, his shirt wrinkled. I looked away and helped myself to some cereal.

The longer I stay out, the more I can fade the edges of my reality, forget what I lost this summer.

I settle into one of the chairs near the fire. The heat burns through my jeans. The boy next to me has wide shoulders, red hair, and freckles. He looks unlike anyone I've ever seen before. He turns to me and asks, "If you could be any animal, what animal would you choose?"

I wonder if he asks this question to every girl who sits next to him. "I guess a dog," I say. "Since humans take care of them so well."

He nods. "Honest, at least."

I resist an eye-roll. "What about you?"

"An anteater," he replies without hesitation.

I can tell he wants me to ask him why, but I don't. There's something satisfying about not giving someone what they want. Instead, I crack open my beer and take a sip.

When he realizes I'm not going to respond, he asks, "You want some whiskey?" He shows me the bottle. "It's small batch. Japanese. You'll never taste anything like it again."

He's trying to impress me. Japanese whiskey probably tastes as terrible as regular whiskey. "Sure," I say. "Thanks."

He pops out the cork and sips, making an "Mmm" sound after. Then he passes me the bottle.

It isn't good, but it burns less than other liquor. I take another sip and another, and then one more for good measure. There's a flicker of annoyance on his face. Maybe his Japanese whiskey is expensive.

"Thanks." I hand the bottle back to him. "It's really good. Where'd you get it?"

He tells me a story about a friend who lived in Japan for three months. We pass the bottle back and forth while he speaks. It's a long story. And eventually I'm giggling–at what, I'm not sure. But my cheeks are flushed, and the redheaded boy is looking cuter by the second. I like his freckles. In the light of the fire, I find myself trying to count how many there are.

The summer air is warm and heavy, like a cloak protecting us from the rest of the world. It feels like this night could stretch out forever, but once we leave it, we'll never be able to find it again. It feels like being alive.

It takes a few more sips of whiskey to realize I'm drunk.

My phone rests in my bag, on silent. I'm not supposed to be out again. It's late, I'm sure. My parents are probably worried. And suddenly I feel very bad about that. They don't deserve to be worried.

I'm a bad daughter.

It's only when I reach over to grab my phone that I realize I'm holding hands with the boy. I shoot him a messy smile, then disentangle myself from his grasp. There are texts from my parents. I squint. It's hard to read when you're drunk. I can't believe people drive like this. The messages are all some variation of "Where are you?" "Are you okay?" "Get home immediately."

I don't want to get home immediately. I want this night to last forever. I feel like we could keep the sun from rising if we keep going, keep drinking, keep the music playing and the fire burning. I glance across the fire pit at Shira, and she gives me a smile so wide I feel it down to my toes.

I text my parents: Sorry, out with Shira. We're being safe. Will sleep at her place tonight.

The party continues. At some point, I end up lying on a blanket. The redhead is on one side, his hand holding mine. We kissed for a while, in the woods, against a tree. But my head started spinning, so I pushed him aside and drew us back to the party. Through my drunken haze, I realized I was lucky he didn't push back. I hate knowing that's something to be lucky about.

Now I'm on the blanket with him on one side and Shira on

the other. A girl named Lilli-Belle is next to her, and I think that's such a pretty name, like a character in a fairy tale, and I told her that earlier, and she kissed me on the cheek and said thank you.

The music is still playing but softer, and the fire is still burning but down to smoky embers, and I realize that the sky is lighter, that we've made it to dawn. My heart fills with a powerful feeling.

I roll over and tell Shira, "Thank you."

She smiles. "No, thank *you*."

We watch the sun rise together, and then we sleep.

Chapter Fourteen

I WAKE UP to knocking on my bedroom door. Disoriented, I roll over and check the time. It's dark outside. After watching TV with Mom, I went to lie in bed for a few minutes before a shower, but I guess I fell asleep. I blink a few times at my phone and see it's past nine.

"What?" I mumble, voice thick with sleep.

"I'm coming in!" Joey announces. My door opens without further warning, and my brother strides into my room, wearing a suit, his wild hair tamed back. "Up and at 'em!" He claps his hands together. "Chop-chop, time to go!"

"Huh? Go where?" My mouth full of cotton, I roll over to a take a sip of water, then chug it. The heat definitely got to me today.

"Back to Bonanza," Joey says, like it's the most obvious answer in the world.

"*Joey*, it's past nine. Bonanza just closed."

"Obviously I know that, *Hannah*. It's the first games of the Olympics! And I can't be late. I'm hosting."

I blink. "Okay . . . so go? Why didn't you just stay after your shift?"

"Because you're coming too, and you're going to love it." He pauses. "And I forgot my suit at home."

I shake my head. "You seriously think I'm going to *return* to my place of work this late at night to watch people play pinball?"

Joey shakes his head. "Nah, it's bowling first." He looks back into the hallway and hollers, "Shower faster, Ethan!"

I wake up a little more at the mention of his name. "You're dragging him into this too?"

"No, he's going of his own accord because he's a supportive best friend and not a naysayer like my dear sister. Now get some pants on and get in the car. Or go without pants. It's your choice."

I don't want to put pants on. I don't want to return to Bonanza, especially for the Olympics.

But now that the fuzziness has worn off, the effects of my nap are kicking in, and I feel wide-awake. If I stay in the house like this, there's a good chance I'll start peeling the wallpaper.

"Hannah! Pants!" Joey screams.

And the path of least resistance with Joey is no resistance at all.

"Fine," I mutter, shoving my covers off and rooting around for a pair of not-dirty pants. Laundry. I should do that one day. "But I'm not promising to have fun."

"Deal," Joey says. "Now let's go."

Twenty minutes later, we're back at Bonanza. I can't believe I was here at the crack of dawn this morning and now late at night. *What is this place doing to me?*

It's warm out and dark, only a few floodlights illuminating the parking lot. With the customer cars all gone, I realize I can now recognize the cars of my coworkers. Gary's Civic Accord. Tony's forest-green pickup truck. Daisey's Jeep Wrangler. After a few weeks at Bonanza, I know other things about my coworkers too. I know that veteran employee Iris eats lunch at the right corner of the concessions so she can see if anyone is going to beat her *Pac-Man* high score. I know Nate always empties the trash cans before they overflow, unlike the rest of us, who seem to put it off until the last possible second, like a disgusting high-stakes game of Jenga. And I know that Patrick, for all his cool bravado, can hold a conversation with a five-year-old kid for ten minutes and actually seem legitimately engaged the whole time.

In only a few weeks, I've picked up and stored all this

information. I wonder what my coworkers have noticed about me, what details have been tucked away. I wonder how much more we'll know about each other by the end of summer.

"Come on, slowpokes." Joey jostles us toward the entrance. "We have five minutes until the event starts, and the bowling alley is a six-minute walk away."

Ethan shoots me an eye-roll and a smile. His hair is still wet, a few beads of water dripping onto his neck. We both put the bare minimum effort into our outfits. Ethan basically has a capsule wardrobe at our house—extra work shirts, jeans, pj's, etc. Tonight, he's in his gray drawstring sweatpants and a faded Bonanza shirt. I'm wearing black leggings and an oversize T-shirt handed down from Dad's concert years. My hair is sticking out in five directions, and I think I reapplied deodorant, but I can't swear by it. Really bringing my A game tonight.

The night air presses against us as we rush inside, and my ankle twinges when I land on it wrong. Wind rustles through the air, kicking up debris, skittering it across the paved lot. Ethan stops to pick up some of the trash, and I join him, gathering an empty chip bag, a plastic water bottle, and a flyer for some band called Motel/Hotel.

We dump everything into the recycling cans by the front entrance and then continue through Bonanza to the bowling alley. The double doors whoosh open, and a wall of noise greets us. I'm shocked by how many people are here. Upward of fifty, I would guess. Everyone is in high spirits, shouting across the room. "Party in the USA" plays over the speakers. Banners and balloons decorate the alley.

"Gotta get ready," Joey says, rushing toward the front counter.

Ethan stays back a second. "Told him I'd help." His eyes scan my face a moment too long. "You good?"

"Yeah." I nod. "Of course. Go on."

Once they leave, I search the crowd for a friend to latch onto. Maybe Nate is here. I spot Brie. She's sitting on the concessions counter with a small circle of friends, including Grand Supreme winner Sophie Flores. As if she can feel my gaze, Brie looks up and catches my eyes. She gives a nod and small smile, and I give a quick wave back. My stomach is in knots thinking about our time with her sisters tomorrow. I hope it goes okay.

I turn away and scan the alley again, relieved to find Nate this time, sitting alone at an empty lane. His nose is stuck in his phone as I approach.

"Hard crossword today?" I ask.

He startles at first, but then he smiles wide enough that his glasses inch up on his face. Nate is cute. It's a shame he finds my brother an obnoxious pain in the butt. "Hello, Hannah. How are you?"

"Oh fine, just spending twelve hours a day at Bonanza, totally normal. Can I sit here?"

"Of course!" Nate replies. "My friend is grabbing us snacks, but there's plenty of room." He pats the bench next to him, and I sit. "And it was a hard crossword today, but I finished before lunch. I'm working on my own now."

"Wait, what?" I ask. "Like you're building your own puzzle?"

His smile grows. "Yup."

"That's so cool. How do you even do that?"

"Well . . ."

"Hannah!" a voice interrupts. Nate and I look up to find Joey standing in front of us, hair gelled back, stone-faced in his suit. "This is a disaster."

I doubt that. "What's wrong?"

Joey huffs out a giant sigh. "Sheena had to drop out of the tournament. She has a stomach bug and doesn't want to puke all over the lanes. I offered her some Pepto-Bismol and Imodium, but she refused both. Can you believe that?"

I tilt my head. "Joey, why do you have Pepto-Bismol and Imodium on you?"

"Because he's out of control," Ethan answers, walking up to join us. He gives Nate a quick hello. "Have you felt his backpack? Thing weighs like fifty pounds."

"It's called being *prepared*," Joey replies. "I'm the host. I take my duties seriously."

"Pretty sure host duties don't include running an infirmary," I counter.

"Well, if I don't prepare, then who will?"

My heart softens for him then. He's just trying to make sure everyone has a good time. I'm about to try to comfort him when, surprisingly, Nate speaks up.

"Joey." Nate's voice is kind and calm. "Everyone will have fun tonight. You're doing great. Don't stress yourself out. It'll be okay."

Somehow, this helps. The panic fades from Joey's eyes. "Right." He clears his throat. "Um, thank you."

I give Nate a grateful look. He shrugs and goes back to his crossword.

"We still need one more bowler, though," Joey tells us. "The prelim rules require an even match for each round, which means we need six bowlers tonight, and we only have five. And no one wants to do it."

"Hannah's good at bowling," Ethan suggests.

I glare at him. "Excuse me, *you're* the one who bowls all the time. Why don't you do it?"

Ethan holds up a laptop. "I'm scorekeeper."

"How convenient for you," I reply.

Ethan grins in response.

"Oh, Hannah," my brother begins, drawing my attention back. Oh, lord. He's pulling out the Pixar-character eyes. "Dear sister, beloved Hannah, please will you—"

"Joey, I said I don't want to participate. . . ."

"It's just a prelim round—"

"I know, but—"

I shouldn't be surprised by what happens next. I have, after all, known my brother his entire life.

Joey gets down on his knees and puts his hands together. "Hannah, the fate of the entire Bonanza Olympics now rests on your strong shoulders. This isn't a favor for just me, your incredible, kind, loving, hilarious, charming, and ridiculously good-looking brother; this is a favor for all Bonanza employees in our fine play-nation." His voice starts rising, and other people look over at us. Ethan holds a hand to his mouth to cover his laughter. Even Nate is biting back a smile. Oh jeez. "Decades from now, we will remember this day. It will be a landmark moment in the turning tides of our relationship, and—" His voice raises even louder. "And we will always—"

"Okay!" I finally shout, now that almost everyone is looking at us. Daisey has pulled out her phone to record, and I have a feeling that it will be sent to ten different group chats. "Okay," I agree, more softly this time. "If you shut up, I'll bowl."

"Done and done!" Joey pops back up to a standing position and sweeps forward to kiss my cheek. "Thank you. You will not regret it. Hey, you might even win. Ethel!" he shouts, suddenly storming in the direction of another employee who's setting up the judging table.

I roll my eyes. I'm not going to win. One morning of practice is not enough. Plus, I'm just filling a spot. I'll perform the bare minimum while eating concession nachos. Maybe I can even count this as my good deed of the day, since I'm helping out my brother.

"How is Joey the host, anyways?" I ask, turning to Ethan and Nate. "He's only been here a year. Isn't it, like, a revered position?"

Both boys shake their heads.

"It's an unpaid full-time job," Nate replies. "No one wants to do it."

"Except Joey," Ethan adds. Then he nudges me. "Hey. Look at you. Participating in the Olympics. And you thought you were too cool."

I roll my eyes. "Congratulations, I've been infected."

Nate nods. "That happens a lot here."

These bowlers mean business. Right out of the gate, two score strikes and three score spares. I feel a hint of pressure trickle across my spine. Plenty of people are still chatting and laughing, but a shocking number are paying rapt attention to the game and judge commentary (while winning the game is based on score alone, there's a panel of judges anyway to comment on form and flair).

And now it's my turn. To bowl. In front of everyone.

I've never had a problem with performance anxiety before, but I've also never bowled in a tournament with only one session of practice. I pick up the same ball I used this morning, then walk to the front of my lane. Joey's voice echoes from the alley speakers. "We now have first-time Bonanza athlete Hannah Klein up to bowl. Hannah is seventeen years old and a rising senior in high school. She trained under the tutelage of our parents, David and Sarah Klein. Hannah showed great talent for ballhandling from a young age—"

The crowd breaks into laughter, and I shoot Joey a look that could probably kill him if only he would meet my eyes.

"Not like that, y'all!" he says. "Minds out of the *gutter*. A bowling pun, if you will. Now Hannah comes from the fair city of Wakesville, Georgia, which by unforeseen coincidence, is the same city from which almost every other Bonanza Olympian hails. A special thank-you to Jack O'Connor from Ireland for making this an international competition. Now, let's tune in for Hannah's first frame of the preliminaries. . . ."

From somewhere in the crowd, I hear Daisey shout, "You go, girl!"

"Go, Hannah!" another voice yells. I spin and find Patrick walking through the alley doors, his hands cupped around his mouth to increase the volume of his cheer. He's looking good, in dark jeans and a black V-neck. I chew the inside of my cheek as he gives me a smile and a two-finger salute. It's hard to explain, but I wish I felt more excited to see him.

I wave at him before turning back to my lane.

That's when someone, whom I can't identify, shouts, "Don't mess up!"

Great. Thanks for that.

And then suddenly, despite the fact that I don't care about the Bonanza Olympics or bowling—my pulse begins to race.

Which is silly. Really.

It's just *bowling*. It's just bowling at my *part-time job* for a silly made-up tournament. It doesn't matter how I perform. There are no stakes to this. It doesn't matter.

And yet. I'm a competitor. I always have been. And although soccer is out of my life, it seems my competitive spirit is still there, eager to break out of its year of hibernation. I can't fight my nature. If I'm going to do something, I might as well fight for the win.

My heartbeat drumming, I take a steadying breath and focus on the pins in front of me. I set a goal for myself. Knock down half the pins. That's a solid number. It might even leave me a chance at a spare as long as I don't split them too badly.

Oh god, what if I split them too badly?

Unfortunately, that's the thought that invades my mind right as I pull back my arm and release the ball. My breath catches in my throat as it rolls down the lane. Time slows. Sounds melt away. For a moment, I feel like I'm back on the soccer field, floating in that eternal second when everything else disappears, and I wait to see if my shot will sink into the net. And then—

Crash.

The ball slams into the pins.

All but three clatter to the ground.

Mild applause breaks out around me. I fight back a smile as Joey begins his commentary again. "An absolutely outstanding first showing from Hannah Klein! Truly a spectacular spectacle to behold. This young athlete is just getting started, and I know we all can't wait to see what happens next. Will she get the spare? Will she—"

Joey continues, but I'm too focused on the remaining pins to listen, too distracted by the adrenaline rushing through me, because that was—well, that was *fun.*

I forgot the rush of competition. The *joy* of it.

A bittersweet feeling surges through me, the thrill of success and a sharp reminder of what I've lost. Bowling might not be my dream sport, but I miss the feeling of competition.

And I want more of it.

Chapter Fifteen

I DON'T GET the spare, but I do knock down two more pins. Still, as the competition continues, I find myself quickly slipping away from a chance of making it through to the finals. Not that I *care* about making the finals. I don't care. I just want to bowl well.

The top three players will go on to compete in the finals two weeks from now. The competition is stiff. Sherry means business and has racked up four strikes already. This guy Charlie seems like he's been bowling since he left the womb. And assistant manager Kristine nails a difficult split. My ego takes a hit with every pin they knock down. Obviously, I can't bowl as well as someone who's been practicing for years, and yet it grates at my competitive nature to be so far from the lead.

I'm in fifth place in the six-person prelim, and that's only because the person in sixth is fighting a massive hangover. The possibility of clinching third place feels more impossible with each passing frame. And my rental bowling shoes aren't helping. My ankle feels unsecure in them, like it could give out with one wrong turn. I glance over at Ronald, who's holding strong in fourth place. Ronald is nineteen with pale skin and beady eyes. People call him Phantom of the Bonanza because he works exclusively in the alley bowels. This is my first time seeing him in person. Before tonight, I've only heard people call him over the radio to "get the jammed pins on six" or "fix the ball return on four."

Sweat beads down Ronald's neck. The competition is getting to him.

At least nerves aren't a problem for me. I know how to compete. I know how to take that mounting energy and funnel it toward the task at hand. The tighter the score, the more focused I am on my goal.

"Hey," a voice says. I turn and find Ethan behind me, laptop in hand. His brown eyes are wide with contagious excitement. "Look at this."

"At what?" I ask.

He steps forward and shows me the screen. "You can move into the finals if you get a strike on your last frame and Ronald over there messes up his. That is, if you care about winning." The corner of his mouth quirks up in a knowing smile.

"I don't *care*," I say. "It's just, you know, if I've come this far, I might as well . . ."

Ethan's smile grows.

"Oh, shut up!" I hold up my hands. "Fine, I care. I want to win. Whatever. Big surprise." I roll my eyes. "But beating Ronald only puts me in fourth."

Ethan leans even closer. He smells good, familiar. I take a quick breath as he says, "A little bird told me Sherry has a family reunion the week of the finals. She's only playing the prelim for street cred and then will drop out."

"*Oh.*" My eyes widen. "So fourth place is . . ."

"Really third place," Ethan finishes.

"Okay, what do I need to do, again?"

Ethan's grin is infectious. "You need a strike. And we need Ronald to mess up. Anything under a spare will clear the way for you. Good news is, his hands look pretty sweaty."

We both turn to appraise Ronald, who is now patting down his neck with a towel.

I turn back to Ethan, chewing my lip. His attention moves to my mouth, only for a moment, but when his eyes flick up to mine, there's something in his gaze that makes my whole body heat. I feel practically . . . undressed.

I swallow, hard.

"Um." My tongue feels stuck to the roof of my mouth. "So. A strike."

"Uh, yeah." Ethan's voice is low, scratchy. "A strike."

Say something, Hannah. Say any normal words.

"Too bad my shoes suck," I blurt out, pointing down at them. "My ankle is not happy. I can't believe customers pay for these."

Ethan winces. "Yeah, pretty sure Bonanza hasn't updated them since the early aughts." He looks thoughtful for a moment before shaking his head. "All right. You've still got this, though. Go get him."

He gives my shoulder an awkward squeeze before sitting on the bench at my lane.

I take a sip of water, then tune back in to Joey's commentary as we move into the final frame. My system thrums with restless energy. I just need an opening. I need a chance.

And then it's Ronald's turn, Ronald with his sweaty hands. He douses himself in powder. It gets everywhere. On his pants, his face, the floor.

It makes a mess but will also keep the ball from slipping out of his hands. *Damn it.* My shoulders tighten as Ronald finishes dusting and picks up his ball. If he manages a spare or better, I'm out of the running.

He steadies his aim, then moves forward and releases the ball. It spins swiftly down the lane. My breathing quiets as I watch it head directly for the center pin, but then at the last second it veers left, *way left*, and—

"Yes!" I shout, very loudly, too loudly.

Ronald knocked down three measly pins.

Red tinges my cheeks as I look around to see if anyone noticed my unsportsmanlike behavior. *Plenty* of people did. A few are laughing at my outburst, including Sherry, but Ronald definitely isn't. He glares at me with the fury of a thousand Georgia summer suns.

Sorry, I mouth with a wince.

I can feel the tension in the room grow as Ronald prepares for his second bowl. Most of the side conversations have dimmed to murmurs, and even Joey's commentary sounds like we're on a golf course, his hushed voice falling over the crowd.

I spot a trickle of sweat running down Ronald's neck, the one place he didn't manage to powder. "Hey, batter, batter," I mutter under my breath so softly only I can hear. "Swing batter, swing batter, batter."

He gets in position, winds up, and—

Again, the ball shoots straight down the lane. My heart sinks as this one stays true to course. I pray for the same mistake to be made, for the ball to veer to the left again, but it's like a magnet is pulling it center. Ronald's measly three pins are going to turn into a spare.

Damn it.

The ball strikes the pins with a resounding crack, and the defeat feels so painful I have to close my eyes. A moment later, there's a warm hand on my shoulder, and without even turning, I know it's Ethan behind me again. "Hannah, *look*. Look at the pins."

I let my eyes stayed closed one moment longer, relaxing under his touch. Prickles run down my spine, the feeling of his hand on my shoulder, his lips close to my ear. Even surrounded by fifty people, it feels like a private moment. Suddenly, there's a *want* in me I've never quite experienced before. I feel entirely out of equilibrium.

Then his hand slips away, and I open my eyes, and I look at the pins, and—

There are two still standing. *Two pins*. Holy shit.

I can win.

Well, win enough to move on to the finals.

"Oh my god." I turn to Ethan, eyes wide. "I can do this."

He smiles. "You can do this."

Adrenaline courses through me.

I can do this, and I want to do this. I tamped down my competitive spirit for so long now that it's chomping at the bit to be in control again.

As Ethan rejoins the crowd, I spot Brie with her friends. She's still here, watching, and I find myself comforted by her presence. She gives me a thumbs-up and mouths the familiar words *You've got this.*

I feel almost buoyant as I stride up to the ball return,

funneling all my energy into the task at hand. Sports are simple at their core. Score a goal. Knock down some pins. And yet, there are multibillion-dollar industries for them. There are international Olympic games for them. There are lifelong, die-hard fans for them.

Because there's something special, something utterly perfect, about the simplicity of their tasks and the drive to achieve them.

As I go to pick up my ball, I notice Ronald glaring at me from his lane. I smile and wave. His glaring intensifies, and my smile deepens. *Oh, this is going to be a fun working relationship moving forward.*

I turn back to my lane and take a slow breath to focus my thoughts. *Knock them all down. Win.* It's wild how badly I want this when two hours ago I didn't even want to participate. But I want that rush. I want that satisfaction.

I lift up my arm until the ball is eye-level and then look down the lane, focusing on that center pin. *You are going to hit that pin, ball. And you are going to be a strike. And Ronald will wail in defeat.*

If I get the strike, I'll only need a few more pins after to place third. And I truly don't think I could get a gutter ball if I tried. *Okay, Hannah. Don't jinx yourself. Just do it. Like the slogan.*

I take one more breath, then throw the ball down the lane with every bit of force in my muscles. The noise is sucked from the room as the ball whizzes down the lane. All I can hear is the hypnotic rolling of the ball, *thwump, thhwump, thwump.*

My eyes are magnetized to the ball, so I'm not even sure where it's going to land until it cracks against the pins and—

They all go scattering down.

"OH MY GOD!" I shout so loud it hurts my own eardrums. I pump my fist into the air as my heart thuds hard and fast. "Yes!"

And then there are arms around me, and for a second I think, I *hope*—

No, it's not Ethan. Ethan wouldn't hug me like that.

I spin around and find Patrick behind me. The disappointment startles me. He's as handsome as ever, lean and attractive in his plain black tee. And his expression is bright as he leans in to kiss me, but on reflex, I pull away.

His arms drop. Hurt reads in his eyes.

"Patrick . . . ," I start to say, not sure where I'm going with it.

He's clearing his throat, running a hand through his hair. "Nice strike," he says. "Uh, Tony and I are heading to a party. Assuming you don't want to join us."

The comment feels like a dig. I've told him I can't go to parties, and I thought he was okay with that. Now it feels like that's all getting thrown in my face, like I've done something wrong.

And I don't even *want* to go to the party. And not only because of my parents. The rules. Mountain Bliss. But because, I realize, that desperate urge to escape has lessened. I had fun tonight—real, actual fun. The adrenaline of competition. I felt like myself again. And I don't want to run away from it. I want to stay. And maybe tomorrow when I see Brie . . . maybe there will be a chance to fix things.

Maybe if I stop hiding, I'll be able to find some of what I lost.

"Um." I tuck a strand of hair behind my ear. "I'm staying here. Then home."

"Right." Patrick nods. The coolness settling between us makes my spine rigid. Something irreversible seems to have shifted. "See you later then, Hannah. Congrats on the win."

"Haven't quite won yet," I reply weakly.

There's a slight bitterness to his tone, like cold coffee. "Yeah, well, you will."

As he turns from me and disappears into the crowd, I take a steadying breath. Patrick is frustrated, and rightly so. Because I've been hiding from a lot of things, not just Brie.

Because Patrick hugged me, Patrick went to kiss me—

But I wanted it to be Ethan.

Last Summer

"This is weird," I tell Shira. "Kids from school are here."

"I know," she replies. "But there was nothing better going on tonight."

We're in the rich part of town, a house with a pool and finished basement and no parents in sight. Some kids are getting plastered, others are eating pretzels and playing Cards Against Humanity. My anxiety notches up as I look at the familiar faces. What if someone from the team is here?

I pick up a bottle of Malibu and fill four shots. "L'chaim," I say, clinking glasses with Shira.

"L'chaim," she responds.

We down two shots each.

An hour and three more drinks later, I'm plastered and in the middle of a conversation about the possible existence of aliens with some kid I had gym class with in middle school. "No, no, no, you see," he argues, holding up a finger. "The Fermi paradox says—"

I cut him off with, "Beer's empty, gonna grab another drink."

It turns out, with enough alcohol, partying with kids from high school is just like partying with kids from college. I'm pulled into a game of flip cup, which I totally dominate. Three rounds later, I feel a hand on my shoulder and spin around to find Shira. She's sipping wine out of a bottle with a crazy straw. Her black eyeliner is smudged at the corners.

"HEY!" I shout. "Where have you been? Come on, play with us."

"Andie just texted me about a party downtown. I've got a DD. Let's go!"

"You go," I tell her. "I'm having fun here."

She shrugs. "Up to you; just find someone sober to drive you home, 'kay?"

"Definitely!" I give her a tight hug before turning back to the game.

The party blurs later into the night. More drinking, more laughing. One guy tries to get handsy with me, but I say no, and when he tries again, a bunch of girls start booing him and taking his picture until he leaves the party. After I thank them, my head is swimming, so I flop onto a couch for a breather.

"Hey!" someone shouts. "I'm sitting here."

When I look over, the room spins to a stop. The person sitting next to me—no, the person I'm practically sitting on—is Brie. My best friend. Her hair is down, and her eyes are lined with shimmer.

"Hannah?" she asks.

Without meaning to, I mock her question. *"Brie?"*

Her face shifts, like she smells something bad.

"What are you doing here?" I ask.

She scoots out from under me, scoots away from me. She's wearing a gold skirt with a plain, off-white tank. "It's Taylor's house," she replies. "It's her party."

Right. Taylor. One of Brie's friends from coding club. I've always found it strange that Brie has time for other things outside soccer–coding, babysitting, a boyfriend.

"Still broken up with Cody?" I ask. Her face flickers with hurt. "He was a dumbass anyways," I say, trying to make it better. "You could do so much better."

Brie's jaw hardens. "Stop it, Hannah."

"Stop what?"

"Stop being an asshole." She takes a short breath, then stands up. "You're drunk. I'm driving you home."

"What?" I ask.

"You can't see straight. I'm not having your death on my conscience."

"I'm *fine*," I say, and even though I fully intend to get a sober ride home later, I take out my keys and shake them. "All good," I sing. "Promise."

"Hannah," Brie says. "Get in my goddamn car now."

I roll my eyes. But as I look around the room, I realize the party is dying down. My options for a ride are limited, and I don't really want to stay here overnight.

"Fine." I huff a sigh. "But drop me off at Shira's. My parents will throw a shit fit if I come home like this."

I'll be in serious trouble if my parents catch me this drunk. My last straw was three straws ago. I'm actually grounded right now.

I follow Brie outside. Summer is winding down, the night air tinged with a fall chill. I stumble to keep up with Brie as she strides to her car at the end of the street, almost tripping on a pothole in the darkness. I left my crutches at home. My ankle burns.

The ride home is silent. Brie's fingers drum on the steering wheel at each stoplight. She's pissed at me, her expression hard and focused on the road. My head pounds from the alcohol. My eyes dip closed, fluttering back open only when the engine shuts off. It's then I realize I'm at my house and not Shira's.

"Hey, what the hell?" I ask, sitting up. "Brie, you know I can't go in there like this."

She won't look at me. "Go in the house, Hannah."

"I'll be grounded. Forever."

"Sounds like a good plan," she snaps. Then her voice softens. She looks at me, eyes pleading. "You're *plastered*, Hannah. You need help. Go inside."

"No."

"Yes."

"No."

"Fine!" she shouts. "Then I'll call your parents. I'll tell them myself that you were going to drive home drunk."

"Stop being so dramatic." I slide down in the seat with a huff. "It's a total drag."

"I'm trying to help you," Brie says.

I know I should feel something when her voice cracks, but I'm already broken in too many ways to react. And when she calls my parents and tells them what happened, I vow to myself never to speak to her again.

Chapter Sixteen

I PUSH BACK my hair as I walk through the arcade doors. It's growing out, summer quickly slipping by. Yawning, I stretch my arms overhead. I slept like crap last night. I blame adrenaline. Securing third place in the preliminaries and then admitting to myself that I like my brother's best friend had me way too wired for a peaceful slumber. I tossed and turned into the early-morning hours, wanting too many things that all feel out of reach.

"Hannah! Hannah!" two voices call out.

Lucy and Riley are sprinting toward me. It's been a year since I've seen them. There's a big difference between eight and nine, and the change makes my throat tight.

Although they're identical twins, I can tell them apart easily by the scar on Lucy's left eyebrow, a roller-skating accident from a few years ago. They're both dressed in white, Lucy in a romper and Riley in overall shorts.

"Hi, girls!" I say, forcing cheer into my voice as they tackle me with hugs. I'm happy to see them, *more* than happy, but last night has my system all out of whack. I want to stop running, but that means facing everything I've been hiding from—including my feelings for Ethan, a much-needed conversation with Patrick, and trying to fix things with Brie. None of which sounds like an easy task.

As the girls step back, I take a breath and clap my hands together. "Okay, what are we playing first?"

"We were just deciding," Brie answers, catching up to us. Her braids are down today, and she's wearing a tie-dye Bonanza shirt. It's cute. Hannah from last year would call dibs on wearing it next.

"I want to play *Mario Kart*!" Lucy shouts. "I'm really good at it."

The competitive glint in her eyes makes me smile.

"Ghost Hunters Six, please," Riley requests, her voice softer than her sister's. "Last time the poltergeist tried to kill me with a chain saw, but I escaped through the torture room."

"Er, delightful," I reply.

I catch Brie's gaze, and we're both holding back laughter.

Riley's horror obsession is both charming and alarming. She caught one of the Saw movies on TV when she was six and hasn't looked back since. You'd think she'd have nightmares, but it's her family who has the nightmares when she says stuff like, "People can die so many different ways!"

"Okay," Brie says. "Sounds like splitting up is in order. Hannah, want to take on *Mario Kart* with Lucy?"

I nod. "Gladly."

"Then off to the horror show we go!" Brie tells Riley, taking her hand.

Lucy drags me to the *Mario Kart* machine, chattering away about everything she's done this summer. We start playing, and she races like a speed demon, while I slip on so many bananas that Lucy accuses me of losing on purpose. I'm definitely *not* losing on purpose. I would never voluntarily let someone defeat me, especially not a defeat this embarrassing. On one race, Lucy legit *laps* me, and I accidentally let out a word that means I'll have to contribute fifty cents to their family curse jar.

"And *no* IOUs allowed," Lucy informs me, before proceeding to come in first place, again.

Eventually, she gets tired of beating me. "I want a challenge," she says, and sighs.

The girls want to play together, so we end up at the *Dance Dance Revolution* machines.

"Dance with us!" they plead.

A pit forms in my stomach. My ankle has been feeling a bit better lately, but it's definitely not strong enough for

DDR. Of course, the girls wouldn't be thinking about that, and the thought of explaining it makes my skin itch.

Out of instinct, I look to Brie for her help. Her eyes meet mine, and I know she can immediately tell what I'm thinking. I'm grateful our best-friend telepathy is somehow still in working order.

She turns to her sisters. "How about y'all play, and Hannah and I will get snacks for after. Sound like a plan?"

Riley pouts. "*Fine*, but then after we're all going to bowl together, right?"

"Absolutely," Brie agrees.

Both the girls smile, then jump on the machine to start playing. Relief sweeps through me as Brie and I head toward the concessions. "Thanks," I say, twisting my fingers together. "I um . . . I couldn't . . . well, thanks."

"No worries," Brie replies. Slowly, her eyes slide toward my ankle. I can feel my muscles stiffen in response. "How—" She hesitates. "How's recovery going?"

I have to say each word carefully so my voice doesn't crack. "Um, okay. Walking has gotten a lot easier."

"That's good." Brie nods. "And hey, congrats on the bowling prelim. That's impressive. Seems like you've made good progress."

"Yeah." My throat tightens. "Thank you."

I want to ask Brie a question in return because that's how conversations work, but I feel stuck. Words used to flow between us with no effort or thought. The only questions I can think of now are ones I don't want answers to: *How's the team? How's practice been going? When's the game against Kensington?*

But I want to try. I want to bridge this gap between us. So, after way too long a pause, I ask, "What kind of toppings do you like on your hot dogs?"

Brie gives me a bit of a funny look before answering, "Uh, ketchup and mustard. You?"

"I don't mind a bit of sauerkraut, if the mood strikes me."

I have never in my life put sauerkraut on a hot dog.

"*Cool.*" Brie draws out the word.

"Yeah."

Oh god, what's wrong with me?

There's a line for EZ Eats. Gary must be out sick because it's only Sherry behind the counter. Brie and I stand behind a couple of preteens who are debating the best Animal Crossing villagers. I've never played the game, but there was a time you couldn't pry Joey away from it. *Look how cute they are!* he would shout as our parents called him to the kitchen for dinner. *I must give them gifts and make them happy!*

I look at Brie, then the boys, and then we both smile. She also remembers Joey's Animal Crossing obsession. He once asked us to de-weed his island because our parents would kill him if he didn't finish his homework first. We said no because we were the older siblings and we did not do manual (virtual) labor for the younger siblings. And then we made salted caramel popcorn and watched *Married at First Sight* instead. That was a fun evening. Brie and I are excellent reality-TV partners. Our commentary gets snarkier and snarkier throughout the episode as we try to one-up each other, and by the end of it my sides always hurt from laughing so hard.

I miss her. I miss *us*.

The feeling hits me like a sack of bricks.

I want my best friend back.

I have to try harder.

I take a slow breath. Then another. And another. This is not the place to do this. The concessions line at Bonanza is definitely not the place to do this. And yet, the words are ready to pour out of my mouth.

"Hannah?" Brie asks, looking over at me in confusion.

"Um." The lump in my throat feels like it'll be lodged there forever.

Seriously, *why* am I doing this now? I've held a grudge against my best friend for a full year. I can't hold out a little longer? These preteen boys are doused in way too much body spray, and it's going to be our turn to order soon, and yet I'm about to drop an emotional sledgehammer.

But I can't stop the words from coming out:

"I miss you, Brie."

Brie seems startled at first, her eyes widening in response, but as I continue to speak, there's a deep softness there. "I know . . . ," I say. "I know last year was a shit show. And I messed up in a lot of ways. And well, you know, you messed up too, so, but anyways . . ."

The preteen boys have stopped talking and are definitely listening to me. This is perfect.

"Crap. Um. Well—"

"Hannah," Brie, *thank god*, interrupts me. She clears her throat, tucks a braid behind her ear. "I want to talk about this too. But the concession stands . . ."

I give a quick laugh. "Not the best venue. I know."

"Yeah."

She gives me a warm smile. My stomach is in absolute knots. One of the boys gives us a weird look, then mutters something to his friend. I have the distinct urge to shove him.

I'm staring down at my feet when Brie asks, "Can we talk about it tomorrow? Maybe after Bubbie's unveiling?"

Her proposal sounds like an awful day, going to the cemetery and then dissecting our relationship.

But I think of that checklist on my fridge. I think of how my parents want me to do better. *Need* me to do better. I think of how I need that for myself as well.

I nod and say, "Okay."

✿

After scarfing down an assortment of hot dogs, nachos, Twinkies, sour straws, and soda, we head to the bowling alley, where we load up on *more* snacks: popcorn, M&Ms, and slushees. And then we lay claim to the best lane in the alley—the wall lane on the left. The one on the right is gross because it's by the bathrooms.

Lucy and Riley request bumpers, so instead of trying to play seriously, Brie and I decided to have fun bumping our balls off them in increasingly more chaotic patterns. We make bets using M&Ms about how many times we can get the ball to careen back and forth while still knocking down more than half the pins. The girls turn out to be *very* good at this newly established sport and end up with all the M&Ms except for the orange ones, which apparently, according to Lucy, taste like "regret."

She's not wrong.

The time flies by faster than it has all summer, and before I know it, the girls have to go home, and we're all saying our goodbyes.

"See you tomorrow," Brie says. My heart skips as she gives my hand a quick squeeze.

"BYE, HANNAH!" Riley shouts.

"We love you!" Lucy adds as they both give me tight hugs.

"Love y'all too," I say, hugging them back.

As they leave out the double doors, I take a steadying breath. Tomorrow will be more than difficult. The friendship autopsy with Brie is intimidating, but it feels like nothing compared to Bubbie's unveiling.

I take a deep sigh and begin cleaning up the remnants of trash at our bowling lane, sorting out the plastic to recycle. I wish I were working today so I could distract myself. At least when I get home, I can spend time with Figgy. As I finish up, I catch someone out of the corner of my eye.

Patrick.

He's walking through the alley doors, Bonanza shirt uncharacteristically rumpled. He's holding a Red Bull in one hand and a stuffed bag from his favorite bakery in the other, signs of a hangover if I've ever seen one. As he turns into the employee locker room, my pulse picks up, and a sick feeling lodges in the back of my throat.

I have to break it off with him. That's something I have to face.

Because I like *Ethan*.

I like Ethan's smile. And his drawings. And his *forearms*.

I like that he took me bowling. And that he told me about his parents. And that I think about him when he's not around.

I breathe in, then out.

It's not right to continue things with Patrick when I'm thinking this much about another guy. Even if there's no chance of anything happening with the other guy because he's my brother's best friend, and I'm deluded for simply having these feelings.

Patrick and I aren't technically dating, but we have made out all over Bonanza. The relationship merits a clear end. I'm not going to be a coward who ghosts him. He deserves more than that.

I take a steadying breath, make my way to the locker room. I find Patrick sitting on a bench, biting into one of his favorites, a sweet bun filled with red bean paste, while scrolling through his phone.

"Hey," I say.

He looks up at me, eyes lightly rimmed with red. "Hey, yourself."

"Um." I clear my throat. "Fun night?"

He sips his Red Bull. "Something like that."

Silence beats between us. I rock back on my heels, unsure how to do this.

And then he speaks again, his voice soft. "It's okay, Hannah. Just say it."

My cheeks tinge red. He's letting me off easy. That's nice of him. "Um." I take a steadying breath. "Sorry. I haven't done this before. Um. Look, you're great, obviously, but . . ." My fingers twist together. "I don't think it's going to work out between us. I'm sorry."

Patrick nods, once, twice. Then he throws me a gut-punch. "It's that Ethan guy, right? You like him?"

How does he know that when I just figured it out myself?

My first instinct is to deny it.

But why lie? What good will it do?

"Yeah," I admit. "How'd you know?"

He shrugs. "Whenever I looked at you, you'd be looking at him."

"Oh." I breathe out the word, heart pounding.

Patrick smirks softly. "You're too much of a good girl for me, anyways."

Not exactly true. Patrick just doesn't understand that last summer I was so bad I'm in repentance mode, like a yearlong Yom Kippur.

But it's easier to let him have it. "Maybe so," I agree. "Um, I hope we can still be friends?"

Patrick rubs the back of his neck. I can't help but notice his bicep flex as he does so. The boy really is that good-looking.

"Don't stress, Klein," he tells me. "We're all good."

The conversation with Patrick was unpleasant, but it could have gone a lot worse, and I'm glad everything is out in the open. He left right after to go help Tony with the go-karts, and I stayed behind to practice some deep breathing, which did not help. As I exit the locker room to finally go home, I spot the Golden Oldies settling into their favorite lane.

The sight makes my heart ache a little. In her later years, Bubbie preferred books and symphonies to sports, but I'm sure she would have fit right in with this group, sending them into stitches of laughter with a single story. She could have had so many more good years.

I decide to see if they need anything before I leave, my good deed for the day. As I approach, I overhear their conversation.

"And that's when I told him," Ginger says, "if he wants to sleep in the house tonight, he's going to have to tie up that loose cow first."

Tears of laughter are coming out of Tashia's eyes. "Imagine!" she hollers. "Bringing home a cow to save on milk money. You lived in the city, for goodness' sake."

"Men." Madeline shakes her head. "Never thinking."

"At least not with the right body part," Ginger adds.

The ladies break into more laughter, and that's when Ginger spots me. "Hannah, dear!" she says. "What a treat!"

"Y'all need anything?" I ask. "I'm not working today, but I'm happy to help."

"We need this ball return fixed," Adele replies.

"Sure!" I say.

"No, no," Madeline cuts in. "No working if you're not

getting paid. Go grab Ethan to help out. I see him right over there. He has such a handsome face. His parents must be proud."

Ethan?

Oy.

I thought he had the day off as well, but I turn and find him organizing shoes behind the counter. My heart rate picks up, pulsing in my ears.

I'd like to know the exact second Ethan got so good-looking. Not just -looking. *Hot.* His hands practically dwarf the shoes as he sorts them into bins. His shoulders seem to grow broader by the day.

It couldn't have happened overnight. It only feels that way because I was gone so long.

"Hannah?" Madeline prods.

I cough into my elbow. "No problem. Be right back."

I'll just grab Ethan. No problem at all. Thank god Patrick left.

I take a quick breath as I approach, my pulse still thudding away.

Ethan looks up from his sorting and smiles widely. "Hey there, bowling finalist!"

"Hi!" I squeak out.

My cheeks warm. Normal, Hannah. Just *be normal.* He doesn't know you like him.

"Um," I say. "The Golden Oldies need you to fix the

ball return. Also, Madeline says you have a handsome face. Think she's hitting on you?" I joke.

Ethan laughs. "Nah, they're trying to set me up with their granddaughters. Apparently one of them even goes to our shul? Naomi. Do you know her?"

Suddenly, my jaw is very tense. "Nope." I pop out the word. "Pretty name, though."

I don't like the idea of him going on a date with Naomi. What if they eat bagels and lox at Schulman's Deli and then fall in love and have a million babies?

Okay, help. Serious help.

Ethan's eyes linger on me a bit too long, like he's trying to puzzle something out.

"Come on." I nod my head toward the Golden Oldies. "They're waiting."

He puts down the shoes and follows me to their lane. Madeline's gold bracelets jangle as she waves at Ethan. Her blond hair looks brighter than ever today. She must have just gotten it touched up at the salon. "Oh, there you are!" she calls. "I haven't seen you in days!"

"Yeah," Adele adds. Her hair is cropped short. A giant peacock brooch is pinned to her shirt. "What gives? You don't like us anymore?"

The other ladies chime in with their own mingled disgruntlements.

"Sorry, sorry." Ethan holds up his hands. "You know

how chaotic this place gets. Plus, I'm on shoe duty."

They make sour faces at this.

Ginger plugs her nose. "So you're bringing a stench over to us?"

"Nah," Ethan replies. "I don't smell. Right, Hannah?"

He leans closer to me, as if he wants me to *sniff* him. There's a dangerously playful look in his eyes. Since I refuse to back down from a challenge, I lean forward and give him a strong sniff.

Damn it. Of course he smells amazing.

"We're all good," I say, cheeks flaming. "He smells fine."

Oh god, why is there a sparkle in Madeline's eye now? This is bad. These ladies can whiff out a crush in a hundred-mile radius, and here I am, serving a giant steaming one up to them on a silver platter.

"Erm." I tug on the collar of my shirt. "Can I get you guys anything while he fixes the return? Waters? Saltines? Peanut M&Ms?"

Adele pats the seat next to her with two hard thumps. "Sit down."

"Yes, ma'am," I say, and sit next to her.

"You, over here," Ginger tells Ethan.

"Gotta fix the return first." He grins. "That *is* why you called me over, right?"

She waves her hand. "Fine, fine."

Sixty seconds later, the return is running. Ethan dutifully shuffles over and sits next to her so we're facing across from each other. Ginger smiles. "Now isn't this nice?"

Ethan laughs. "Yeah, but I'm supposed to be working."

Madeline waves her hand. "Oh, but this is all part of the job. Keeping loyal customers happy. Now tell us, what's the hot gossip around town? Any fights? Any breakups? Any hookups?"

If my cheeks were red before, they're now all-day-on-the-beach-without-sunscreen burnt. Fights and breakups and hookups oh my.

Ethan's gaze flicks to me, and everyone notices.

"Really?" Madeline asks, interest piqued. "Hannah, dear, tell us what you've gotten yourself into."

"Oh, leave her alone," Adele says. "The girl can have a private life. It's none of our business."

"Adele, you make *everything* your business," Madeline snips.

"Oh really?"

Ethan and I exchange a look while they go at it. I'm relieved the attention is off me for a moment. Ethan shakes his head at them, and I roll my eyes, and then we're both smiling, and unfortunately, that's when Madeline says, "*Oh.*"

"Oh what?" Adele asks, snapping her attention back to us.

Madeline looks between Ethan and me, and so do the rest of the Golden Oldies, and that's when Madeline lets out a low whistle, and every particle of my skin sets on fire.

"Oh, yes," Ginger agrees. "I see it now."

"Oh, absolutely," Adele chimes in. "What a cute pair."

"Can't believe I didn't notice it before," Madeline adds.

"Um." I squirm in my seat. "I should get back to work."

"You're not working today," Tashia says pointedly.

Please let me get out of here before they say anything too blatant.

"Y'all would make the *cutest* couple," Adele tells us.

Damn it. Too late.

"That is," she continues, "if you're not already dating? Are you? Oh, tell us." She claps her hands together. "What a treat that would be!"

I'm not looking at Ethan. I'm not looking at anyone. I'm looking at the floor, wondering if I try very, very hard whether I might suddenly be granted the power to fall through it.

And that's when Ethan says, so softly I can barely hear it, "We're not dating. Hannah is taken."

I chance a look up at him. There's something in his eyes, something that makes my stomach stir and my breath catch. And I find myself replying, "Actually, not anymore."

For a moment, it's like the air has been sucked from the room. Every nerve of my body feels electrified as Ethan's eyes search mine. A tether pulls taut between us, ready to snap.

"Well." Madeline loudly clears her throat, jolting me away from Ethan's gaze. "That's enough of that. Are we going to sit around gossiping all day, or are we going to bowl?"

Ginger stands up. "We're going to bowl. And I'm going to whup your butt."

"Don't count your chickens," Tashia says. "You only won last time because you got the split by luck."

"Not *luck*! Skill!"

"Mm-hmm, just like you're skilled at playing slot machines."

"Oh, will you two stop?" Madeline asks, pulling her ball out of its pink bag. "We all know I'm the best at—"

The conversation becomes impossible to follow, and I take my chance to escape. Ethan follows right behind. We walk in unbearable silence. I can feel him glancing at me, quickly, out of the corner of my eye. My skin heats, and I try to break the tension with a joke. "You should probably keep your distance," I tell him. "Or next thing you know, they'll be spreading rumors that we're engaged."

He smiles. "You're not wrong." He takes a pronounced giant step to the right. "That work?"

I laugh. "Definitely have them fooled now."

And then, because I'm a person who apparently hates herself, I say, "Ridiculous thing for them to come up with. It's not like *we* would ever date."

Hannah.

Why.

Why.

There's a long pause, and when Ethan finally replies, his voice has gone all stilted. "Yeah. Right." His eyes are anywhere but on mine. "I'm gonna head over to whirly ball. Joey said he'd need backup later."

"Right." I nod. "Great. See you! Have fun! Bye!"

My face is in my hands before he even leaves.

"Madeline?" I ask.

After my disastrous interaction with Ethan, I decided I needed to park my butt on a bench outside of Bonanza, my brain obviously too boiled to drive home yet.

"Everything okay?" I ask, checking my phone.

It's only been half an hour since I saw her inside.

Madeline looks over at me, her eyes squinting in the sun. "Oh, Hannah dear! You startled me. I'm fine. Just a stomachache. Decided to drive home in case things get too risky for the public facilities." She sighs. "Can't eat spicy food like I used to. Be sure to take advantage of that steel stomach while you can, sweetheart."

I laugh. "Will do. Want some help getting to your car?"

"I don't need it, but I'll certainly take the company," she agrees.

We walk together. The top of her head barely reaches my shoulder. Apparently, she was taller in her youth. "Shrinking by the second," she complained last week. The wind whips her perfume in my direction, and the scent reminds me so soundly of my bubbie that I take a sharp inhale. Her unveiling is tomorrow. Eleven long months without her. The thought makes me light-headed. I'm not ready to say goodbye again.

I spent sixteen years with one of the most special women on the planet. Bubbie was a force of nature, and her love for me was as strong as a hurricane. And then she slipped through my fingers while I was barely paying attention. The guilt burns. I lost her, and I've let her down ever since then. How can I possibly face that?

We make it to Madeline's car, and I pull open the door for her. "Want me to put your walker in the trunk?" I ask.

"Sure, dear," she agrees. "Thank you."

I put away the walker and am about to say goodbye when she tells me, "Come, sit with me a minute. I'll run the air."

"What about your stomach?" I ask.

"*Sit*," she commands, patting the seat. Her nails are lacquered with lavender polish. "Keep an old woman company."

I bite back a smile. "I thought you called yourself 'vintage,' not 'old.'"

"Oh, can it," she replies.

I slide into the car with her. The leather seats are worn-in, smooth and buttery. Madeline cranks the AC and Stevie Nicks plays from her speakers.

"Go on, then." She turns to me. "What's weighing so heavy on that mind of yours?"

"Um, what do you mean?"

She gives me a hard look.

I slide farther into the seat, biting on my nail. "Um, your perfume," I say. "It smells like one my bubbie wore. She, uh—" I pause, my throat tight. Madeline's eyes stay concentrated on mine, their warmth making my voice wobble. "She passed away almost a year ago now. Her unveiling is tomorrow; that's a Jewish thing, we—"

Madeline nods. "Yes, I've been to a few unveilings for friends of mine."

"I'm sorry to hear that." I look down at my shoes. There are tears threatening to surface when I say, "My bubbie and me, we were really close. It's hard."

"I'm sure it is," Madeline agrees. She takes my hand and gives it a squeeze. "I'm sure you miss her, and I'm sure she's so proud of you."

I let out a laugh, short and sharp. It surprises us both enough that even Madeline looks startled. "What?" she asks.

I look out the window, heart squeezing. "I don't know how proud she'd be of me right now."

And then I tell her everything.

I'm not sure why I open up to Madeline. Maybe it's the perfume. Maybe it's my exhaustion from a long day. My walls are crumbling, and I don't have the fight left in me to hold them up. So I let it all out.

I tell Madeline all about Bubbie, how she was an Olympian, how she was brilliant, smart, funny, caring. I tell Madeline how much I wanted to be like her. I tell her—

I tell her the overwhelming guilt I feel that I wasn't there for her. That I spent her final hours on a soccer field instead of at her side. That I was too focused on my own goals to realize how sick she'd gotten. And that after she passed away, instead of making her proud, I broke my ankle and lost everything. I disobeyed my parents. I partied and drank and put them through all sorts of stress.

My voice is tight, tears clogging my throat as I admit, "I've been dishonoring her memory from the day she died."

Tears follow. Not loud sobs, but a steady stream down my cheeks. My face flushes. And I breathe heavily.

"Oh, darling," Madeline says. She reaches over and wraps my hand in both of her own. Her silver rings are cool against my skin. "That's all right now, that's all right. Sweet thing. I can't imagine how hard that must have been to lose her and then the sport you love so much. I promise, if she were here, all she'd want to do is wrap you in a giant hug."

"I'm not sure about that," I whisper.

"She's your grandma," Madeline says firmly. "Your warrior. She's there to protect you, to understand you. I'm sure she took a wrong step or ten as a teenager too. We all did, sweetheart. It's called being young." She leans closer with a sly smile. "And I'll let you in on a secret: we keep messing up as adults, too."

Madeline continues talking as my breath and tears calm. The woman, bless her, never runs out of words. "Your bubbie loved you. There was nothing but a deep well of understanding there. And you loved her, and I'm more than sure she knew it. And you know what, darling?" she asks. "One of the best ways to honor her memory is to be a little easier on yourself. That's what she would want. You understand?"

I nod, dried tears on my cheeks. "I think so."

Slowly, her words make an impact through my web of guilt. I think—no, I know—Madeline is right. My bubbie had all the compassion and love in the world for me. She wouldn't want me to dwell on what I've done wrong. She'd want to give me a hand and pick me back up.

"You should talk about these things more often," Madeline tells me, passing me a soft tissue from her purse. "You can't keep this all to yourself. It's too hard on the heart. What about your family? I'm sure they miss her too."

I think of that night weeks ago in my room with Joey, when he brought up Bubbie and I shut down the conversation. I loved Bubbie, but she didn't belong only to me. That pain is shared.

"You're right." I swallow hard, then nod. "I know just who to talk to."

Last Summer

"You're grounded," Mom says when I walk through the door.

"Duh," I respond.

I glance behind me. Brie's headlights retreat from the drive-way. My parents made her promise to text when she got home safe. My parents thanked her for getting me home safe. I cannot believe the mess she's gotten me into.

"Drink this water; go to bed," Dad orders, voice leaving no room for argument. "We'll talk in the morning."

With the way the room is spinning, I'm not sure I'll be up by morning, but I shrug my shoulders and say, "On it, Captain," with a clumsy salute.

I take the glass of water and walk back to my room, almost tripping when my ankle gives out. "Goddamn stupid broken bones," I mutter, hobbling down the hallway.

"Hannah?" a voice calls out.

I blink, look to the left, and realize Joey's door is cracked, lamplight trickling into the hallway. I push open the door and peek into his room. He's on his bed, sitting crisscross applesauce, with a PlayStation controller in his hand. He looks five years younger than normal, his eyes wide and worried. It angers me, though I'm not sure why.

"What?" I ask, accidentally shouting the word. Alcohol and soft-spoken do not go hand in hand.

He flinches, like I scared him. And I feel even angrier then. What right does he have to judge me? He has no idea what I'm going through.

"What?" I snap, my voice coming out even harsher.

He glances over at his TV. Some video game is on pause. It must be easy being Joey, spending all his time playing games and goofing around, an easy life handed to him on a silver platter. He doesn't have to try at anything.

"Where were you?" he asks, his words so soft I can barely hear them.

"A party," I answer. "Obviously."

"Again?"

I roll my eyes. "What? You auditioning for the role of Mom and Dad?"

He glances down at the floor, then asks, "Do you want to go with me to the cemetery tomorrow? I'm going to visit Bubbie."

The question feels like an attack. A judgment. I'm out partying while he's the good kid, bringing stones to Bubbie's grave site.

The thought of her there, underground, alone, makes my stomach turn. I hate it. I hate myself.

Joey's stare disarms me.

He doesn't get to do this. He doesn't get to make me feel guilty for coping in whatever way I can. "Jesus, Joey," I say. "You look like a wounded animal. It's pathetic." I straighten up against the doorframe. "I'm going to bed," I tell him. "I'll see you later, baby bro. You do you, and leave me alone."

Chapter Seventeen

IT'S LATE WHEN Joey gets home from Bonanza; our parents are already asleep, Dad's snores filter into the dark hallway. Joey stayed out until right before curfew to host the go-kart preliminaries. In the dim living room, I can see the bags under his eyes. I know he loves hosting the Olympics, but I hope he's not pushing himself too hard to make them a success.

"Hey, brother," I say. "Where's Ethan?" It's unusual to see one walk through the door without the other.

"Sleeping at his place," Joey responds, flopping down onto the couch. He lets out a yawn so giant Figgy stirs from her sleep, blinking at him with annoyed eyes. "Sorry, girl," Joey says, reaching down to pet her.

"Oh," I respond. My stomach twists at the thought of Ethan in his own home. I hope his parents are sleeping so he can rest well. My fingers itch to text him, but I don't know what to say. And besides, I have another task at hand.

"Hey, Joey?" I ask softly.

He looks up at me, cracking another yawn, this one tiny and cute. I smile. Even though we're only a year apart, I remember Toddler Joey clear as day. Chock-full of energy. He was on the go nonstop every day until he'd run himself into the ground, falling asleep anywhere—restaurant booths, preschool floors, a nice patch of grass in the backyard.

We were so close as kids, always playing together and sharing friends. Even when soccer controlled my life, we still had this natural bond.

And then I tried to push him away. I was cruel, and for some reason, he still stuck by me.

"Yeah?" Joey asks, blinking heavily. He's no longer a toddler. He's all grown up, taking on more responsibility than I could imagine. He's kind of incredible.

"I'm sorry," I tell him, taking a steadying breath. "I'm sorry about last year. I was going through a hard time, but so were you. You lost Bubbie too. And I wasn't there for you." My voice hitches as I repeat, "I'm sorry, Joey."

He's silent. Which is unsettling for Joey.

The room quiets. I can hear Dad's snores again. I can hear the ticking clock. If I strain my ears, I can hear wind outside, rustling though the trees. It's going to storm tonight.

When Joey finally meets my eyes, he looks older, no

longer my kid brother. He's a full-fledged human with all the lines drawn in.

His response surprises me.

"Did you know I came out to Bubbie first?" he asks.

I shake my head. "I didn't."

"A week before I told you guys, we were at the park, trolling for dogs." Bubbie loved a sunny afternoon in the park, always on the hunt for cute dogs to pet. "Bubbie asked me if I wanted to get some lunch, and I just blurted it out. 'You know I'm gay, right?'" Joey lets out a soft laugh, eyes far off, like he's back in the park with Bubbie right now. "I don't know why I blurted it out. I guess I blurt a lot of things, but I didn't expect to let that one out so quickly. Well, Bubbie just looked at me and said, 'I know now. And I love you. And what do you want for lunch?'"

Joey turns to Figgy again, scratching behind her ear. "I knew I was lucky. I knew y'all would accept me. But coming out still wasn't easy. Not at all. I'd been wanting to say something for a long time. It was building up inside me, and with Bubbie, I felt so safe. I felt so absolutely seen and loved. So I told her first. And I'm really glad I did."

My throat clogs with emotion. Bubbie made us all feel so deeply loved. A comfort blanket. A source of light. "I'm glad you did too," I tell Joey. "I'm really glad."

Figgy nuzzles closer to Joey, letting out a soft whine, like she knows we're talking about Bubbie. "Later that day," Joey continues, "back at Bubbie's house, she asked if I wanted to talk about it; she asked what she could do to support me best. I felt so secure. That was the thing about Bubbie, you know? When she said something, you believed it. The woman was unbreakable." His voice falters. "Until she wasn't." My heart squeezes as he looks at me. "I miss her so much."

"Me too." I breathe deeply. "Me too."

And then I walk over to the couch and sit next to him, shoulder against shoulder, leg against leg.

"I'm sorry," I say, tucking my head against Joey's shoulder. "I'm sorry for your loss. I'm sorry I acted like the loss only belonged to me. I'm sorry I was kind of an asshole last summer."

"Thank you." Joey knocks his knee into mine. "You know I love you, right?"

I laugh, and there are tears in my eyes, just a few, light and warm. "I know now. And I love you, too."

It's cool today. We should be grateful for that.

It stormed all last night, thunder booming and lightning crackling in the sky. I tossed and turned all night, dipping into sleep for only a short moment before a crash of noise startled me back awake. My dreams were brief, scattered. Pieces of my bubbie, her laugh, her scent. A feeling of dread, loneliness.

I didn't know what it was to truly miss someone until I lost her.

At nine in the morning, Mom raps softly on my door. "We're going to leave in half an hour, all right?"

"Yes," I call back, my throat dry.

There's a pit in my stomach as I get dressed. The black dress from last summer fits better now that my muscles are smaller, but it still looks like something more appropriate for a twelve-year-old girl than me; it's too frilly, too cutesy. I push hangers around in my closet until I find a forest-green dress Mom bought me for synagogue. It's silk and flowy with a small row of buttons in the front. I slip it on and look in the mirror, trying to see if I can find my bubbie in the reflection. Everyone tells me I have her smile. I wish I could see it.

Thirty minutes later we're in the car. Mom and Dad sit up front, and Joey is in the seat next to me. It feels strange that Ethan isn't with us. Everything feels a little off-balance without him. I hope he slept okay.

Joey looks over and gives me a small smile. I squeeze his hand, relief flowing through me. I didn't realize how much I missed my brother, even when he was right in front of me.

A few cars have already arrived when we pull up to the cemetery. Some of Bubbie's friends, some distant relatives, and Ethan, leaning against his car, thumbs tucked into the pockets of a suit he seems to have just outgrown. My heart thumps as I take him in. His stance is the slightest bit stilted, like he feels out of place. His parents aren't here. Were they at the funeral? Surely they must have been. Ethan is my brother's best friend. He practically lives at my house. And yet I can count on one hand the number of times I've interacted with his parents.

It's my impulse to go right up to him. I'm about to do so when my parents call me, telling me to come greet this relative and that. It reminds me of shiva. I hate small talk, and the mourning version of it is so much worse, musings on the weather mingled with condolences so sweet and sincere they make my skin itch. I say hello to distant aunts and uncles and friends my bubbie had for decades. As I talk, my eyes skim over the site where she's buried. I hate to think about her there, underground, instead of up here with us, where she should be.

After a few minutes, another car pulls up. Brie and her family. They don't hesitate at the top of the hill like Ethan. They walk down the grassy knoll and head straight to us. I haven't seen Brie's parents in more than a year, but they look just the same, and I'm grateful when they smile at me with warmth.

"So good to see you, Hannah," Mrs. Bradley says, wrapping me in her arms. She smells comforting, clean and cozy, and I let myself relax into her hug.

"You too," I say, my voice coming out a mumble.

I shake Mr. Bradley's hand and then lean down to give Lucy and Riley shoulder-squeezes, and then it's just Brie left. She's wearing black slacks and a gray long-sleeved shirt, even though the temperature is already pushing ninety. Like she knows my exact thoughts, she smiles and says, "Didn't have anything appropriate to wear. You know me."

I smile. "Oh, I know."

Brie hates clothes shopping. Her mom buys her a fresh stack of jeans each year so her old ones don't become more holes than pants.

Brie glances around the milling crowd, then back to me, her voice soft. "You still want to talk after?"

I'm so glad I fixed things with Joey. It'd be nice to have my best friend back as well.

Though my pulse is racing, I nod and say, "Definitely."

I'm pulled away again to greet more relatives, and then the service starts. I sit between my mom and brother as the rabbi talks about my bubbie's wonderful life and how lucky we were to have her for so many years.

But it wasn't so many years for me. It was only sixteen.

It doesn't feel fair that a person I loved so deeply will be gone from my life so much longer than she was in it.

But I am grateful to have already had a person in my life I connected with so deeply. I'm grateful to have had a person in my life who loved me so absolutely. I turn to Joey and link my hand with his.

"She was the best," I whisper.

He nods. "The very best."

I want to say hi to Ethan after the service, but by the time the crowd around us clears, he's gone. And then it's time to meet Brie for coffee. We pick a little café ten minutes away from the cemetery, order drinks, and settle into seats.

"So you think people just come here, like, all the time?" Brie asks, curling her legs under her. There are all sorts of people in here, working on laptops, chatting with friends, scrolling their phones, and reading. "Can't imagine having time for it," she says.

"Yeah." I fiddle with the straw of my peach iced tea. "Well, you're really busy, so."

The words come out bitter by accident. I cringe. Not a good start.

Brie pulls on her own straw. She's drinking a frozen coffee and uses the straw to scoop up the whipped cream on top. With the utmost grace, she ignores my comment. "It was a nice service," she says. "I miss Bubbie."

I nod. "Me too."

When we were younger, sometimes Bubbie would pick us up from practice. She'd take us to McDonald's for dinner and let us order McFlurries with our nuggets and fries.

I loved those evenings, all three of us in cahoots.

"Um." I shift in my seat. The velvet covering makes my legs itch. "So . . ."

I take a steadying breath, then look up at my best friend. She's beautiful, always has been. Warm eyes and a full smile. She has this way of looking at you and making you feel like everything is going to be okay. I hope that's true. I hope it will be.

"I'm sorry," I say. "I'm sorry for how I treated you last summer. I'm sorry, for uh, well, I'm sorry for being a bitch."

Brie laughs, hard, eyes lighting up. "You put that bluntly."

I grin. "Figured that was best."

I fiddle with my straw again, looking down at the notched wood floor. "I'm sorry I was a bad friend. I'm sorry I didn't care about your problems, how I treated everything with Cody. It was wrong and unfair and you deserved better, but—"

My breath hitches. It would be so easy to leave it at that, to just apologize and move on. But that's not enough. I need Brie to know I felt hurt too.

"But." My voice cracks as I take a short breath. "You hurt me, too. You didn't give me a second chance. I was a mess, Brie. My bubbie died. I broke my ankle. I lost everything. And then you ratted me out to my parents. I know

I was being a bad friend, but you didn't have to turn me in like that. It felt vindictive."

"Hannah." Brie's voice falters as well. My heart is in my throat, wondering what she'll say. "I was *scared* for you. I wasn't sure if there'd be a second chance. You were so drunk that night and threatening to drive home—"

"I was kidding!" I interject, all that anger rushing back to me. "Of course I wasn't going to get behind the wheel."

But as I say the words, they feel hollow in my mouth. How can I know for sure what drunk Hannah would have done?

"I couldn't trust that. I couldn't risk—" She takes a shaky inhale. "I couldn't risk losing you."

"Oh," I say.

My heart squeezes, tears threatening.

"I wasn't turning against you, Hannah," Brie tells me. "I was just trying to keep you safe."

I look down at my ankle. The pain has continued to fade, but the damage from last summer is still there.

"You were protecting me," I say softly.

"Of course I was." She sighs deeply. "Okay, yes, I was angry at you for your aforementioned bitch behavior, but I'm not petty like that. I've always had your back. I only turned you in to protect you. I swear."

My voice is wobbly. "I should've suspected the best from you and not the worst."

"Yeah." She gives me a small smile. "You should have."

My body feels heavy, with the exhaustion of last summer, with the relief of finally talking about it. "I'm sorry," I tell her again.

"I forgive you."

Those three words land with incredible impact, an enormous tension easing from my muscles. But still, something is off, unresolved. We're not Hannah and Brie. Not that I thought we'd just snap back to normal, but I know there are still things left unsaid.

Brie knows it too, and she speaks first. "The thing is . . . ," she says, clearing her throat. "I want to be your friend again, Hannah. I mean, I am your friend. But I don't know how to do that with soccer." My stomach clenches as I draw back from her. "See?" she asks. "You flinch just at the word. How can we be close friends if I have to hide such a big part of my life from you?"

"I don't know." My throat feels way too swollen. "I wish . . . I want to say that you can talk about the team whenever you want, but it *hurts*. I don't want it to, but it does."

"I know," Brie says. "And I'm not mad at you for that. Not at all. I'm sorry. I feel for you. I really do. I can't imagine how hard it must be. I know how much you loved soccer." My eyes threaten to water. And then Brie's hand is there, holding mine, soft and warm. "Hey," she says quietly.

"I'm here for you. I promise. I just don't know how to be *us*, like we used to be, if I can't share my life with you."

"Maybe we can't," I say softly.

There's a pause, a long one. Then Brie blows out a gust of air. "Well, that sucks."

This time her bluntness surprises me. I laugh. "Yeah, it really sucks."

We grin at each other, and I feel a fluttering in my chest. I love Brie. I always have and always will. Our relationship isn't what it was, but it's wonderful to have her back, even a little bit.

"So we'll figure it out," Brie says. "How to be this kind of friends. Okay?"

I give her a small smile. "Okay."

I can't believe I agreed to work this evening, after all *that*.

Not my best decision. But because I'm exhausted, I allow myself the indulgence of watching Ethan Alderman fix a ball return. As his forearms flex, I wonder what it'd feel like to hug him. And I mean *hug* him. Not a friendly, one-arm-thrown-around-the-shoulder hug. I mean a full-on, two-arm, breathe-in-and-out, feel-each-other's-warmth *embrace*.

My skin flushes just at the thought.

He fixes the return, then picks up four balls to carry over to a cart. Much like his suit from this morning, he seems to be outgrowing his Bonanza shirt as well. As he sets down the bowling balls, the shirt pulls tight against his back muscles.

I bite my lip and look down at the counter I'm supposed to be cleaning. I spray it and scrub, *hard.*

And then, he's walking toward me. My heart flutters as he approaches. Maybe I should spray myself with this bottle.

"Can't get it off?" Ethan asks.

"*Excuse me?*" I sputter.

His cheeks redden deeply. "Oh," he quickly says. "Um, never mind. You were just, uh, scrubbing the counter hard. That's all."

Realizing the miscommunication, I force a laugh. "Right, right."

He laughs too, his eyes softening. "How are you feeling after today? It was a nice service."

There's a little tick at the back of my throat when he asks that. I'm feeling better than I have in a while, but clearing the fog also reveals the full depth of my loss.

"I'm okay," I tell him truthfully.

His eyes are warm and trained on mine. How does he make me feel like that? Safe and unsteady in the same moment. "We should go bowling again," he says. "Get you ready for the finals."

Early-morning bowling with Ethan sounds dangerous. And very appealing.

I *do* need to practice, or I'll make a fool of myself at the finals.

"Sure," I say, my heart skipping. "I'm in."

Ethan smiles. "Good."

I try to find something in his expression, a clue to what he's thinking, this guy I've known my entire life. But maybe his thoughts aren't clear enough for me to read.

Maybe I'm not the only one trying to figure us out.

Chapter Eighteen

THE NEXT FEW weeks pass in a blur of activity as I fall deeper into my groove at Bonanza. My first week here, I barely stayed afloat, spinning on the periphery of chaotic action. But now I've found my place in the machine. I mainly work at the prize counter, puzzling out crosswords with Nate in spare minutes. Or the bowling alley, enjoying my time with the Golden Oldies and muddling my way through kids' birthday parties. Occasionally, I'll help Joey with whirly ball. It's nice to see him in his element there, the master of the court. All the kids look up to him with stars in their eyes.

I've even done a few shifts at the mini-golf course with Brie. Our relationship is definitely stilted, but it gives me a warm feeling that we're both trying, that we don't want to lose each other.

And then there's Ethan.

Ethan, who works at the alley with me. Ethan, who splits his soft pretzels with me, extra salt. Ethan, who drives us to Bonanza in the cool morning hours to bowl.

I look over at him now in the lane next to mine. He doesn't even have a shift this morning. He woke up just for this. His hair is a mess, sleep rumpled, a cowlick in the back. His favorite gray sweatpants fall low on his hips. And his forearm pulls taut as he picks up his ball, eyes trained on the lane.

My pulse flutters.

I thought my crush might abate over time. Reality would set in, and I would remember that Ethan is Joey's best friend, practically part of our family, that having romantic feelings for him is ludicrous.

But over the past few weeks, my feelings have only grown.

I feel at ease with Ethan. He's patient, never pushing me too far. Instead, he gives me the room to push myself.

As he's ready to release the ball, he turns to me and grins. "Watch this."

I raise an eyebrow, expecting an impressive trick. I've improved over the past few weeks, but Ethan has acquired some formidable skills over the past year. But then, he drops the ball into two hands and chucks it granny-style down the lane. The ball rockets toward the pins, spinning and spinning, until it slams into them, knocking every single one down.

I laugh as he turns back to me, grinning. "Pretty good, huh? Madeline taught me. Too bad she can't use the move in her league."

"Impressive," I agree.

His grin widens. "You next."

"Seriously? Like that?" I roll my eyes, but pick up a ball. "I'm supposed to be practicing real bowling, you know."

"Yeah." His eyes are bright. "But this is more fun."

"Fine, fine," I say with a dramatic huff.

I walk up to the front of the lane, hunch over, and toss the ball with two hands.

It immediately heads straight for the gutter.

"Wow, you suck," Ethan says.

"*Ha-ha.*" I turn to him while I wait for everything to reset. "Seriously, though, I need to practice my splits if I have a chance at not embarrassing myself at the finals."

"You are terrible at them," he deadpans.

"And *you* are just *so* funny," I reply. "You should give my diaphragm a break from all the laughter."

His eyes crinkle. "I'll see what I can do." He glances toward the locker room, looking slightly nervous. "I think I do have something to help, though. Wait here?"

"Okay," I agree.

He'll probably come back with some kind of joke, like a

tub of protein powder or a toddler-size ball. Or he'll pull up the bumpers for our lane. But when he returns, I see he's carrying a shoe box in his hands. My stomach does a tiny flip as he settles in the seat next to mine and hands me the box.

"What is it?" I ask, arms down by my side.

"Open it and see?" Ethan suggests.

"Hmm," I say, unsure.

He laughs. "Hannah, just open the box. It's not going to bite."

The thing is, though—I'm not scared of it biting. I'm scared I know exactly what's inside that shoe box. I'm scared of it being perfect. I'm scared of my feelings for Ethan to be written all over my face.

"Fine." I straighten my posture, then flip open the lid. Inside, I find a pair of brand-new bowling shoes. But these aren't just bowling shoes. These are bowling shoes that match my favorite ball, black with swirls of deep purple.

My heart lodges in my throat as I stare at them.

How did he—

Why did he—

Heat sweeps across my neck. I need to say something. Soon, preferably.

"Well," Ethan says. His brown eyes fill with hesitation. "You like them? You mentioned your ankle felt unstable in the rental shoes. . . ."

I nod. Once. Twice. Then I turn to him and blurt out, "I didn't get anything for you."

He laughs. "It's not my birthday."

"It's not my birthday either," I shoot back.

His eyes are right on mine, his smile soft. My heart flutters wildly. I can't believe him. I really can't.

"I guess I'll try them on," I say.

"Seems like a good idea." He nods. "You need help?"

"*No.*"

The last thing we need to add to this equation is him slipping a shoe on my foot like I'm freaking Cinderella or something. I clear my throat, then pull out the shoes, fresh, crisp. They make me ache with the memory of brand-new cleats. The fabric is tough, but soon it will wear in, become pliable, a perfect fit. I tug on the shoes, then yank the laces tight. My ankle feels swaddled, secure.

My throat tightens with emotion.

"What do you think?" Ethan asks as I stand up. "Do they have the magic power of the split?"

"We'll have to see . . . ," I respond. Then, taking a deep breath, I turn to him and say, "Thank you. For the present. That was very nice and very unnecessary."

He waves his hand in dismissal, but his cheeks have gone red. "Don't worry about it."

I bite the inside of my lip. *Does he like me? Why else*

would he buy me bowling shoes? I'm pretty sure Joey has never bought Brie so much as a soda.

"Go on, then," Ethan says. "Show us their power."

Thirty minutes later, we discover the shoes don't quite have magic powers, but they are effective. I feel good wearing them, strong. My technique improves, and I begin to feel even more excited about the bowling finals.

"Thank you again," I tell Ethan as another frame resets. "These are great, really."

He smiles. "No problem."

There are faint circles under his eyes, making his gaze soft and sleepy. "You gonna go nap at our house after this?" I ask.

His expression changes slightly. But I can see it, his guard going up. "Nah, got to swing by the house. I have to do laundry."

My stomach pinches. I try to make light of it. "We have a machine, you know. Excellent dryer, too."

"Yeah, thanks."

"Ethan—" I start to say.

"Your ball is back," he cuts me off. "You should practice more before your shift. Finals are in a few days. I'll refill our waters."

I bite my lip as he walks away. He runs a hand through his hair, rumpling it further. I shouldn't let him shut me out like that. I know all too well how much it hurts to keep the bad feelings inside. I should make him take his wall down, even if I have to tear at it brick by brick.

It's the mini-golf finals tonight, the first finals of the Olympics. The games have been a whirlwind of activity over the past few weeks, making Bonanza feel more like a summer camp than a workplace. It's more than a little cool to see all Joey's hard work come to fruition.

I'm exhausted after early-morning bowling followed by a double shift. But mini golf, with three preliminary rounds, is the most competitive game in the Olympics. And with Brie in the finals, I have to support her.

It's late, but Bonanza's neon lights illuminate the dark night, swathing the course and faces in Technicolor. There's a big crowd, and the air buzzes with excitement as everyone mills about, chatting and laughing. I love Bonanza at night, when all the guests have departed. There's something magical about the space belonging to just us.

I'm wearing shorts and a sweat jacket over my T-shirt. I've slid out of my work shoes and into flip-flops. Night has cooled off the air, and through the neon lights, I can see a dappling of stars in the sky. Someone hooks up music, and an indie-pop playlist feeds through the speakers.

I scan the crowd for Brie and find her by the entry booth. She's changed from her work outfit into black leggings and one of our team's jerseys. The image jolts me. I miss the ritual of my uniform. Pulling on my jersey, tying back my hair, lacing my cleats. My team colors made me proud, *confident*. That jersey straightened my spine.

I take a steadying breath, then work to keep my smile full as I approach. "Hey, Brie," I say. "Wanted to wish you luck out there."

"Thanks, Hannah." She gestures down at her jersey. "I wanted to feel in the competitive zone."

I nod. "Totally. I get that." I push through my discomfort. Brie deserves all the support tonight. I'd love to see her win. "How you feeling? Need anything?"

She smiles. "I'm okay, thanks. A little nervous about the castle." She gives a fake shiver. "That's where I'm going to lose. I know it."

The castle is the final and trickiest hole on the Bonanza golf course. You can choose two different paths—either shoot around the castle on putt one and then aim for the hole behind it on the second putt, or you can try to go through the world's smallest and most awkwardly angled opening on the castle itself. If you sink the ball just right, you'll get a hole in one. Since the competition is so tight, the castle hole in one will likely be the deciding factor for the gold medal.

"Are you going for the hole in one?" I ask.

Brie sighs. "I think I have to. I mean, I guess I could take the easier route and shoot for a lower medal. But, well . . ."

She gives a knowing smile, and I smile back. "You want gold," I say.

She laughs. "Yep. I want gold."

We're the same. In so many ways, we're the same. If there's a goal, we want to hit it. We want to win. I miss the joy of competing at Brie's side. There's nothing else like it.

"Well," I say. "I know you'll do great. I'm excited to watch you win."

She nudges me in the arm. "Thanks, Hannah."

There's no doubt in her smile. I know she's happy to have me here.

"Shots! Shots! Shots!" everyone shouts.

A game has started, as is always the case at Bonanza.

Bonanza: Why be relaxed when you can turn literally anything into a game?

It's been decided that after the competitors finish each hole, we'll hold a shot contest. Not *real* shots, of course, at least not officially, because no one is looking to get fired. Whoever can down three shots of Coca-Cola, put their forehead to a club and spin around ten times, and then putt a ball into the hole first will win.

After the fourth hole and round of this game, Daisey cajoles me to the front to compete with her. She was just on vacation for a week with her son and her parents, and I missed seeing her around Bonanza, so even though it's my impulse to protest, I say yes.

Also, well, it seems *fun*.

"Come on!" She pulls me through the crowd. She's wearing a long-sleeved black shirt, the fabric soft and ripped purposely at the shoulders. There's a new streak of blue in her hair.

The guys we're competing against have clear liquid in their shot glasses instead of soda. I spot one slipping a small bottle of vodka back into his pocket. I'm not judging. They're over twenty-one, and it's a Friday night. But I'm happy to drink soda. I don't want to blur tonight's edges. I want to experience it all unfiltered.

"We need one more!" Daisey tells me as she lines up our shots.

I scan the crowd, searching for someone to pull in, hoping to spot Ethan. He came back for an evening shift, but I barely saw him. He's probably keeping Joey company now as he provides commentary on the night.

But I do spot Nate, hanging out with Laney, a soft-spoken girl who works at EZ Eats. I think Gary and Sherry like her because she has less "attitude" than the rest of us teenagers.

"Nate!" I call out, waving my arms. "Nate!" He looks up on the second shout. "Come join us! Shot contest." His expression wavers, and I clarify, "Not *real* shots."

He nods and says something to Laney, then walks over to me. He adjusts his glasses. "Look at you." He grins. *"Participating."*

I roll my eyes. "Oh, whatever."

He laughs and lets me drag him toward the folding table.

A minute later, we're all ready with our shots. The guys next to us, a pair I only vaguely know since they work at the go-kart track, look red-faced. They might already be a few drinks in. It's only hole four. These guys are in for a reckoning if they're going to try to keep this up.

Hopefully it'll make them easier to defeat.

Gary does our count-off: "Three! Two! One!"

"Shots! Shots! Shots!" everyone screams as we begin to knock them back. The Coke fizzles down my throat and makes my head buzz, but I get my three down quickly, then stand up and pick up my putter. I give myself some space, put my head against the top of the handle, and then spin around. By spin five, I'm dizzy and laughing, and around me, I can hear everyone else having fun with it as well. After spin ten, I stand up and almost stumble over, but my ankle is stronger now after being in use all summer.

I pick up my club and dizzily power-walk to the starting line for my putt.

Daisey and one of the guys are close behind me. Nate is done spinning, but is holding out his arms to gain balance. With barely any lead at all, I put my golf ball down on the ground and look at the hole. Oops. Still dizzy, I placed the ball in the entirely wrong position.

Daisey laughs and hip-butts me, putting her ball down in a better spot. "CLEAR!" she shouts, making sure no one is in the way of her putt. She gives her ball a hard tap, and it goes . . . straight off the course. Drunk Guy #1 and I then attempt to putt at the same time from opposite starting points. Our balls converge near the cup and knock each other away from the hole. Daisey is prepped to go again, shooting one off, while Nate has finally made it to the course, and Drunk Guy #2 is throwing up in a trash can.

I let out a laugh. It's chaos. Delightful chaos.

Nate finally gets his shot set, then in a loud and determined voice shouts, "CLEAR!"

He gives his ball the gentlest of taps, but suddenly all mesmerized, everyone stops what they're doing and watches it slowly crawl toward the cup, until—

"SCORE!" everyone shouts.

"SHOTS! SHOTS! SHOTS!" everyone shouts.

"Keep it down, would you!" someone yells from the course ahead of us, probably one of the actual mini-golf finalists.

We all laugh and stumble forward to the next hole. This place is ridiculous. I love it.

It's the last hole of the game. I'm slap-happy from exhaustion, having participated in three more rounds and winning one. By now most of us are done messing around and are actually paying attention to the real competition—or some are drunk from the game and have wandered off to pursue more illicit activities. I'm not saying Gary and Sherry were giving each other *looks*, but uh, it felt like a very private moment to observe.

Daisey has gone home because she has to pick up Owen early the next morning, and Nate has also bid me a good night. I thread through the thinned-out but still healthy-size crowd in search of a friendly face to watch the final hole with. Brie, Patrick, and aptly named Birdie are all tied for first place, so it's all down to the tricky castle shot, just like Brie predicted. As my eyes scan the crowd, I spot a tall boy with rumpled hair, and smile.

"Hey," I say as I approach.

Ethan turns to me. It's hard to read his eyes in the dark. He's standing alone, thumbs tucked into his pockets. For the first time I can remember, he doesn't smile at me, like his face is too tired to muster the energy. "Hey," he replies.

My stomach twists. He's hurting. And I can't stand it.

I bite the inside of my cheek and take half a step closer to him. "Ethan, what's going on? Talk to me."

"I'm all good." He shuts me down with a very-unlike-Ethan bro voice. "Gotta use the bathroom. See you later." He turns and heads off the course. I want to chase after him, but if he's really using the bathroom, that would be weird. Plus, I want to support Brie on her final shot. I chew my lip, pulling out my phone to text Ethan but having no clue what to say.

Sighing, I turn back to the action. I'll find Ethan after. I'll make him talk to me.

I tune in to Joey's commentary. His voice is hoarse at this point. One month of Olympic commentating on top of his already vocal job of wrangling kids has really done a number on him, even with some substitute hosts taking his place when he needed a night off. Still, there's as much charm and enthusiasm to his commentary as always.

"Well, here we are, folks," he says as I make my way closer to him. He gives me a puppy-dog wide grin. I wonder if he knows Ethan is upset, how often they talk about his home situation. "The final hole of the night, the formidable, the daunting, the all-impressive Princess Castle. We cannot call it Cinderella's Castle due to copyright law, but let's just say the resemblance to Cinderella's Castle is uncanny. Now, as the scorings stand, we currently have a three-way tie for first place. Someone will need to make a bold move to secure that golden medal. Who will it be? Or will all try for the victory shot? The difficulty level of this hole in one rates at a ninety-eight percent according to the *Mini-Golf Courses of America* guide published in 2006. Let's tune in to the action. Patrick Cho is up first. Patrick . . ."

As Joey continues to speak, I look over at Patrick. Yesterday, he was called into the alley to help, and we registered a party of twelve preteens together. After, he went to grab a snack and asked if I wanted anything. It was a nice gesture, an olive branch. Or, a french-fries branch. I'm glad he's not upset with me. Not that he should be mad at me for expressing my feelings. But still, I'm grateful things are okay between us, if only a little awkward.

I hope he golfs well—but I hope Brie wins.

Surprisingly, Patrick doesn't go for the hole in one. Instead, he lines up his ball to shoot around the castle, which he accomplishes in one easy stroke. "Perhaps aiming for silver, Patrick Cho takes the safe route. Let's see if he can secure himself a medal, folks."

He sinks the ball easily on the second tap, and everyone imitates a polite golf-clap.

"Very nice stroke work," Joey says. Laugher echoes throughout the crowd, and Joey grins. "I'm sure he practiced for many hours."

"All right, that's enough," Patrick says, laughing good-naturedly. He catches my eye and smiles, and I give him a little clap and a thumbs-up. It feels awkward and silly, but also nice.

Birdie is up next. She's one of the oldest Bonanza employees. I've only met her a few times, as she works in the Bonanza security office, watching live feeds all day. Her job mostly consists of calling in backup for massive spills or kid tantrums. I can't imagine what would happen if there was actually a security breach. She'd probably call for Tony to tackle them.

Birdie is pulling no punches tonight. She aims for the small hole in the castle, pulls back, and takes the putt.

"Look at that aim," Joey commentates. I quickly glance over at Brie. Her face and muscles are tensed as the ball rolls toward the castle opening. "Is it going to—yes, Birdie has gotten the ball through the hole, but wait—" He's running around to the other side of the castle. "There was too much momentum! It might—yes, it has skipped over the cup and gone off course. Oh no, dear Birdie, we thought you had that one."

Birdie is flustered now, and it takes her two more putts to sink the shot. "That's all right, that's all right," Joey tells her. "We'll still be seeing you on the podium tonight. A job well done, Birdie."

Birdie grunts.

And then—it's Brie's turn.

She could shoot around the castle and tie for gold with

Patrick. But tying for first isn't *really* first, not when you're as competitive as we are. I watch as Brie carefully walks onto the course. Her shoulders are taut, eyes concentrated on only the surroundings that matter. I know that look. When Brie gets that look on the field, there's no getting past her. She's a defensive juggernaut. When Brie gets that look, I know we're going to win the game.

A hush falls over the course as she lines up her shot. When she putts, the sound of the club hitting the ball breaks the quiet, a soft yet resolute *thwack*.

It rolls and rolls and rolls.

Even Joey is silent.

The ball makes it through the opening in the castle, and I hear the faintest whisper of Brie letting out a breath.

We all race around to the other side, and then—

"Brie Bradley, everyone!" Joey shouts. "Our mini-golf gold medalist!"

There are cheers and applause, and the smile on Brie's face is so wide, I can feel her joy down to my toes. I shout and clap along with everyone else. It feels great to support my friend again. It feels *right*.

And suddenly, it clicks—

I should always support her. She's Brie, my best friend, my person.

I find her in the crowd and tackle her with a hug. She lets out a surprised "Oomph," and for a moment, I'm scared she'll reject me, but then she hugs me right back.

"I'm sorry," I say, my voice muffled in her jersey.

"For what?" she asks, pulling the slightest bit away.

"You should talk about soccer," I say. "As much as you want. It's part of your life, and that's something I care about. I don't want you to hide yourself from me. Okay?"

Her eyes brim with emotion. "Are you sure?"

"Absolutely," I say.

She tackles me with another hug, and we stumble to the ground laughing.

Chapter Nineteen

BRIE INVITES ME to grab Blizzards with everyone. Joey has already been hustled into a car and is en route to Dairy Queen. Although I'd love to celebrate with Brie, the thrill of her win is fading, and I'm reminded that Ethan has disappeared.

I promise Brie I'll join next time, and then I make my way back toward the Bonanza building. It's nearly deserted, just a few people scattered around to clean up and shut things down. As I walk through the double doors, it feels like I'm the only person in the building. The lights are half-dimmed, most of the arcade games turned off. It's cool and unsettling, like getting stuck in a mall after close.

I make my way toward the bathrooms, even though Ethan mentioned them half an hour ago. I should text him instead of searching the Bonanza catacombs. What if he even left already?

I'm pulling out my phone when I hear the sounds of a pinball machine. The pinball finals are next week. Someone's probably getting in extra practice. Curious, I round the corner to see who's playing.

"Ethan?" I ask.

He's focused on the machine, shoulders rounded, hands tensed. A tall shadow in a dark room, lit only by the neon lights of the machine. He hits the ball a few more times, then steps away and lets it sink.

Ethan steps back and turns to me. "Hey, Hannah."

He looks different under the dim lights, both older and younger, dark circles and wide eyes. He looks lost. There's a gnawing feeling in my stomach as I instinctively step toward him.

"What's going on?" I ask. "Talk to me. Please."

Ethan looks down at his shoes, plain white sneakers, scuffed with a summer of work. His voice wobbles the smallest bit when he speaks. "I guess, uh, well." He looks up at me, and the vulnerability in his eyes makes my heart ache. "I don't know where to go. I've spent so many nights at your house, but I don't want to go home. I'm so—" He breaks off, and I notice his fist clenches at his side. "I'm so angry at them, you know? We'd all be better off if they divorced, but they don't see that. They're stuck in this toxic loop and keep dragging me down with them."

My chest feels tight, pained. I want to take his hand and release the tension in his grip.

"I'm sorry," I tell him. "You know you can *always* stay with us, right?"

He nods. "I know."

"I mean it," I say, my voice firm. And this time I do reach forward and grab his hand. My heart skipping, I unfurl his fingers and then lace them through mine. Something flutters through me at the warmness of his grip, and my chest winds tight. "My parents love you. We all love you. You're always welcome. *Okay?*"

His eyes are so dark. I feel like I can barely breathe.

"Okay," he whispers.

I release his hand and step back. The distance clears my head, just barely. "I'm sorry," I say, taking a breath. "I'm sorry you have to live like this. It's wrong and unfair, and if you want me to give your parents a talking-to, I'm happy to do that."

Ethan laughs, light appearing in his eyes. "A *talking-to?*" he asks, one eyebrow hitched.

I roll my eyes, grinning. "Oh, whatever. I've been hanging out with the Golden Oldies too much. Leave me alone." I pause. "But seriously, if you want me to talk to them, or I guess it'd make more sense for my parents to talk to them, or if you want us to go with you while you talk to them, we can do that, okay?"

"Thank you, but—" He sighs, shrugs his shoulders. "I don't think it will help. I've tried in the past. Your parents tried too. I think I've got to just ride it out until college and then let them figure it out on their own—or continue to make each other miserable." His voice softens. "Thanks for talking to me, though. I know it's not good to bottle this stuff up. I just don't know how to release it. Sometimes at night, I get so restless, sleep feels impossible."

I think of that night a few weeks ago, out in the backyard, under the moonlight with Ethan. I think of how nice it felt to talk with him, to confide in him. I think of how we're better versions of ourselves when we're together.

"We should do something," I say suddenly. "To let the anger out. We could . . . bowl more?"

Ethan laughs. "What about whack-a-mole?"

I shake my head. "What about . . ." And then, whack-a-mole sparks an idea. A smile draws to my lips. "I know the *perfect* thing."

The Bonanza graveyard is empty.

And *dark*.

"Do you see it?" I ask Ethan, stumbling into him. Our phones only provide so much light, and it's hard to hold mine steady with two golf clubs in my hand.

"Yeah, I think it's right—" There's a small click, and

then suddenly the graveyard is swathed in artificial light. "Here."

As Ethan turns to me, my heart begins to pound. We were standing close in the dark, and now Ethan is right in front of me, his smile as warm as the heat emanating from his body. I let out the smallest shiver, wishing I could burrow closer to him.

My voice comes out thick. "Nicely done."

His eyes linger on mine. "Thanks." And then he steps back, running a hand through his hair. "So what are we doing here? Making a barrel fire? Burning our secrets on pieces of paper?"

"Nah." I wave my hand. "That's boring. Plus, I don't want to burn down the place."

"Good call," Ethan agrees. "What is it, then?"

I grin at him. "Come on."

My skin feels alert, sensitive to every change of the wind as Ethan follows me around the graveyard. I take us all the way to the back, behind the red vinyl couch and broken record machine, then down a small dirt path. Daisey showed me this hidden section a couple of weeks ago, a place where the *real* trash collects, items so battered they're not even worth setting up in the graveyard.

The path opens up to piles of castoffs, everything from old box TVs, to furniture broken beyond repair, to go-karts rusted in weeds. Out here, the floodlight still provides enough illumination to see, but the stars in the sky also make their presence known, blinking in the dark night.

I pass Ethan a half-bent golf club and say. "Wait, here."

"You're being *very* mysterious, you know," Ethan says.

"Is it annoying?" I ask, walking forward into the trash heap.

"Only a little," he replies.

Smiling harder, I pick through the debris. There's a great selection, but I settle on a broken box TV. It's heavy, but my muscles have regained some strength after a summer of hauling bowling balls. I heave the TV into my arms, then walk back toward Ethan. I place it on a wobbly stool and turn to him. "Okay, you're up first."

He raises an eyebrow. "Up first at what?"

I point to the golf club, then the TV. "Smashing, obviously."

"Seriously?" he asks, his smile betraying him. "We'll get in trouble."

"No one's here," I say. "And it's just junk."

"I don't know. . . ." He stalls.

I grab the club. "Well, if you're going to avoid the task at hand, I guess I'll have to go first."

Adrenaline beats through me as I walk up to the TV. This seemed like a good idea. A release. But I'm a little nervous now. What if we do get in trouble?

I've never really been the type of person to back down, though.

I lift my arms, pull back the club, and then, with all my might, I swing.

Bam.

The sound cracks the silent night. The TV flies off the stool, landing a few feet away with a loud thud, its glass splintering into pieces.

That was satisfying, *exciting.* I turn back to Ethan. His eyes are wide, magnetic.

I grin. "Your turn."

He scans the pile of junk. Quiet folds over us. It feels all too good, all too right, to be alone out here with Ethan. His smile grows as he pulls out an old cash register. "Bet I can hit this farther than your TV," he says as he sets it on the stool.

I cross my arms. "Bring it on."

He swings back and hits the register with such force that it shoots back at least twelve feet before crashing to the ground. *Damn.* Ethan glances at me with a smug smile. "Sorry, I'm so awesome."

"Oh, it's *on.*"

I pick up another TV next, thinking I can perfect my craft, but it's too heavy to hit Ethan's cash register mark. Then he goes for a glass beer stein, which makes a satisfying sound, but the spiderwebbed glass cracks in too many

Laura Silverman

pieces to go far. Then I spot an old trophy from one of
Bonanza's many tournaments. I stretch back and blast it far
past Ethan's register. We go back and forth, combing the
pile for satisfying items to destroy. The more we hit, the
more adrenaline rushes through my veins, the more my
heart pounds, the more I feel awake and alive, so far from
the numb state I curled myself into over the last year.

Ethan seems awake as well, alive, almost frantic. When
he laughs, it's loud and full, a release of everything he's
been holding inside.

I want to help him get it all out.

"How does it feel?" I ask as he sets up a cracked bowling
pin. "To be so angry at them?"

Ethan turns to me, face shifting. "My parents?"

The look in his eyes makes my throat tight. "Yes."

"Awful," he tells me, his eyes dark in the night.

I step closer to him. "Do you want to scream?"
Something sparks in me as his voice catches on the word:
"Yeah."

"Okay, then." My pulse is racing. "I'll scream with you."

I move closer to him. He's so *tall*. He towers over me
now, neck tilted so he can meet my eyes. I want to know
what it'd feel like to be wrapped up in his arms.

"Ready?" I ask.

He nods.

I swallow hard. His fingers fidget.

And then we scream.

Hesitant at first, laughing at ourselves in the process.

But then louder, straight from our stomachs.

Our shouts echo through the dark night, and when our eyes lock, a million emotions pummel me. I hate that his parents fight. I hate that my bubbie died. I hate that I broke my ankle. I hate that life is so much harder than this for so many people.

We scream and we scream until my jaw aches and my eyes water and my fists hurt from clenching them.

When we stop, our heavy breathing is the only sound in the night. And I'm even closer to Ethan now, his fingers within reach of my own. His gaze is on me. My heart drums, loud and steady. Does he want this too? Does he want *me* too?

His hand reaches out, tentative. When his skin brushes against my own, I almost jump, and when his fingers lace through mine, my pulse pounds in my ears.

I know what it is to want something badly.

And I want Ethan Alderman badly.

I lean forward, and so does he, and—

Something crashes.

We both jump. A pile of our junk settling. Ethan's hand slips from mine, and he steps back, clearing his throat. His voice is thick when he speaks, eyes clouded. "We should try to clean some of this up," he says.

I nod because I don't want to hear what my voice sounds like right now.

And then my phone is ringing. Frazzled, I grab it from my bag. I panic when I see my mom on the caller ID and the time. It's past midnight. Past curfew.

Hand shaking, I press accept. "Hello?"

Mom's anger is tactile. "Where are you?"

Last Summer

We're sitting in the dining room. We *never* sit in the dining room. Unless it's like Passover or something.

Mom and Dad are on one side of the table. I'm on the other, my head still pounding from last night. They didn't seem to care about that when they dragged me out of bed at nine in the morning. It's possible I might still be drunk.

I lean back in my chair and stare at my parents. "This feels like *a bit much*, you guys. I know I'm grounded. I don't need a formal council to go over the terms."

"Hannah." Dad's voice is firm, but he keeps fidgeting with his wedding band. "You were *already* grounded. That obviously didn't work."

"Okay . . . ," I say. "So now what?"

I crack a yawn as Mom speaks. "We think you need some time to reset," she says. "We know it's been hard for you, dealing with the loss of your bubbie and soccer–and, well–" Her voice trembles, but my head aches too much to feel sympathy. "And well, we're at a loss too. We just want to keep you safe, and we haven't been doing that. So." She clasps her hands tightly. "So we think it's best if you get some time to really heal. And we've heard wonderful things about Mountain Bliss Academy, and–"

It takes a few seconds for the name to click. Mountain Bliss, Mountain Bliss . . . wait, wasn't Shira's friend sent there after she tried to sell drugs on campus?

I stand up from the table, then immediately regret it, my head feeling light. I push through anyway, gripping the table's edge with my fingers. "Boarding school?" I ask. "You are not sending me to boarding school. For what? Having a few drinks? Don't you think that's a little over-the-top?"

"Hannah, sit down," Dad says. From the other room, Figgy whines in response. I slump back down into my chair as he speaks. "You've been drinking for weeks, getting *drunk* for weeks, missing curfew, ignoring your grounding. You were–" He takes a heavy breath. "You were going to get behind the wheel last night. Don't you know how dangerous that is?"

"No, I wasn't!" I shout. "I was just messing around."

"I'm sorry," Dad says. "There's been too much lying already. We can't trust your word."

It's a gut-punch.

I've always had my parents' trust. And now it's gone.

"I know this may seem extreme," Mom continues. "But we

love you, and we want you to be safe and happy. That's our first priority. We think this could be good for you, I promise. We wouldn't be sending you, otherwise. We think it'll help. And it's a great place."

They continue to talk, trying to tout all the great programs at Mountain Bliss, from yoga to sustainable farming, promising it's all really nice, that the time will fly by, but I barely hear them as my thoughts turn inward.

I've lost everything.

Bubbie. Soccer. My best friend. And now, my parents' trust.

It's all gone.

I have nothing.

Chapter Twenty

"IT WAS MY fault," Ethan says as soon as we step through the door.

Mom and Dad are standing in the living room, arms crossed. Joey is sitting on the couch, munching on a bowl of popcorn. Figgy is begging by his feet.

"This isn't a show," I tell Joey.

"It's better than what's on TV," he replies through a mouthful of popcorn.

"Hannah is right," Mom says. "Joey, go to bed."

He sighs and stands with a huff. Before retreating to his room, he gives us a weird look. "What were you two doing, anyways?"

Figgy pads behind him, following the popcorn, and then Ethan and I are left alone with my parents. The room grows silent. My palms grow sweaty.

"Seriously," Ethan repeats. "It was my fault we were out late. I'm sorry. Hannah didn't do anything wrong."

"That's very kind and a nice try, Ethan," Dad says. "But Hannah is seventeen years old and perfectly responsible for her own actions. She has a curfew, and she broke it. You don't get to take credit for that." Dad narrows his eyes. "*However.* You shouldn't be out this late either. It's unacceptable. You sleep under this roof, you arrive home before midnight. Mess up again and that curfew becomes ten. Understood?"

I swear Ethan's eyes are almost smiling in response, like it's nice to be lectured, like it's nice to be *seen*. "Understood, sir."

"Good." Mom nods. "Now go to bed and let us talk to Hannah alone."

He turns to me and mouths, *I tried.*

I smile at him, my cheeks warming. "I know."

Once he leaves the room and I turn back to my parents, all that warmth disappears. Reality sets in. I broke curfew. It was just once, and I wasn't doing anything bad (well, except for technically smashing company property to pieces), but what if that doesn't matter? What if one toe over the line means back to Mountain Bliss?

The kitchen clock ticks, louder than ever before. Nerves gnaw at my stomach.

"Hannah," Dad says slowly. His eyes are weary. I think of

how much I've aged my parents. How their worry for me has sagged their shoulders. "We found something. In your room."

"We weren't snooping," Mom adds quickly. She's wearing her favorite pj's, the Peanuts ones. I remember buying them for her Hanukkah gift years ago. "We were just cleaning. Your dad was vacuuming, and—"

"I noticed a loose floorboard, and—"

The blood drains from my face as Mom continues, "You know how he is about fixing things right away. . . ."

"We found these."

My stomach drops as Dad pulls out the Altoids tin, vodka, and lighters. I've been so busy lately that I forgot all about them. Guilt and regret claw at me. Why didn't I just throw them away in the first place?

My instinct tells me to run from this conversation.

But I know that instinct is wrong.

I know my parents deserve better, and—

I deserve better too.

My entire body is a tensed knot. I take a breath in, *one, two, three*; out, *one, two, three*. When I meet my parents' eyes, there's no anger there. Only concern. It makes my heart squeeze.

"I'm sorry," I tell them, anxiety racing through me. "I promise those are from last summer. I know I was supposed to throw everything away, but . . . I swear I haven't used any of that stuff. And Ethan and I were just at Bonanza tonight. We lost track of time. We weren't drinking or anything. I swear." I glance down at the floor, my hands twisting together, my heart beating so loud I'm sure they can hear it. "Do you believe me?"

"Yes," Mom says simply.

"Of course we do," Dad replies.

Their answers stun me.

When I look up, Mom's eyes are full of love. "Come, *Hannah*," she says, pronouncing my name the Hebrew way, digging into the *H*. "Sit with us."

We all sit on the couch. I curl up against one of the armrests, knees tucked to my chest.

"I don't want to go back to Mountain Bliss," I whisper. There's a tremor to my voice.

"We don't want that either," Dad says. "We want you right here with us."

His gaze is steady and kind, and I feel my muscles relax the slightest bit.

"Let's start with why you were out so late," he continues. "We know the finals ended. Your brother has been home for a while."

"Um." I look down at my knees as my mind whirs with excuses—*the car wouldn't start, I said I'd help with cleanup duty and it took forever*—but when I look back up at my parents, I know that's the old Hannah talking, the old Hannah lying.

And I realize I still have one more relationship to repair—my relationship with my parents. And the only way that will happen is if I tell the truth.

"The truth is . . . ," I begin. "Ethan and I were out late because we were hitting trash with golf clubs at the Bonanza graveyard."

Silence beats through the room.

Then Mom laughs, short and high-pitched. "I'm sorry, you were *what?*"

I go on to explain the whole thing, tiptoeing around Ethan's struggles since that's his story to tell, sharing only enough to let my parents know he needed someone there for him tonight. And then I tell them about everything I've been working through as well, that I fixed things with Joey and Brie, and that I'm slowly turning a corner with my grief for Bubbie, and that although I've been bowling, I still haven't found a new passion.

"And I don't know if I will," I say. "Soccer . . . it meant everything to me. My whole life. I worked so hard. I could—" I take a steadying breath. "I could see myself there, on the Olympic podium, just like Bubbie. And then it was taken from me. And I'm dealing with that. I am. But I don't think I'll find a replacement. I can't just get a new passion, but I don't want you to send me away again, okay? Please don't send me away again."

As soon as I finish talking, I hear a whine. I look down

and realize Figgy has left Joey's room and made her way to my side. I smile and reach down to hug her. "You are the *goodest* girl," I murmur into her fur.

"Yes, she is," Dad agrees. When I look back up at him, he seems like he's barely holding it together. His eyes shine with tears. "Hannah, we're so proud of you."

"We're not sending you back to Mountain Bliss," Mom says, then smiling a little, adds, "We wouldn't want to put poor Figgy through that again."

"Keeping me home for the dog?" I joke.

"No," Mom replies firmly. "We're keeping you home because we love you and because you've made so much progress this summer and because we are too selfish to spend more time away from you. We want you where you belong—home."

"Really?" I ask. My body is still tense, like it can't quite believe the words. All summer, I've been scared of not doing enough, of not being enough, of getting sent away again.

"Really," Dad tells me. "You've become such a hard worker, you're closer with Joey again, and most importantly, well, you seem *happy*."

I realize it suddenly.

He's right. I *am* happy.

I have a job I love, a brother I love, a best friend I love. I lost so much last summer, but in a way, that makes me more appreciative of what I do have now.

"Yeah." I smile. "I guess I'm doing okay."

"We love you, kid," Mom says. "So very much." Then she claps her hands together. "Now that we've gone over that, you still did break curfew. And you have drugs in your room."

I grimace. "Oy vey."

"'Oy vey' is right," Mom agrees. "Why did you keep that stuff?"

"I was scared to let it go, I guess." I hesitate. "Just in case I needed it." I think back to that night after my fight with Ethan, how unanchored I felt, how easy it would've been to slip back to old habits.

But I'm better now.

Even if my future is unsure, I trust my own two feet again.

"Let's throw it all away, okay?" I ask.

"Right in the trash," Dad says. "I think we need a new curfew as well. What do you think, Sarah? Home by ten?"

"Sounds reasonable to me," Mom agrees.

"But the Olympics!" I say. "I have my bowling finals, and Joey is hosting, and—"

They exchange a look, parent telepathy doing its most.

"Okay," Mom says. "Home by ten *with the exception* of Bonanza Olympics activities, in which case you must arrive home with or before your brother. Deal?"

I bite my tongue about my younger brother having a later curfew than me. "Deal."

I can't sleep.

I fixed things with my parents. I'm staying home permanently. And it's three in the morning after an incredibly long day. I should be exhausted, knocked out into a hard slumber.

But I can't sleep. Because I'm thinking about Ethan. The way he looked at me tonight, the way his fingers felt laced with mine.

What would have happened if that pile didn't crash? If my parents didn't call?

Would he have kissed me?

It can't just be in my head. He feels something too. You don't look at someone like that without feeling something too.

I want him.

My stomach flips at the thought. The worst part is that he's right down the hall. He's here, but he's not with me. I reach for my phone, and my heart starts beating out of my chest before I even unlock it.

I'm not doing this. Of course I'm not doing this. I'm not—

I pull up my text chain with Ethan, mostly a thread about bowling and carpooling to work.

My fingers type out the message while I pray these palpitations don't lead to a heart attack: Are you awake?

It takes all my willpower not to throw my phone at the wall after sending that message. Instead, I put it facedown on my bed. I'll wait two minutes before I check it. In two minutes, he'll respond, or he won't, and I'll know he's sleeping and not twisting around in bed thinking of me as well.

The house is silent, save for Dad's snores, barely audible through my door. My head swims. *Has it been two minutes yet? Should I check my phone?*

There's a knock on my door.

Wait.

Was there?

Yes, a knock. Another now. A light double tap. And then a whispered voice: "Hannah?"

Holy shit.

I feel like I'm hallucinating as I peel back my covers and slide out of bed. I'm wearing an oversize T-shirt, so large it almost touches my knees. My hair is a mess from tossing and turning. I pad with bare feet across the floor, avoiding the creaking floorboards, and then open my door.

Ethan is there, eyes dark in dim hallway. "Hey," he says, his voice low, barely audible.

My stomach pools with warmth. Every nerve of my body feels alert to his presence.

I can't think of what to say, what to do—so, I stop thinking.

And instead, I reach forward and pull him into my room.

I close the door behind us, clicking it shut quietly. When I turn to Ethan, his gaze seems to be everywhere—on my eyes, my lips, my bare legs. My heart pounds. His hand is still in mine, and I squeeze it tightly. I want to say *yes*. I want to say *please*. But I can't form words.

I step closer, and he does as well, until we're standing with only a centimeter between us. He lifts up his free hand, and then more gently than I could have ever imagined, he brushes his fingers against my jaw. My skin heats. His touch is too much and not enough.

I've always been an impatient girl.

I lift up on my toes and kiss him.

Ethan's lips are soft, and he responds right away, pulling closer to me and kissing me back at a painfully slow pace. His kisses are light, unhurried. His teeth nip my bottom lip. I inch closer to his warmth until there's no room left. A noise escapes his throat as my hands dig into the muscles on his back.

I'm kissing Ethan Alderman.

And it's not enough. I want more.

I pull away enough to speak. My voice comes out husky. "Bed?" I ask.

He nods. "Yes."

We crawl onto it, both moving onto our sides, which feels safer, a little bit slower. And then we're kissing again. And kissing. *And kissing.* His hands sweep across my upper back, then up into the nape of my hair, and I feel myself arch against him as his lips find my neck, and this makes him groan. Every action has a better reaction. I could do this forever. I feel like stopping would be the very worst thing in the world.

I don't know how much time passes. We kiss and kiss more. Our hands explore, soft noises made when his fingers touch my bare thighs, when my teeth bite at his lips. I've never felt like this before. I've never wanted someone like this before. It's thrilling, exciting, and—a little overwhelming.

I pull away a small fraction. This is Ethan. *Ethan.*

His breathing is hard, his eyes dilated. Concern flickers through them. "You okay?"

"Yeah, definitely." My hand is intertwined in his. I squeeze it. "It's just, uh, well, this is different."

He laughs, soft and a little awkward. "True."

Anxiety flails through my chest for a quiet moment.

"Do you want to stop?" he asks. "Do you want to talk?"

What does this mean? How does he feel? What does he want?

What do I want?

I search his eyes, kind and steady. I glance at his lips, red and swollen.

"Tomorrow," I say, leaning closer. "We'll talk tomorrow."

And then I kiss him again.

Chapter Twenty-One

THE NEXT MORNING, Ethan and I are silent for the fifteen-minute car ride to Bonanza. Joey has been the only one speaking, rattling off "behind the scenes" stories about the tournament and gossip from the Dairy Queen trip after. I'm up front next to Joey, and Ethan is in the back, and we have decidedly not given each other a single glance inside this car, because I'm sure if we do, last night will be written all over our guilty, chapped lips.

Last night—a delirious, wonderful blur that blended into this morning. Ethan didn't leave my room until the sun was threatening to rise. We mumbled sleepy goodbyes, too tired to say more. Thank god we didn't fall asleep in my bed. What a nightmare that could have turned into.

I crashed afterward, a hard and satisfying sleep, and only woke up to Joey banging on my door saying we'd be late for work. I scrambled into the shower, threw on wrinkled work clothes, and grabbed a granola bar. By the time I made it outside, Ethan was already in the back seat, his head ducked toward his phone. My cheeks heated as I climbed into the car.

I bite my lip now, resisting the impulse to glance at him. We need to talk about what happened, but we certainly aren't going to have that conversation around Joey.

We pull into the Bonanza lot. Joey parks, then turns to both of us, scrutiny in his eyes. "Okay, what is going on, y'all?" he asks. "You two are quieter than crypt-keepers."

My face stays impressively neutral as I ask, "What's a crypt-keeper?"

I can't see him, but I imagine Ethan smiles at this.

"Oh, shut up," Joey says. "You two are acting weird, and you know it. Why did you both come home late last night? What were you doing together? Wait, were you—"

My muscles tense. He figured it out that fast? I guess we weren't exactly covert.

"Were you planning me a surprise birthday party?" he shouts.

Relief floods through me. Thank god. Joey doesn't know. I don't want to keep secrets from him, but Ethan and I definitely need to talk before Joey gets involved. We don't need a commentator around while we try to "define the relationship."

Ethan laughs. "Joey, your birthday isn't for three more months."

"So, maybe you want to be prepared," Joey says.

"Maybe so," I reply.

Joey groans. "Ugh. Fine. Keep your secret-y secrets to yourself. I have plenty to do today. Last week of the Olympics!"

I can't believe that's true, but it is. The summer has flown by faster than I could have ever imagined. The Bonanza Olympics end in a week, and summer comes to a close just a few weeks after that. The pinball finals are tonight, and I'll be bowling in my finals in two days. The medaling and closing ceremonies are on Friday. It's all gone by so quickly, and I have to admit, I'm not ready to move on. I wouldn't have survived this summer without Bonanza. I wonder if there's any chance Pete will let me continue working during the school year.

We all get out of the car. I take my first glance at Ethan, and immediately my cheeks burn. Every inch of him is a reminder of last night—my fingers threaded through his soft hair, his lips trailing along my jaw. Ethan looks just as flushed and turns away from me quickly.

"Okay, seriously?" Joey asks, suspicious eyes whipping between the two of us. "Y'all are definitely hiding something. And I'm going to figure it out." He blows out a gust of air. "What a pair of freaking weirdos."

I'm hoping to pull Ethan aside at the bowling alley, but five minutes into my shift, Brie texts and asks if I can help with a birthday party on the mini-golf course. Right as I reply, Yes, another text comes in. This one is from Ethan. I'm working at the front counter, and he's helping someone open up a lane. I see him glance over at me as I read the message:

Chat later?

His smile is sweet, shy. My pulse flutters. *He likes me, right? Last night surely wasn't just a one-time thing.*

I'm glad he wants to talk. We *need* to talk. This is more complicated than my string of make-outs at parties last year. This is even more complicated than kissing Patrick all over Bonanza. This is *Ethan.*

I text back: yes, definitely

It'll be fine.

Or, it won't.

One or the other.

With a deep breath, I make my way to the mini-golf course. It's a scorcher today, the sun bright in the sky. Sweat beads down my neck as I walk.

I hear the birthday party before I can see it. Never a good sign. I round the corner to discover a horde of seven-year-olds in an assortment of costumes and birthday hats. I find Brie and make my way over to her.

Her eyes are wild, frazzled. There's a bucket of golf balls in one of her hands and a fistful of tiny pencils in the other. "Fifty kids!" she cries. "*Fifty*. I don't know what Pete was thinking." She looks around in terror. "We're going to need more backup."

She picks up her radio and calls for additional help.

Half an hour later, we have eight Bonanza employees wrangling this giant birthday party into order, including Ethan, which makes concentrating on what size putter every kid needs totally easy. I'm not distracted at all when he gets on his knees to console a seven-year-old about a small bruise on his arm. I don't even once think about the fact that he'll probably make a really good father one day.

We fall into a groove. I pass out putters and balls, Brie is on score sheets and mini pencils, Joey gets kids started on the first hole, and Ethan, once done with the crying kid, handles the parents. Nate and Daisey scout the rest of the course, clearing any potential hazards, like hole number fourteen, our camp theme. They turn off the animatronic bear and cover it with a sheet. Kids are big fans of hanging on to its arm, trying to be pulled up into the sky. It's been broken off on more than one occasion.

The party is Bonanza chaos at its finest. There's yelling and laughing and screaming and chasing. One kid is climbing the windmill, while his parents scream for him to get down. Another takes it upon herself to rearrange the rock garden at hole seven, lifting heavy stones close to her own body weight and almost dropping one on her brother's head. Two kids try hitting the golf balls at each other instead of into the holes. One kid screams that he wants to bowl instead and starts throwing his golf ball instead of putting it. Another covertly passes out Pixy Stix like drugs, and soon all the kids are sugar-high.

The hours melt by under the blistering sun. Every now and then, I catch a glimpse of Ethan through the melee. He never loses his patience. In fact, he seems to be having fun, laughing as a kid putts a ball into the cup backward. He picks up the club and tries to do the same thing, the kid clapping at his side. My cheeks warm. It takes all my willpower and a good deal of nail-nibbling to turn away and get back to work.

Somehow, by a miracle of god, we get every kid through the course. At the eighteenth hole, we hand out ice cream sandwiches and cheap plastic trophies—the Bonanza Elite Birthday package. All the kids are sticky-faced and oversugared and trying to fight one another with their golf clubs. Parents coax them into leaving one by one until *finally* they're all gone, and only the staff is left.

We all collapse. Ethan slumps onto a bench, Joey right next to him. Daisey sits up against the castle, her legs splayed like a rag doll. Nate may or may not be snoring on the other side. Brie and I lie down on the fake grass, head to feet. My pulse calms as quiet descends. My ankle is lightly pressed against Brie's head. Her fingers tap the ground near my hip.

"I can't believe summer is almost over," I tell her, my voice soft.

"I know. Then one more year of high school. Then *college*. It's all so surreal."

"You still planning on UNC?" I ask. We always hoped to attend the same college on soccer scholarships. UNC has one of the most elite teams in the country.

"Hopefully," Brie says. "They have a good coding program too." She hesitates. "What about you?"

I bite my lip. My future is an open book now. I feel directionless with no goal posts to hit. "I don't know," I admit. "I'm sure I'll figure out something."

She reaches for my hand and squeezes it. "I know you will. And *hey*, we have an entire year left. Senior year. With my bestie."

I smile at this, feeling a burst of warmth and gratitude. I'm grateful to have Brie back in my life. I'm grateful for the privilege to continue to grow alongside her.

I scoot closer to her, then yawn, eyes dipping closed. Every inch of my body feels drained but at peace.

And then—I feel something wet on my face. And then

on my arm and leg. I blink my eyes open and look up to find rain sprinkling down. Brie shifts as well, and then everyone is rousing from their drowsy states.

"Is it raining right now?" Joey asks.

"That is the moisture coming from the sky, yes," Nate replies.

We all laugh, including Joey, as he shoots Nate an eye-roll.

The rain starts to come down faster, fat drops soaking the ground.

"Shit. I'm too tired to move," Daisey moans. "Inside is so far away."

"She makes a strong point," Brie agrees.

I shrug. "So we'll just get wet. Summer rain is nice, anyways."

It's true. I love summer rain, its coolness cutting the heat, the sweet smell it brings. Sometimes the rain would come right at the end of practice. We'd run muddy sprints down the field, laughing in our soaked clothes.

"It *is* kind of nice," Daisey agrees. "Relaxing." She stretches out her arms as if to catch the drops. A light wind rustles through the trees. "Hey," she says. "Remember that time we had to work a birthday party of fifty kids?"

Brie laughs first, a little snort. Then Joey laughs, quick and hard, almost like hiccups. And then we're all laughing, cackling, holding in our stomachs as the rain above pelts down harder, soaking our clothes and hair.

"What's wrong with us?" Brie asks, hysterical. "Why do we work here?"

"Because it's the best," I reply, sitting up to shake my wet hair. "The very best."

There are agreeable murmurs in response. Then, Daisey speaks again. "Well, y'all, we did it." She glances over and grins at me through the downpour. "Hannah Klein has been converted. Welcome to the Bonanza cult."

"You can do this," I tell Daisey.

"Right." She nods. "Totally. I've got this."

Daisey cracks her knuckles, again. She looks even more badass than usual tonight, having changed out of her wet clothes and into a sleeveless gray Bonanza shirt. A leather-studded bracelet adorns her wrist. Her small gauges are steel, and her lip ring is aquamarine.

"Pinball wizard," I tell her.

She nods. "Pinball wizard."

I pat Daisey on her shoulder, and then she walks up to her machine, cracking her knuckles once more. In the corner, I notice Patrick giving Tony a pep talk of his own, massaging his shoulders like he's about to start a prize fight.

It's just past nine. I'm exhausted, but there's a frenetic energy buzzing in the air. The arcade is packed, everyone excited for the finals. My eyes search the room. I spot Ethan and Joey talking. My breath hitches as my eyes sweep over Ethan. Is it possible he got more attractive since this afternoon?

"You okay, Hannah?"

I jump, then flush when I find Nate next to me. Even though he couldn't hear my thoughts, I feel like they must be written all over my face.

"Yep." I cough. "Totally fine."

"*So,*" he draws out the word. "You excited for your finals?"

I've been practicing as much as possible. My wrist is sore, my neck cricked. But I've definitely improved, especially with the help of my very own bowling shoes. Hopefully it's enough to save myself from embarrassment. And I might just be delusional enough to think I have a chance at medaling.

It feels silly, going after a fake Olympic medal when for my whole life I've wanted to compete for the real thing. But even though I've lost soccer, I've come to realize I haven't lost myself. I'm still a girl who likes to win, no matter the game.

"Definitely." I smile at Nate. "You going to come out and watch?"

He smiles back. "Wouldn't miss it."

"How's the crossword-building going?" I ask.

"Oh, catastrophically difficult." He laughs. "But that's what makes it fun."

We catch up a bit more before we're cut off by Joey's opening commentary. "Ladies, gentlemen, and nonbinary folk, welcome to the *PINBALL FINALLLLLLLS!*" He warbles his voice to make a fake effect. It's impressive. Joey could have a future in voice-acting. "Tonight, we watch Tony Cho, Daisey Liu, Veronica Metcalf, Susan Greenland, and Isiah Baker compete for their place on the podium. We've used a random number generator to assign players to machines. The rules are simple—the last player standing wins gold; second-to-last, silver; and third-to-last, bronze. Now, if our champions are ready, let's begin!"

After a count-off, everyone starts their machines. Nate moves forward for a closer look. I heard Tony is pissed he's on the X-Men machine since he prefers the Star Wars one and practiced on it more. Daisey never let herself have a favorite to begin with, so she wouldn't be thrown off by the random assignment. At least Tony has the advantage of an empty aisle. Daisey is boxed in by other players on both sides.

When I glance back at Ethan and Joey, Ethan quickly catches my eye. My heart jumps as he leaves Joey and threads through the crowd toward me. It's all I can do to keep my hands to myself as he approaches with a soft smile.

"Hey," he says, his voice graveled from lack of sleep. "Want to go talk?"

"Yeah." My pulse drums. "Definitely."

We peel off from the crowd. I lead us outside, hoping it will allow us enough privacy and quiet. The automatic doors whoosh open, and we walk off toward the mini-golf course, now cloaked in darkness. Crickets chirp in the bushes as nerves lodge in my throat.

We settle onto a bench at the third hole, a horrible knockoff of the Trevi Fountain.

"Okay." I nod and turn to Ethan. "Let's talk."

"Yes, good," Ethan agrees. "Perfect. Let's talk."

But then my eyes are on his lips. And then his breathing tightens. And then my hand reaches for his. And then we're kissing again, fast and greedy this time, like it's been a decade, not a day, since last night. I scooch closer, but it's not enough contact, so I kick up my legs and put them over his lap. He pulls them closer to his stomach. My skin prickles as his hand skims across my bare ankle. *God, that feels good. How does something so simple feel so good?*

My lips fall to his neck. His fingers trace the hem of my jeans shorts. My skin is on fire. "We should . . . ," he says, voice muffled, strained. "We should talk, actually talk."

"Mm-hmm," I agree, kissing his jaw. "Definitely. In just one more second."

One more second turns into ten minutes, but finally we

pull apart. Ethan's eyes are dark, dilated, his lips swollen. If we walked back into Bonanza right now, everyone would know.

"Hi," he says, voice husky.

"Hi." I smile at him.

I just kissed Ethan Alderman. *Again.* My legs are on Ethan Alderman's lap. My *tongue* was—

"Oy vey." I cover my face with my palms. "Oy vey, oy vey."

Ethan laughs, soft and kind. "Just the reaction I want after I kiss a girl."

I fake-punch him in the shoulder. *"Ha-ha."*

His gaze grows more thoughtful. "What are you thinking?"

I take a careful breath, trying to steady my thoughts. "I'm thinking I just kissed my brother's best friend. And that I *liked* kissing my brother's best friend."

He grins. "That's good you liked it."

"I thought it was pretty obvious."

"Confirmation is always a plus."

We're both smiling, but I still feel threads of anxiety. Ethan takes my hand. His touch is so tender I might just keel over. And then he really does me in.

"I like you, Hannah Klein," he says.

My heart is pounding in my ears.

"Are you sure?" I ask.

He laughs. "Yeah, I'm sure."

I duck my head down, trying to hide my wide smile. Ethan Alderman likes me. And he's holding my hand. And that feels nice and warm and *right*.

I bite my lip, then say, "I like you too, Ethan. How weird is that?"

We can't stop grinning. "Very weird," he answers. "Very weird and very nice."

"How did this happen?" I ask.

"You tell me," he says. "When did you start liking me?"

A blush rises to my cheeks. Somehow talking about this feels more intimate than kissing. "Um, I guess at the beginning of summer. I noticed you, um . . ." My blush grows. "Well, you certainly looked good. And then our late-night talks, bowling in the morning. I just liked being around you. I felt like myself again." I glance at him. "What about you?"

He coughs. "Um, like, two years ago?"

"*What?*"

Ethan laughs and holds up his hands. "Don't freak out. It's not like I was pining for you the whole time, but do you remember that yellow dress you had? With the little straps—I, uh, well, you looked very nice in that dress. And suddenly I was aware that you weren't just Joey's older sister—you were a girl. A very pretty girl who was independent and funny and strong, and so I noticed. I noticed you."

"Two years," I repeat, my words a little breathless.

"*Okay.*" He laughs again. "Don't get a big head. The crush ran hot-and-cold. Sometimes you would steal all the hot water in the morning before the rest of us could shower, and then I wouldn't like you as much." I laugh at that. "And then, well, then last summer happened. And you went away. And I met Emma, and that was good for a while."

My smile falls some at the thought of last year. "Sounds like I missed out on a lot," I say. "But I'm glad to be here now."

"I'm glad you're here now too."

We smile at each other, so genuine I can feel it in my every fiber.

"So," Ethan says. "You like me."

"I like you."

"And I like you."

"Correct."

"So should we—" He clears his throat. "Do you want to go on a date with me?"

I hesitate, and in that short moment, his smile falls. I quickly grab his hand. "It's nothing bad," I say. "I *do* want to go on a date with you. I'm just—are you sure?" I look down. "What if things go badly? I want you to always feel comfortable at our house, you know? Are you sure this is what you want?"

There's silence for a long moment. Then Ethan squeezes my hand and says, "First of all, I definitely want to date you. Second of all, if things go badly—which, let's not put that possibility into the air—I'll still be comfortable at your house. I promise. After all, I'll get Joey in the divorce."

I laugh. "Fine, but Figgy's all mine."

"If you insist."

"Okay," I agree. "It's a date."

Ethan draws me closer and kisses me again.

We return to the arcade to find only Daisey and Tony still playing. Isaiah secured the bronze medal. Ethan gives my hand a squeeze before I thread through the crowd for a closer look. We agreed to tell Joey later tonight. The rest of Bonanza is sure to figure it out soon enough. I don't exactly want everyone in our business before our first date, but privacy really isn't an option here.

As I make my way to the front of the crowd, I can still feel Ethan's lips on mine, his fingers brushing against my skin. I can't believe I get to do that again, kiss him again. It all feels like a strange, lovely dream.

At the front of the crowd, Daisey is cursing, loudly, while Tony's jaw is set in an increasingly firmer line. They've both passed the records on their respective machines. The crowd moves with them, oohing and aahing and gasping breath. Daisey's hands are clutched to her machine in a death grip, while Patrick wipes sweat off Tony's temple. Their fingers jam the buttons. Tony will probably have to repair the machines tomorrow after all the abuse.

I'm on the tips of my toes when Tony suddenly lets out his first and only giant curse: "SHIT!"

It takes us all a collective moment to realize his ball sank into the gutter. He lost.

Which means: "Daisey Liu wins gold!" Joey shouts.

The arcade erupts into cheers and applause, but Daisey is too in the zone to realize she's won. She continues to play, hitting the ball again and again. I rush forward and put my hands on her shoulders. "Daisey! You did it! You won."

Slowly, she relaxes her grips, then lets her arms fall to her sides. The ball sinks into the gutter. She turns to me with a smile of disbelief. "Holy shit. *I won?*"

"You won!" I tell her. "Pinball wizard!"

She winks. "Pinball witch."

Almost everyone is happy about the result, except for Tony. He starts muttering about an unfair competition, how he was put on a tougher machine. Patrick is trying to talk him down, but Tony shrugs off his attempt and strides up to Joey. "I want a rematch," he demands. "The competition was rigged."

Joey looks startled at first, then annoyed. "Well, there are no rematches. Daisey won. Fair and square."

"She had the better machine," Tony says, voice rising.

Joey blinks. And suddenly, I see the fog of his crush evaporating. His voice comes out firm. "It was a random draw that you agreed to. And one might argue you had the easier machine because you weren't boxed in on both sides."

Tony shakes his head. "That's bullshit, man."

"You lost," Joey replies. "Deal with it."

"Whatever," Tony mumbles, waving Joey off and stalking toward the doors to outside.

Joey turns to Daisey and says, "Sorry about that. Hope he didn't spoil your win."

Daisey smiles. "No worries, Joey. I never let men ruin my night." She scans the crowd. "Now, who's down for a game of shots?"

"What?" Joey asks.

He's sitting on his bed, hands laced in his lap, staring up at the two of us as we stand in front of him. *"Seriously, what?"* He looks at me, then Ethan, then back to me, like we're a science experiment gone horribly wrong. *"How? Why?"*

"Um," I say.

"Well," Ethan says.

"Attraction is . . . ," I continue.

"We realized that . . . ," Ethan adds.

We glance at each other. The light panic in Ethan's eyes makes me smile. It's possible everything he does makes me smile.

I turn back to Joey. "We just realized we liked each other. That's all. So we're going to see what happens."

Joey nods, and very slowly asks, "So you've, like, *kissed*?"

"Anyways!" Ethan says loudly, clapping his hands together. "Long night. Time for bed."

"Like *bed*, bed, or Hannah's bed?" Joey asks.

I groan. "Why is this a nightmare already?"

Ten minutes later, I've escaped from Joey's room and am washed up and in my pj's. I'm about to turn off my lamp when there's a knock on my door. My pulse skips. *Ethan?* Part of me feels excited to see him again, to kiss him again, but part of me is ready to decompress and get a good night of sleep.

I slip out of bed and open my door to find Joey standing there, Figgy by his side. Joey has always been her favorite, even though the rest of us refuse to admit it. He gives me a little two-fingered wave and then steps into my room, Figgy padding in next to him.

"Hello," I say slowly, giving Figgy a few good pats. She looks up at me with a gentle tail-wag. Sweetest girl.

Joey's gaze tracks across my room. "It's so empty in here now," he says.

I glance around as well. "I guess so."

"You used to keep everything. Your room was an archeological dig. And then last summer, boom, twenty trash bags out of the house, off to Goodwill and the dump."

He's right. I used to be—well, not a hoarder, but a clinger. I liked my things, liked combing through old soccer uniforms and school assignments and printed pictures curled at the edges. I liked my walls, plastered with posters of Megan Rapinoe and Marta Vieira da Silva, with ephemera from team trips, flight vouchers, and fast-food receipts.

But after I broke my ankle, I felt like I needed to erase my past, not to think about what would've been my future.

Joey traces a finger across my comforter, then looks up at me with a little smile. "So, you and Ethan, huh?"

I bite back a grin. "It's new. I don't know." I glance down at my feet. "It's a little scary, I guess."

"How so?"

Joey sits at the foot of my bed, and I move to my desk chair, tucking my legs up against my chest. I used to sit like this all the time as a girl. It felt safe, secure. "I like him," I say. "So much that I'm scared of it going badly. He's such a big part of our lives. I don't want to mess that up."

"You think you're going to run off my best friend?" Joey asks.

"I guess, a little bit."

Joey laughs, hard.

"What?"

"Hannah, if Ethan were easy to run off, I would've done that years ago. If the boy can handle me as a best friend, he can handle anything."

I smile. Ethan did promise something similar. He's not going anywhere.

"You're not *that* bad," I tell Joey.

He snorts. "Thanks. What a compliment."

I extend my left leg and nudge him with my toe. "Seriously. You're a great friend. And funny. And smart. And sweet. Ethan is lucky to have you."

"Stop it or you'll make me cry." Joey's tone is joking, but his smile lets me know he appreciates my words. He shifts back and says, "So Tony's a douchebag."

I laugh. "Yeah. I don't think he's the one for you."

"It's a shame, with the muscles and everything."

"Mm-hmm."

Joey glances at the ceiling, pondering. "You know, that guy Nate is pretty cute, though. You're friends with him, right?"

I raise an eyebrow. "I am. He's great. My favorite Bonanza employee."

"*Hey!*"

Nate and Joey are different, but just like his best friend, Ethan, I think Joey could use a more introspective partner to balance him out. Though the thought of Joey trying to sit still for more than a few minutes with a crossword puzzle does make me laugh.

"What?" Joey asks.

"Nothing, nothing." I wave my hand. "I say go for it. Just, you know, approach with caution. If you start sniffing around him too much, you might scare him off."

"Yeah, yeah." Joey rolls his eyes but is smiling. "So you gonna win tomorrow?"

My pulse skips. It's scary to want something, to go after something. But that's who I've always been. That's who I'll always be.

I nod. "I'm sure as hell going to try."

Chapter Twenty-Two

"I CAN'T BELIEVE y'all came!" I rush up to the Golden Oldies and give them all hugs. The full contingent is here tonight, and they're wearing their sparkling gold bowling shirts, reserved only for their own tournaments.

"Wouldn't miss it for the world," Madeline tells me.

Ginger winks. "We've got to cheer on our girl."

"Still, it's late," I say. "Y'all are awesome."

Tashia waves a hand. "We're old, not dead, sweetheart. I might like a good early-bird special, but that doesn't mean I'm asleep by nine."

"Speak for yourself," Adele replies. "I had to drink an espresso to stay up for this. But it was worth it. You gonna do us proud, darling?"

My stomach does a little flip. "I hope so."

I feel weirdly emotional standing in front of all of them.

Very few non-employees show up for our Olympics, but the Golden Oldies are here. They're here to support *me*. It reminds me of Bubbie, at every game to cheer me on. I wonder how loud they can whistle.

"Go on, darling," Madeline says. "It's about to start."

I give them all one more round of hugs and then maybe wipe some moisture from my eyes. Then I walk over to my lane, where Ethan is waiting for me with snacks.

"Ooh," I say, taking in his offerings: Oreos, french fries, and soda. "Thank you."

"Gotta keep the athlete fueled," he replies.

"There is something to be said about a sport that allows eating while playing." I pick up a fry and give it a generous dunk in ketchup.

Ethan laughs. "Agreed."

Then his eyes flick to my lips.

"What?" I ask.

He reaches out a hand. "Ketchup."

"Ew, don't." I scoot away from him and wipe at the ketchup myself. "I've never understood the appeal of couples wiping each other's faces. It's like, that interaction should be reserved for parents to toddlers, you know? *What?*"

Ethan's smile is wide and teasing. "*Couples?*"

My cheeks go deep red. "Not that we are—we are not a 'couple.' I just mean . . ."

He laughs hard. "You're cute."

"That is off topic."

"That is *never* off topic."

I roll my eyes but can't wipe the grin from my face. "Enough of that. I've got to focus now."

"Okay, okay."

He gives my hand a quick squeeze and then joins Joey as he begins his opening announcements. I scan the room, my nerves pulsing. Brie is here. She wished me good luck earlier and is now hanging out with her mini-golf coworkers, splitting a mega-size plate of nachos. Nate is here as well, hanging out with a few friends. Their necks are craned over his laptop in concentration.

And then—then there's my competition.

My competition that includes Patrick. He earned first place in his preliminary. Even though things have been friendly enough between us, it feels strange to compete against him. To help alleviate potential awkwardness, I walk over and say, "Hey, Patrick."

He's polishing his bowling shoes, a pair that look cool and vintage. The boy has good taste. But I still prefer my galaxy-purple ones. He looks up and nods. "Hey, Klein. Congrats on making it to the finals."

"Thanks." I shrug. "Just luck."

His eyes glint. "Now, we both know that's not true. You've got skills."

"Yeah," I admit. "You're right. I am awesome. And

congrats to you, too. Sorry I missed your prelims. I heard you were great."

"No worries." Patrick straightens up, running a hand through his perfectly tousled hair. Then he glances over at Ethan, who's now in conversation with Joey. "So you and him, huh?"

I hesitate. "News spread already?"

He grins. "It's Bonanza. Of course it did."

"Yeah, well . . ." I dig into the floor with my shoe. "We're giving it a shot."

I look down at the shoes Ethan gave me, so different from my cleats, yet familiar in a way. It's nice to be in gear again. It's nice to feel like me again.

"What about you?" I ask Patrick. "You single and ready to mingle?"

He laughs. "Klein, you've been hanging out with the Golden Oldies too much."

I gasp. "Impossible." Then I reach out my hand to him. "May the best bowler win?"

He gives me a solid shake. "May the best bowler win."

I'm not going to win.

This becomes apparent early on when Patrick and Sophie Flores pull so far ahead, the rest of us are left trailing in their hand-powder dust.

But to my satisfaction, I discover my practice has paid

off—because I'm once again in a battle for third place. And this time, third place means bronze.

Third place means *medaling.*

I want that medal. I want it because the Golden Oldies showed up to support me. I want it because Brie medaled and Daisey medaled. I want it because it would make Bubbie proud. I want it because one day I'll tell my grandchildren about the time I competed in the Olympics, the *Bonanza* Olympics.

We bowl another few frames. My determination grows. Nerves kick up for the other contestants, but I never falter, inching out more of a lead frame by frame. The competition thins, until it's just me and Nick left with a shot at bronze. Nick, the kid who caught Patrick and me in the closet and spread the gossip around right away.

I want to beat him. I'm *going to beat him.*

Patrick glances at me from his lane and smiles at the look on my face.

"Folks, the competition sure is getting heated as Nick and Hannah prepare for their last frame," Joey announces. "Gold and silver are out of reach for these two, but bronze will belong to one of them by the end of the night."

Unfortunately, I'm up first.

I'd prefer second, to have an exact goal to hit. Going first means I need to bowl perfectly or possibly lose. I've already snagged two strikes this game, so a third feels unlikely.

Nick has played erratically: four strikes, one gutter ball, a couple of splits he couldn't finish off. I have no idea what to expect from him next, but I do know one thing—an unpredictable opponent is a dangerous opponent.

I pick up my ball and focus on the pins. Joey switches to his quiet golf-commentator voice. "Hannah Klein approaches the top of her lane, trusty ten-pound midnight-purple galaxy sparkle ball in hand." Joey's voice is barely a whisper. "A hush falls over the crowd as she steadies her aim."

This is untrue. Unless a "hush" means twenty people having ten different conversations at once while music blasts through the speakers.

It's hot in here. The adrenaline is raising my body temperature. Joey dragged me into this bowling tournament, but now I want to win. I *really* want to win.

I visualize the ball crashing into the pins. Everything else drops away, until the crowd is only a faint shadow behind me. I feel my ankle, laced securely in my new shoes; I feel my muscles set for action.

And then I pull back, my arm strong, and launch the ball down the lane.

I drop to one knee to watch as it rolls and rolls, headed on a straight course. It's a perfect trajectory. One I should be proud of. But is it good enough?

My chest tightens as the ball heads straight for the

pins—but at the last second, it leans left. Suddenly pins are clattering, and I'm left with a seven-ten split, two pins in the back on opposite ends. "Crap," I curse. I'm terrible at splits, and this is a tricky one.

Frustration roils through me as I stand up. I could have done better. I should have better. Why am I not—

"Hey," a voice says, warm hand on my shoulder.

My muscles ease as I inhale the scent of Coconut Beach Dream. I turn and find my best friend behind me. She's wearing jean shorts and her tie-dye Bonanza shirt.

Brie smiles. "You're stressing, Hannah."

I nod. "I am stressing."

"Well . . . ," she says. "Just don't."

She cocks her head, and then we're both laughing. "Thanks, excellent advice," I reply.

She grins. "You've got this. I know you do." She glances over to the other lane. "Plus, that Nick guy is the worst. I've never seen him take out the trash. And he's always skirting bathroom duty. He's the opposite of a team player. Beat him for all of us, okay?"

I nod. "I will do my best."

"Your best is more than good enough." She shoots Nick a sour look. "Looking forward to his demise and your victory."

She gives me a solid hug, then returns to the crowd. I take a short breath and pick up my ball. Joey narrates the difficulty of my split as I focus on the pins. I'm pretty sure he's reading straight from a Wikipedia page.

I did practice this split, though never successfully. Still, I know the technique. Aim for the inside edge of one pin and hit it with enough force to crash the pin into the wall, then bounce across the deck and take out the other.

Easy, right?

I steady my breathing, draw on a bit of luck, and toss the ball. My breath catches in my throat as the ball spins down the lane. It's heading directly for the left pin I planned. Maybe—just maybe—

My ball crashes into the pin, and it clatters sharply against the wall, but the angle is off. One pin remains standing.

Damn. I just left Nick a wide-open window for bronze.

"Too bad, so sad," he tells me from the next lane.

I roll my eyes. *Kindergartener, much?*

"Best of luck," I tell him in the most genuine voice I can manage. "I really hope you win." Sometimes the low road is pretending to take the high road. Sure enough, my good sportsmanship throws him off, and he gives me a funny look.

He shakes his head, then picks up his ball, forest green and his very own that he brought here in a leather bowling bag. Joey narrates once more, explaining that Nick only needs nine pins to win. Nick turns and waves to the crowd with a giant smile, like they're all here to celebrate him. Then he turns to his lane, steadies his aim, and tosses the ball with an absurd amount of force. It rattles down at an insane speed before popping off into the gutter. Someone laughs, hard. I swear it sounds a little like Ethan.

A dark cloud falls over Nick's face, while my heart leaps.

He prepares to go again. He shifts left, then right, lining up the ball and checking and adjusting and checking. Time moves slower than the molasses syrup we use to make Bonanza's Super-Fun Drink! Finally, Nick seems satisfied. He breathes in and out and throws his ball.

This shot is better. Much better. Good speed, strong trajectory. My pulse rockets as the ball clatters soundly into the pins.

At first, it's hard to see what happened. But then, the sight clears:

Seven pins down, three left standing.

"HANNAH KLEIN WINS THE BOWLING BRONZE!" Joey shouts. "MY SISTER, THE MAGNIFICENT ATH-LETE, COMING FROM BEHIND WITH MINIMAL BOWLING EXPERIENCE, CLINCHES A PLACE ON THE PODIUM! CONGRATULATIONS, HANNAH!"

Holy crap.

I won. I *won.*

Well, I won bronze. But it sure as hell feels like gold.

Everyone rushes me: Joey, Brie, Ethan, Daisey, Nate,

the Golden Oldies, and more. There are hugs and congratulations. "Shots! Shots! Shots!" someone screams.

Before I know it, I'm getting pulled into the bowling-
alley version of shots, which is a lot more dangerous since
bowling balls weigh much more than golf balls. I lose three
rounds in a row but don't care in the least. I congratulate
Patrick on his gold and laugh as Nate and Joey spin around
too many times and dizzily half fall into each other. Brie
points at Ethan to challenge him, and they tie in a head-to-
head match.

It's delightful. It's chaotic. It's the very best of times.

Chapter Twenty-Three

THEY'RE GOING TO love you," Madeline tells me.

"How do you know?" I ask.

"Because they love anyone under the age of forty who isn't being paid to spend time with them. Come on, then, enough dilly-dallying."

I'm with Madeline outside Hillside Homes, a senior community that's a combination of permanent residents and visitors like Madeline who like to spend the afternoon playing bridge. Madeline can bring an opponent to tears— at least that's what she told me. And I, without a doubt, believe her.

Helping out the Golden Oldies started as an easy way to check off my daily good deed—walk them to their cars, go above and beyond with food service, sit and listen to their twenty-minute stories, which was never really a good deed since their stories are better than anything I've ever read in school. But quickly, that's what I discovered about all my interactions with them. It never felt like a chore because I enjoyed the time we spent together. It was mutually beneficial.

Their stories excite me. They make me want to have an adventure, to lead a grand life. Their stories remind me of Bubbie, of her passion, of her determination. The Olympics might no longer be in my future, but there's still plenty of life out there for the taking. I'm only seventeen, after all. I'm just getting started.

Madeline and I enter the senior center. She introduces me to Bryson at the reception desk, a man in his midforties wearing a green polo. Bryson smiles and welcomes me effusively, telling me how happy he is to have a new volunteer.

"Happy to be here!" I respond. "How can I help?"

"Oh, let's see." Bryson pulls out a clipboard. "It's time for the morning snack, if you'd like to help hand those out. Come on, I'll show you over to the cart."

"I'll see you soon, sweetheart." Madeline squeezes my shoulder. "I've got to see about a man who owes me money."

"No shakedowns, Madeline!" Bryson calls out.

"I would never!" she replies, then winks at me.

I tamp down a laugh as Bryson leads me to the pantry. Inside, there's a large refrigerator stocked with juice, water, seltzer, pudding, and Jell-O cups. The pantry also holds shelves of snacks, from breakfast cookies to Goldfish and pretzels. Bryson tells me to stock the cart with a variety, then stop by each room, knocking if the door is closed.

"What if they don't answer?" I ask.

"Don't worry about that. These residents are serious about snack time. They'll answer. Start with the residential rooms first and then visit the common areas. If you step into the rec room first, the cart will get raided in about five seconds."

"Got it, thanks!"

As I push the cart down the unfamiliar hallway, a few nerves trickle in. I'm reminded of my first day at Bonanza, overwhelmed by the chaos, by all the new faces. The senior center is certainly calmer than Bonanza—and has fewer weird smells—but it's still untraversed territory. It's still a step out of my comfort zone.

But trying new things, even if awkward at first, has only turned out well.

I take a steadying breath, then knock on the first door to my left. "Hello?" I ask. "Would you like a morning snack?"

Handing out snacks to seniors is just as easy as handing out snacks to kids. Actually, easier—less mess. Everyone loves snacks, and it's easy to make friends when you're the one providing them. It takes me ages to get down the hall because most residents want me to stay and chat, which I'm happy to do. I learn quite a few things: that I look like three of their granddaughters, that the AC always runs too cold, and that Betty Hampton and Roger Davies are having an affair in room 301. Finally, I make it out of the residential hall and into the rec room, and then just like Bryson warned, my cart is instantly raided.

Now *this* chaos definitely reminds me of Bonanza. Everyone greets me at once, asking my name, my age, where I want to go to college, what my parents do for a living. I answer as many questions as I can. Eventually the rations on the snack cart disappear, and the crowd abates, allowing me to chat in smaller groups of people. After a while, I smell a familiar perfume and turn to find Madeline next to me. She loops her arm through my elbow and says, "Darling, I'm going to teach you how to eat chumps for breakfast. Now pass me a seltzer."

Three hours later, I leave happy, exhausted, and the enemy of the bridge players at table seven. I drive home and face-plant onto my bed, a warm feeling bubbling up inside me. When I was sent home from Mountain Bliss, I was asked to find a new passion. And while I haven't quite found a replacement for soccer, I have found so much that does make my heart happy—from working at Bonanza to reconnecting with the people I care about most to now volunteering. And I think that's okay. To have a lot of little things that make me happy instead of just one big thing. I think that might actually be better.

My alarm goes off at nine at night because I'm now certifiably indoctrinated into the Bonanza cult. My bed is warm and cozy, and I feel like I could roll over and fall right back asleep until morning, but no, I'm going to peel off my warm layers of blankets and drive to Bonanza late at night to participate in the closing ceremonies.

And I *know* I've officially lost it because I *want* to go. I have a bronze medal to receive. Plus, Joey worked his butt off all summer, and I want to show up and support him. And Ethan and I have a surprise for him.

It was a frenzy the past few days, pulling this present together, but thankfully everyone was on board to help, saying it was one of the best Olympic games ever, all because of Joey.

I roll out of bed and get dressed, opting for a Bonanza T-shirt since most employees will still be dressed from work and because my brain doesn't have the horsepower now to "put together an outfit." Plus, it feels patriotic. Then I kneel, lift up the dust ruffle on my bed, and grab the scrapbook stashed underneath. It's absolutely stuffed. Yesterday, I had to filch a jumbo rubber band from Pete's office to secure it.

I hug the book to my stomach as I walk to my car, a strange feeling washing over me. There are still a few more weeks until school starts, but in a way the closing ceremonies mark the end of summer. I know I've made a lot of progress, but it will still be strange to return to school without the identity I held for so many years. I'll no longer be the athlete, the jock, the star soccer player. I'll just be—

"Hannah!" Mom calls. "Wait for us!"

I turn in the driveaway and narrow my eyes as I see my parents scurrying toward me, both wearing jeans and Bonanza shirts. Did they buy those from the *gift shop*?

"Wait for you?" I ask. "What do you mean?"

"We're going to the closing ceremonies, of course!" Dad says.

"We heard that everyone is invited," Mom continues, "and seeing as we have a bronze medalist and a host in our family, we figured it was our duty and honor to show up!"

"Duty and honor?" I ask, one eyebrow raised.

"Oh, stop being such a teenager," Dad tells me. "C'mon. We'll drive."

"Is that an actual *digital camera*?" I ask as I follow them to their car.

Ethan approaches me before I have a chance to warn him. He sweeps me into a hug, kissing my lips softly. My cheeks are red as he pulls away and says, "Hey."

I cough and slip out of his embrace. *"Hey."* I pause. "So. My parents are here." I turn around. "Like, right here."

Ethan's eyes widen as he looks at the two shocked faces behind me. We've been trying to figure out the best way to tell my parents we now make out on the regular, seeing as they might not be thrilled hearing that while knowing we sleep under the same roof.

"Uh." Ethan practically chokes on the word.

"Right. So." I turn to my parents and force a smile. "The news is out. Ethan and I are dating. Or, technically, going to date. We're going on a date this weekend. Sound good?"

My parents exchange an unreadable look. My bravery wavers.

Then Mom says, "We're going to have to get locks on the bedroom doors."

"Maybe little bells or alarms," Dad adds.

"Security cameras too?" Mom asks.

"Not a bad idea," he agrees.

Ethan and I look at each other in surprise. And then, I laugh. It bubbles out of me. And then Ethan laughs too. And then some people turn and stare at us, which just makes me laugh harder. And suddenly, Dad lets out a giant guffaw, a full-on belly laugh, and Mom is laughing as well, slapping her knee.

"Seriously?" Dad asks, practically wheezing. "You two are going to date?"

"Yeah," I say, wiping away tears of laughter. "Sorry about that."

Ethan shifts on his feet. "But um, really, is that okay?"

"Oh, well, we love you, Ethan," Mom says, squeezing his shoulder. "If you want to take on Hannah, that's your choice—"

"Hey!" I shout.

"There'll have to be some ground rules, of course," Dad says.

"*Many* ground rules," Mom agrees.

"What are you psychos doing?" a voice interrupts.

We all turn around to find Joey standing there, and the laughing begins again.

"Does he know?" Dad asks.

I nod, then tell Joey, "Cat's out of the bag."

"Who even uses that expression?" Ethan asks, laughing harder than ever.

"We are never going to be normal again," Joey says.

"Oh, we never were normal." Mom throws an arm around his shoulder. "Now, don't you have a closing ceremony to host? Come on. Lead the way."

"Okay, okay." Joey shrugs out of her hug, but then kisses her cheek. "After me."

"Hannah!" someone calls out.

I turn around to find Pete behind us. *Huh.* Pete never attends the Olympic events. He walks up to my family holding a clipboard and *three* pens, BlackBerry buzzing on the hip of his khakis.

"Hi, Pete," I say. "What's up? Do you need me to take an extra shift?"

"Quite a few extra shifts, actually," he replies, clicking a pen. "If you'll have them. I'd like to offer you a permanent position. We can start at twelve hours a week."

I pause as his words sink in.

"Oh." A warm feeling spreads though my limbs, and I can feel everyone smiling behind me, like this is some big deal. And, you know what? This *is* a big deal.

I was hired as a seasonal employee and off the back of my brother's recommendation. But now I've proved myself as a Bonanza employee, proved myself enough that Pete officially wants me on the team. And I'm pretty damn proud of that.

"I accept!" I say. "Thank you."

Pete, being Pete, simply scribbles something on his clipboard and tells me to come by his office tomorrow to sign paperwork. As he walks away, I turn to my family, and not only are they all smiling, but they start clapping, too.

"Oh my god." I laugh. "Please, stop."

They do—eventually.

❧

The Bonanza Olympics closing ceremonies are being held in the graveyard. "For ambience," Daisey explained the other day.

Mom and Dad exchange some mumbled words as we trip down the dim path. But I can see their smiles through the darkness. Soon light breaks through, and the graveyard is revealed.

"Wow," I breathe.

The place looks incredible. The setup crew must have worked on it all night. In addition to the floodlight, candles line the perimeter. Two trash-can fires are roaring strong. All the broken furniture has been positioned into a circle around an impressive podium. The podium that Tony, after he apologized to Daisey about being a sore sport, built out of scrap wood as repentance.

Most people are already here, dressed in their Bonanza shirts, creating a sea of color. Excitement crackles in the air, voices softer than usual, murmurs and whispered conversations. Stars blink in the night sky, a light wind rustling through the trees. My skin prickles. Tonight feels like something special, like a memory I'll hold on to for years to come.

I spot Brie and tell my family I'll be right back. "Gold-medalist superstar," I say as I walk up to her. She's wearing her team jersey and on-theme gold earrings.

"Bronze-medalist superstar," Brie replies.

I curtsy. "Thank you."

She nudges my foot with hers. "I'm glad you'll be here this year. School sucked without you."

I nudge her back. "Thanks. I'm glad I'll be here too."

We say hello to more people, mingling in the warm night. Instead of blasting the crowd with his loudspeaker, Joey lets the crowd find silence on its own. Eventually we all settle into seats. I'm between Ethan and my parents, aware of my thigh pressed against Ethan's on the small vinyl couch. His pinkie rests an inch from mine. I reach out and link them together.

He glances over at me with a smile so warm I feel it from the inside out.

"Good evening, everyone," Joey says. The light breeze cools off the heat. I lean closer to Ethan. "Welcome to the closing ceremonies of the Bonanza Olympics. To no one's surprise, this summer we have witnessed incredible feats of bravery, good grace, and pure athleticism. I'm so proud to be a part of this incredible staff—" There are a few chuckles at this, because the maturity level of Bonanza employees hovers around thirteen years old. "Thank you, everyone, for your participation and your heart. Without further ado, let's begin."

Since we all live in the same country, each gold medalist picks a different "anthem" for their medal ceremony. Daisey picks "Anarchy in the UK" by the Sex Pistols. And Brie picks one of our favorite workout anthems, "Good as Hell" by Lizzo. Songs are sung, pictures are snapped, and everyone claps at the end of each anthem. My parents wave Brie over and insist on taking pictures with her medal.

And then Joey is calling up the bowling medalists. Ethan gives my hand a quick squeeze. My parents give me a thumbs-up. Against all logic, I feel a little pinch of nerves as I walk over to the podium. Some eyes follow me, while other people chat with their friends. Patrick arrives at the same time. He's wearing his favorite gray beanie. I smile and say, "Hey, *you*. Congrats on gold."

"Hey, *you*." His eyes crinkle. "Congrats to you, too."

"What song did you pick?" I ask.

He winks. "You'll have to wait and see."

I laugh. "Okay, okay, build the suspense, then."

I can't believe just weeks ago we were making out. It's strange how far away that feels, how fast things can change. I can't see Patrick as anything other than a friend now. I'm grateful that instead of losing him I just found him in a new way.

We climb onto the podium along with Sophie Flores, who is wearing her cape. Joey gives out our medals. Patrick's gold, Sophie's silver, and my bronze. Joey pauses when he reaches me, handing over the medal slowly. Tears brim in the corners of my eyes as I look down at the design. It's a cheap thing. Nothing like a real Olympic medal. Nothing like Bubbie's. A thick plastic disc with the year and a Bonanza logo imprinted on it. A child's party favor.

But it's mine. I earned it. And that's a wonderful feeling.

And I think it'll look nice on the mantel next to Bubbie's.

"You did good, Hannah," Joey says, the emotion in his eyes transparent under the moonlight. "I love you."

I swallow hard. "I love you, too," I tell my brother.

He returns to his microphone to start Patrick's anthem.

We hold our hands to our hearts, and I take a solid breath, trying to calm the emotion running through me. And then the music starts playing, and—

I burst into laughter as Patrick gleefully belts the song at the top of his lungs. *Of all things*, Patrick picked the Bonanza theme song. Of course he did.

I sing along as well, and so does the rest of the crowd, everyone hollering the words, trying to outdo each other. My lungs burn for air as I shout the lyrics.

The stars are bright and shining, and so are my coworkers' faces, and I'm standing on the Olympic podium with my family cheering me on, and I'm really, *really* proud of myself.

More tears brim. I don't rub them away. I just sing louder.

"Oh, how we love Bonanza!
It's the best place in all the land!
We want to spend all day here,
Oh, that would be so grand!"

"And on that note," Joey says after playing "Time of My Life" to end the ceremony, just like the end of any good bar- or bat-mitzvah party, "I am wishing you all a good night."

"Wait!" I call out, standing up from the vinyl booth as Joey finishes his speech. "We have something for you!"

I grab the scrapbook, and Ethan and I rush up to the podium while everyone looks on. Joey seems confused at first. "You what?" he asks.

"We have something for you. Here." I present him with the scrapbook. "It's a thank-you gift. For being the best Olympics host anyone could ever ask for."

"The very best!" someone screams from the crowd.

"You rock!" another voice calls.

"Joey for president!" a third voice calls.

My brother looks genuinely overwhelmed as a bunch of people start clapping for him. His cheeks flush, and his eyes well with emotion. Joey has never been the bashful type, but he sure looks the part right now.

"Here," I say, my voice softer, giving him the book. "Open it up."

Joey takes the scrapbook, and I take half a step back toward Ethan. He smiles warmly at me as Joey flips through the pages with tentative hands. The moisture in his eyes wells more. "This is . . . ," he murmurs. "This is actually incredible."

"*You're* incredible," I tell Joey.

"Yeah, you're fine," Ethan jokes. We all laugh as Ethan adds, "Seriously, you're amazing, Joey. Everyone helped make this to say thank you."

Each employee decorated their own page. Some just scrawled messages, others pasted in pictures and memorabilia, like arcade tickets and party favors. A few people have left coupons: ONE FREE SHIFT CHANGE and ONE FREE CONCESSION POPCORN and ONE FREE BATHROOM DUTY. I notice with pleasant surprise that Nate left a coupon for ONE FREE LUNCH TOGETHER. The strangest page includes a lock of hair from a girl named Annie with a note that says, *Thank you for giving me the courage for my long bob.*

And on the first and most special spread of the book, there's a hand-drawn portrait. Ethan drew a panoramic of every employee at Bonanza, spread out among the bowling alley, mini-golf course, the arcade, and more.

"It's perfect," Joey says. "Thank you."

"Thank you, friend," Ethan replies, hugging Joey tight.

I join the hug as well, saying, "Just don't expect anything good for your birthday."

"Fine, fine. I've been warned," Joey says.

And when he laughs, it sounds like summer nights.

Epilogue

"ARE YOU SURE you packed enough snacks?" I ask Dad.

"What?" He looks up in panic. "You think we need more?"

I laugh. "That was a joke, Dad. We're *definitely* good."

"Well, if you're sure . . . ," he says, looking over his bounty: cookies, crackers, PB&J sandwiches, popcorn, clementines, and chocolate. Not to mention the cooler full of drinks, cubed cheese, and kosher dill pickles. The game is only two hours long and we already ate lunch, but Dad will be Dad.

He sneaks Figgy a piece of cheese, which she snaps up with a tail-wag.

Five minutes later, we all pile into the car. I'm stuffed into the middle seat between Joey and Ethan because even though I'm tall, they're now taller. A lot certainly changes in a year. Ethan gives my hand a light squeeze, and Joey nudges my shoulder. Mom glances at me in the rearview mirror and smiles. My pulse skips. I'm glad they're all here with me for this.

We arrive at the field and tumble out of the car, grabbing the snacks and stadium seats. It feels surreal to be on this side of things, to be holding a cooler instead of lacing my cleats. It feels wrong, and my stomach knots.

"Hey, Hannah girl," Mom says.

The boys are walking ahead to claim seats, but Mom's eyes are fixed right on me.

My hand is clenched, nails digging into my palm. Mom scoots closer and grabs that hand, and I let her lace her fingers through mine. Her skin is soft from moisturizer. "I'm proud of you, mamaleh," she tells me.

Tears prick at my eyes, because no one has called me "mamaleh" since Bubbie passed away; because Mom is proud of me; and because I know Bubbie would be proud of me too if she were here with us now.

"Come here," Mom says, wrapping me up in a hug. I inhale her mom scent, and my pulse calms.

After a minute, I pull away and wipe at my eyes. "Thank you," I whisper.

"No thanks needed." She puts an arm around my shoulder. "You ready?"

I nod, and we walk down to the field's edge together.

Mom then joins the boys in the stands, while, my heart drumming, I walk onto the field itself. My old team is there in their signature uniforms. There are a couple of new girls I don't recognize, but most of them I could spot anywhere. They stretch and chat and eye the opposing team—Kensington. It's the most important scrimmage of the summer.

I'm relieved when Brie spots me first. A wide smile breaks over her face. She rushes up to me with a hug. "You're amazing," she says. "Thank you for coming."

"No problem," I say, voice a little shaky.

"You want me to walk over to the girls with you?" she asks.

"Yes, please."

With Brie's arm looped through mine, I feel stronger. We head over to the rest of the team. Silence falls over the group as they notice me. My skin itches under their scrutiny, and it takes all my willpower not to run away. Elizabeth is closest to me, but her eyes are looking anywhere but at mine.

"Hey, y'all," I say weakly.

Nina, always the team leader, greets me first. Her skin is tanned from a summer of practice. She steps forward and gives me a one-armed bro hug. "Nice to see your face again," she says. "You look good."

"Thanks," I tell her, hoping she can hear how much I mean it. "You too."

And then a few more girls step forward, old teammates and new girls alike. It's awkward, but less awkward than I'd feared. It's hard to see them all in uniform like this, to know I won't be on the field with them, but I'm glad I'm facing that fear. I'm glad I'm here to support them.

Eventually, I've said hi to almost everyone, and only Elizabeth is left. She's kneeling on the ground, knotting and unknotting her cleats with intense concentration. I clear my throat and kneel down next to her. "Need any help?"

Elizabeth is silent at first, staring down instead of at me. Finally, she lets out a tiny "Okay."

With a small smile, I take her laces and pull them tight, knotting them in my signature loop. The method comes to me as easy as ever, like it's been ingrained into my DNA. When I'm done with both of them, I give her feet a pat and say, "You should be all good now."

Again, she's silent. I stand up and nervously wipe my hands on my shorts, wondering if I should leave. And then Elizabeth stands up too. And then, without warning, she launches herself at me, a blur of limbs and hair. Laughing, we almost topple to the ground, but my ankle is strong enough to hold us up now.

"I missed you," she says, breathing into my shirt.

"I missed you, too," I reply. "I'm sorry I was a shitty friend."

"I'm sorry shitty stuff happened to you."

"Thank you," I murmur into her shoulder.

We hug for a few seconds longer, all the tension releasing from my muscles.

Then it's time for their warm-up. I wish everyone good luck and promise to cheer them on. I start walking to the stands, but on the way, I hear someone shouting my name.

"Hannah! Hey, Hannah!"

I spin and find Lily Thompson approaching me, Lily Thompson of the Kensington team, Lily Thompson who broke my ankle.

My stomach drops as she stops in front of me. I want to escape, but it's like I'm stuck in wet concrete.

"*Hey,*" she says. Lily's eyes are wide and brown. Frizzy blond hair escapes her ponytail. Her cheeks are tinged pink, from emotion or the sun, I'm not sure. "Hannah. My parents said I couldn't apologize to you when it happened because you might sue me or whatever, but I don't care. I'm sorry. I'm *really sorry*. I've been wanting to tell you that for a year."

My heart pounds in my ears. "That's okay." I rush the words. "It was an accident."

"I know it was," Lily says. "But I can't imagine—" She breaks off, like she's on the verge of tears. She squints up at the sun, then takes a breath and says, "I can't imagine what I'd do if it happened to me. I ruined your life. I'm so sorry, Hannah."

And then, somehow, the tightness in my throat goes away. A calm washes over me.

Because Lily didn't ruin my life. She really didn't.

And I tell her just that. "I'm okay. I promise."

She looks unconvinced, worry in her eyes. "Are you sure?"

"Positive. I'm good." I glance down at my Bonanza T-shirt, then back at my teammates on the field, then up at my family and Ethan in the stands. And then I turn back to Lily and say with complete honesty, "I'm really good. Actually, I'm kind of great."

I wish her luck in the game, and then I make my way to my family. Mom and Dad scootch over and pat the bench between them, so I'm squeezed in by my parents on both sides. Joey hands me an ice-cold drink, and Ethan gives me a warm smile. I sit back under the summer sun and turn my attention to the field, excited to cheer on my team, ready to whistle as loud as Bubbie.

Acknowledgments

Mom and Dad, thank you for all your love and support. This book was mostly written during the pandemic. Although it wasn't the best of times for anyone, I am incredibly grateful for all the extra months we got to spend together. I love you both so much.

My friends and family, thank you for filling my life with warmth, love, and laughter. Writing a book isn't easy, and I'm thankful I'm not in it alone. Thank you to: Papa Bobby, Bubbie, Kayla Burson, Kiki Chatzopoulou, Alison Doherty, Brittany Kane, Deborah Kim, Katie King, Alex Kuntz, Elise LaPlante, Katherine Menezes, Anna Meriano, Lauren Sandler Rose, Ariel Russ, Melissa Sandler, Amanda Saulsberry, Lauren Vassallo, and Kayla Whaley.

Sensitivity readers and consultants, thank you for taking the time to read this story and help me improve it. Your feedback was generous and helpful. Thank you to Theresa Bremer, Jonathan Goldhirsch, Michelle Lee, and Amanda Saulsberry.

Jim McCarthy, book number seven! It's hard to believe it! Thank you for being a wonderful agent and partner in this business. I'm looking forward to many more stories together.

Kate Prosswimmer, it was a genuine pleasure working with you again. You are a brilliant and kind editor. Thank you for your insightful ideas and your patience. I hope we get to work together many more times in the future.

Ana Hard, thank you for this absolutely stunning cover. I love it more and more every time I see it. Thank you for bringing my characters and Bonanza to life!

McElderry, thank you to everyone who worked so hard to put this book together. Thank you to: Justin Chanda, Nicole Fiorica, Brenna Franzitta, Bridget Madsen, Irene Metaxatos, Nicole Russo, Debra Sfetsios, Valerie Shea, Caitlin Sweeny, Karen Wojtyla, and Anne Zafian.

Readers, teachers, librarians, and booksellers, thank you for supporting books. Our stories need you, and I'm forever grateful for all your passion and support.

Summer jobs, this book is an ode to you and all your messy and exhausting fun. Here's to work crushes and favorite customers and gossiping coworkers and sneaking food and staying way past close.

Thank you all,

Laura Silverman